Also by Natasha D. Frazier

Devotionals

The Life Your Spirit Craves

Not Without You

Not Without You Prayer Journal

The Life Your Spirit Craves for Mommies

Pursuit

Fiction

Love, Lies & Consequences

Through Thick & Thin: Love, Lies & Consequences Book 2

Shattered Vows: Love, Lies & Consequences Book 3

Out of the Shadows: Love, Lies & Consequences Book 4

Kairos: The Perfect Time for Love

Fate (The Perfect Time for Love series)

With Every Breath (The McCall Family Series, book 1)

With Every Step (The McCall Family Series, book 2)

With Every Moment (The McCall Family Series, book 3)

The Reunion (Langston Sisters, book 1)

The Wrong Seat (Langston Sisters, book 2)

The Missing Link (Langston Sisters, book 3)

Non-Fiction

How Long Are You Going to Wait?

Published by Encouraging Works

Printed by IngramSpark in the United States of America

ISBN: 979-8-9895509-1-3

This is a work of fiction. Names, characters, businesses, places, events and incidents are either the products of the author's imagination or used in a fictitious manner. Any resemblance to actual persons, living or dead, or actual events is purely coincidental.

Editor: Chandra Sparks Splond

For autographed copies, please visit:

www.natashafrazier.com

Acknowledgements

Once again, my Heavenly Father has given me the capacity and the provision to do one of the things that I love—write a story to share with the world. Thank You, Jesus!

Secondly, I must thank my family. Though God gives provision, the words on the page couldn't happen if my family didn't give up a moment or two of their time with me here and there. My husband, Eddie, and my children Eden, Ethan, and Emilyn—thank you for your love and support.

My parents and sisters, Courtney and Amber —Thank you for your encouragement and spreading the word! ☺

Chandra—Thank you for your editing expertise. This story wouldn't be as amazing without you.

Special thank you to my sisters, Tiera, Toccara, and Shenitra, who have prayed with me and encouraged me in my journey.

Page 35— I am thankful for your encouragement and feedback throughout my writing process. Thank you for making me better.

My CBLR family—Thank you for your support, readership, and love. I appreciate each of you.

And the Dream Team—Thank you for listening, providing feedback, and brainstorming with me.

Book clubs and Indie bookstores— Thank you for shining a spotlight on my books with your readership. I appreciate you.

Dearest reader—Thank you for supporting me by reading, reviewing, and sharing my books with others. (Please don't stop.) You're all I think about as I write. This story has been baking for almost four years, revised multiple times. Shortened. Lengthened. And lengthened again. Ginger and Brock's story is long overdue. So, here's to you, my dear reader! Enjoy!

Natasha

Batch

Of

Love

Natasha D. Frazier

Chapter One

It had been two years, two months, and eight days since Ginger Evans opened her bakery, Ginger's Goodies. And she should be proud of the fact that her business was still operating, but it wasn't the dream. And it was far from what she imagined when she promised her mom she'd pursue her passion. But she couldn't allow her emotions to crumble like crispy cookies. Not today.

As she'd done every morning since she moved back home after college graduation seventeen years ago, Ginger stopped in the kitchen to double check her father's medication for the day. She ran a finger over the pill boxes and took a deep breath before opening them to check each slot. He could do the task himself, but she insisted on taking care of him. She couldn't lose him, too. The least she could do was ensure he'd have his medication while she was away at work. In the Katy Mills outlet mall food court—as far away from her dream of having her own building as the east is from the west.

Satisfied every pill was in its proper place, Ginger closed the containers and reached for the recipe book she and her mom started and never got the opportunity to finish. She turned to the last page and skimmed the cake recipe using coconut flour—a recipe they tried ages ago when gluten-free baked goods weren't too popular. A knot formed in her throat. To force back the emotion that threatened to take over, she snapped the book shut, stuffed it in the island drawer, gathered her purse and keys, and headed out of the kitchen toward the front door.

"Glad I caught you before you left for work," her father, Kenneth Evans, called out.

Ginger jerked, spun on her heels, and clutched her chest with her free hand. She gasped like a swimmer whose head had been under the water for too long. "You scared me. I thought you were still in bed."

He cocked his head to one side and raised an eyebrow. "I'm awake early for the same reason you are. Figured it'd be a good idea to check in on you before you left for the day."

Ginger closed her eyes for a second and released a steadying stream of air. Today's date was etched in her mind like the engraving on her mother's tombstone. At thirty-eight years old, she'd think it would be easier to get through today, but seventeen years later, her mother's death date still numbed her. Made her recall every promise she made and failed to fulfill—like buying her own building and perfecting the cake recipe they started together.

"I'm okay, Dad."

As her father, Ginger knew he saw through her façade when he nodded and opened his arms wide. Ginger stepped closer and accepted his embrace. "Your mother would be proud of you and the journey you've taken, just as I am."

Fighting back tears, Ginger took a heavy breath before responding, "Thanks, Dad."

And somewhere deep down inside of her, Ginger knew her father was proud, and her mother would be as well. But sandwiched between two fast food restaurants in the mall's food court wasn't her idea of fully realizing her dream or anything like what she and her mom talked about. And today was a reminder of that fact.

Thirty minutes later, Ginger parked in the near empty parking lot in front of entrance seven outside of Katy Mills mall. Patrons traveled from within the city limits of Houston, TX, and surrounding areas to visit the outlet mall. Foot traffic hadn't been an issue for her growing company. In fact, she should be grateful for how much Ginger's Goodies had grown in the past two years, but couldn't help the drowning feeling of coming up short since she didn't reach her goal of having her own storefront a year after opening her business as planned. Her emotions intensified because of today's date.

Ginger pushed past her feelings of disappointment and strolled through the mall to the pink and white Ginger's Goodies designated space inside the mall's food court. She smiled at the sight of it. *Do not despise small beginnings,* her mother would always say, quoting Scripture. An overwhelming sense of peace washed over her, and she took that as a sign her mom was smiling down on her. It wasn't what she imagined, but at least she'd taken the steps to get closer to what she pictured for Ginger's Goodies, right?

Ginger was always prepared for the morning and lunch crowds with cookie dough she'd made, rolled into balls, and stored in the freezer the prior day. All she had to do was pop them into the oven when she came into work the following morning. Scones, muffins, and croissants were usually prepared the same day. Today was similar to most days with her serving customers almost non-stop until the end of the lunch hour.

However, she relished the time she could sit for a few moments to rest her feet.

"Ginger, any more of those chocolate chip cookies?" Lisa Atkinson called out, approaching the counter. Lisa's parents owned a bookstore, Between the Lines, about ten minutes away from the mall, so she stopped by the food court most days during lunch to support Ginger. She and Ginger became fast friends in college, bonding over their love for books and pastries.

"Always for you. What's new today?" Ginger used the tongs to grab Lisa's cookies from the warmer and rang up her order.

Lisa tapped her card on Ginger's machine. "I saw an advertisement on Facebook this morning I think you'd be interested in."

Once the payment processed, Ginger sent the receipt via text as she usually did. "Can we really trust anything we see on social media?"

"Don't be a petty Betty. This is right up your alley." Lisa held her phone in Ginger's line of view and hit the side key to illuminate the screen.

Ginger's belly dipped. Could this be for real?

A baking competition.

Twenty-five-thousand-dollar grand prize.

She needed every dollar.

Her breath caught in her chest while images of how she'd put the prize money to good use came to mind. A down payment on her new storefront.

There were three rounds. Every baker who desired to enter the *O Taste and See* baking competition had to first submit a video entry of them baking a triple-layered cake. The winning bakers would advance to the local competition, where they would bake in front of a live audience. Finalists would bake on live television, and the winner would receive a trophy, title of Master Baker, and a check for twenty-five thousand dollars. She could do without the title. The trophy would look nice in her new building, but what she really wanted and needed was the check and the publicity.

"So, what are we thinking? Are you going to do it?"

"This could be the break I need. I clearly need the money if I want to elevate my business." Could she trust this baking competition was legitimate though? There were too many scams happening nowadays and she didn't want to get caught up in one because she'd been blinded by what she wanted—her own storefront.

"I thought you'd be a lot happier about this. Seems I'm more excited than you. As soon as I saw this ad, I hopped in my car to come show it to you because I wanted to see your face. And I have to say, I expected a little more excitement from the woman who could probably bake in her sleep." Lisa leaned against the counter, broke a piece of cookie, and popped it into her mouth.

Ginger massaged her forehead and darted her eyes around the area to ensure no customers were approaching. She clasped her hands together, hung her head, and took a deep breath. If she could express her vulnerability to anyone, it would be her best friend, Lisa. "Just a bunch of jumbled up emotions, I guess. Today is the anniversary of my mom's death, and I can't help but wonder if I've made her proud." Even as the words tumbled from her lips, she knew that was a lie she'd repeated so much that had now taken on an identity of its own. But still, she couldn't help but wonder if there was some truth to the fable.

While she wanted and needed to seize this opportunity, in the pit of her belly, an uneasiness settled there. What if she didn't win? Would her dream of having her own building be further out of reach than she hoped?

"Oh, sweetie." Lisa gently squeezed Ginger's shoulders. "Lift your head and take a good look around you. You may not be where you want to be or have your own building, but you've done a pretty good job. And even if you don't win, I think the experience is everything. You've got this."

Ginger nodded and blinked back tears. She threw her head back and took a full heavy breath.

Pull yourself together.

Lisa jammed her fist onto her hip. "Now you know I'm not going to let you miss out on a chance to win twenty-five thousand dollars. And I'm sorry Mrs. Lily is no longer here with you, but the best way to honor her memory is to get out there and show them what Ginger's Goodies is all about. That's all she wanted for you."

"Yeah, you're right." Ginger's eyes glistened and she could feel a more confident smile tugging at the corners of her lips. She'd never forget the conversation she had with her mom where she promised to pursue her dreams of owning her own bakery. And after walking away from her engineering career in corporate America after fifteen years, there was no turning back. *I can do this.*

"So, is it a done deal? You're signing up, right?" Lisa tossed one of those you-need-to-get-your-act-together looks with twisted lips, wrinkled eyebrows, and her head cocked to one side. Standing eye level with Ginger at five feet five inches, Lisa could be intimidating sometimes.

"Done deal." Ginger's smile reached her eyes this time.

"Yes," Lisa squealed and wiggled her hips. "Twenty-five-thousand here we come."

Ginger chuckled at her friend's antics. "Thanks for the encouragement."

"Honey, you know I've got you." Lisa glanced down at her phone screen. "Ooh, let me get back to the bookstore so my mom can take her lunch break. Great chatting with you as always. You've got this baking competition in the bag. I can't wait to celebrate your win." Lisa pursed her lips in an air kiss.

Ginger threw a palm in the air to catch it and covered her heart. "Thanks, Lisa. You're the best."

"Nope, these are," Lisa waved the Ginger's Goodies package in the air and strutted out of the food court.

Ginger took a deep breath to calm her nerves. "I can do this. I can do all things through Christ who strengthens me." Ginger continued speaking softly, encouraging herself while she wiped down the countertop and mentally reviewed every ingredient she needed for her contest entry. She rummaged through her stainless-steel cabinets in her commercial kitchen to set aside coconut and almond flour. Ginger didn't like walking through the dark parking lot at night, so she planned to complete her contest entry at home where she wouldn't have any distractions. While in the food court, she needed to focus on her customers.

At closing time, she hurriedly rounded the corner into the walkway and crashed into a man's chest that had to be made of steel, knocking the cell phone out of his hand.

"Oh my gosh, I'm so sorry." She knelt to pick it up, but a strong hand on her wrist stopped her.

"No, no, you're okay. I should've been watching where I was headed. I was a little too preoccupied." He waved the phone in the air. "You're…good." His dark brown eyes widened.

"Ginger." Her name came off his lips in a whisper, a mixture of disbelief, recognition, and a plethora of other emotions she was certain.

Ginger's eyes trailed up to his and air trapped in her chest. Her eyebrows raised above her glasses, and her eyes fluttered. She suddenly needed water, and for a moment, she couldn't decide whether to run and scream or throw her arms around Brock Pearson's neck because she hadn't seen him in over twenty years.

"Brock," she'd finally said, still unable to complete a full cycle of breathing. All of a sudden, her brain ceased sending signals to the rest of her body as she stood in the middle of the food court, unable to take her eyes off him.

And him her.

The light chatter in the distance, the music humming from the PA system, and mall patrons all faded as she struggled to pull her thoughts together. Granted the Houston metro area was large enough not to run into the same person twice, but to see Brock after nearly twenty years tossed her off her axis. What was he doing there? Had he moved back to town? What was he doing with his life? All valid questions, yet Brock was none of her concern anymore.

She'd spent the entire summer before her freshmen year in college getting over their breakup.

"It's good to see you," he finally said. He had to be in as much shock as she was because his gaze remained fixated on her— a spiral of emotions flashing in his eyes. And she almost hated to see it because something stirred within her.

"Same," her voice croaked. That was all she could muster.

Before she knew it, he'd stepped forward and pulled her into a tight squeeze, the kind of hug one gave a precious friend they hadn't seen or talked to in ages. But that wasn't their story. And in the brevity of the moment, she forgot how things ended between them and succumbed to the strength of his arms and the memory of the warmth they provided her, even as a teen.

And she wouldn't doubt he had a momentary lapse in judgement as well because after a about fifteen seconds, his body stiffened as if reality crashed his remembrance. Their relationship ended on not-so-friendly terms. Although they were young, the pain was real.

He pulled back and so did she.

Brock's gaze lingered on her again. "Twenty years," was all he said.

Ginger repeated. "Twenty years."

"Look, Gin, I'm—" he paused and gathered his thoughts. For a moment, Ginger thought he was about to give an overdue twenty-year apology, but instead, he said, "I'm glad to see you're doing well."

"Same."

At this point, Brock probably thought she was losing her mind and that she'd forgotten how to speak. And maybe that was so. Ginger hadn't expected to see him after all this time. Her heart took on the speed of her whisk beating eggs into cake batter, betraying her mind that held tight to the grudge she had against Brock Pearson. But in that moment, her heart remembered what it was like to be loved by him. And she despised the recollection.

Ginger filled her lungs with air, released a steady breath, and took three steps back. "I'm sorry for almost knocking you over.

Umm, have a nice day." She pushed her glasses back in place and hustled out of his presence and the mall corridor, chastising herself. She'd just made an awkward moment even more awkward. But in her defense, what was she supposed to say? What was she supposed to do? She'd succumbed to a moment of weakness when she nearly melted into his arms, and that shouldn't have happened. Walking away was probably the smartest move she made since bumping into him.

Her heart galloped, creating an ache in her chest, but not from speed walking. Seeing Brock after all this time shouldn't affect her the way it did, but here she was engaged in an internal battle to push thoughts of him away.

Again.

His caramel skin reminded her of her favorite treat, but also reminded her of the face she'd fought hard to forget for the last twenty years. And of course, he'd be dressed in a tailored suit looking twice as good as he did since he broke her heart.

Ugh.

By the time she made it to her car, she could still smell his scent–masculine, like a combination of citrus and cedar. She hated she noticed, too, and being close to him caused a ripple to travel up her spine. A shiver ran through her at the mere thought of having that kind of reaction to selfish, self-centered Brock Pearson—the man who trashed her heart like a batch of burnt cookies.

Ginger buckled her seatbelt and started the engine, but couldn't bring herself to shift the gear into drive. She dug through her purse for her phone, tapping and swiping until she opened the contact card for Lisa. She hit the call button, but ended the call before it started.

What am I doing?

She couldn't allow Brock to affect her in the same way he'd done in the past. Her heart didn't have any shelf space for him so she couldn't give him space in her mind either. Twenty years had gone by without him in her life. She'd be just fine if she didn't see him for another twenty.

But even as the thought drifted through her mind, she knew that was another fable she'd learned to believe.

Chapter Two

What possessed him to wrap his arms around Ginger? Hugging her had been an impulsive move, one which he almost regretted. But having experienced the fragility of life through the death of friends he'd met in college, Brock understood how precious every breath was. And for that reason, he'd come close to apologizing for his part in their break-up. Although their relationship ended twenty years ago, the pain was real. And just like he'd never truly let go of his feelings for Ginger, he could see in her eyes that she still cared for him, too.

But he couldn't bring himself to say he was sorry because her actions were what tore them apart. And just as she'd walked away from him twenty years ago, watching her run away from their encounter five minutes ago left him with the same feeling of powerlessness.

No power to convince her to stay.

No power to find the right words to plead his case.

And no power to reel in his emotions for the one woman who had his heart on a hook.

He hadn't moved from the spot where they bumped into each other. More than ten shopping malls in the Houston metropolitan area, and the one time he visited Katy Mills, he ran into Ginger. What were the odds? After their breakup shortly after high school graduation, he hadn't seen her again. And he'd long convinced himself it was for the best since she changed the plan and chose not to attend The University of Texas at Austin where he had a baseball scholarship. Where they were supposed to start their lives together, graduate, get married, and build their family. Her choice changed the trajectory of his life.

Another person bumped into him, knocking him out of his reverie, and reminding him that he'd come into the mall to clear his mind. But instead, seeing Ginger did nothing but disorient him.

After that two-minute encounter, her presence lingered with him.

Her brown almond-shaped eyes drew him in like a camel to water. He'd spent many nights as a teen staring into them after their Friday night movie dates. Her large eyeglasses appeared too big for her face, yet they seemed to be perfect for her. After all this time, she retained her slender figure, and her mocha skin appeared as if it had never known a pimple. Her perfume—light, fresh, and powdery.

Brock took several steps back before turning on his heel to continue in the direction he was headed before the Ginger moment. That's when he noticed the pink and white counter and the large Ginger's Goodies signage, but the neon light wasn't illuminated, indicating that her shop was closed. His heart swelled, seeing that she'd taken the leap and started her own business. Despite their history, Brock was proud of her. Back when they were in high school, she'd bake cookies for him as gifts. A smile filtered across his lips at the memory.

But that was ages ago, and there was no reason for him to get stuck in the past. Brock shook his head to rid himself of the thoughts and continued his stride through the corridor. He needed to get out of the office and give himself time to decompress. The future of his law career was on the line.

His mentor, Andrew Hutchinson, planned to announce his retirement from Decadent Dough the next day. Brock had his own set of plans—to make a play for Andrew's seat as head of the corporate mergers legal team. At thirty-eight years old, he'd be the youngest person in their corporate office in a senior leadership position, but he'd been under Andrew's wing since he started at Decadent Dough eleven years ago. No one could question his abilities.

While in the mall, he searched for a new power tie. Though he had at least ten in his bedroom closet, this seemed like the perfect occasion to grab a new one. He had a reputation around the office for his great taste in ties. He had to look the part, make a good impression, and personify his work ethic. Aware of the rumors that his family's wealth and status got him in the door in the first place, Brock was up to the challenge to prove everybody wrong once he landed this promotion. He graduated law school at the top of his class and had just as much right to be there as anyone else. He could've joined his father's law firm, The Pearson Group, but he'd wanted nothing more than to prove he was as good of a lawyer as his father, and he could do it on his own merit.

Blood rushed through his fingertips when he walked through the entry of Jos. A. Bank. He browsed their selection of silk red ties to find one that complemented his style. One that communicated his readiness for whatever the executives at Decadent Dough would throw his way tomorrow.

He'd been waiting on this opportunity since his decision to join Decadent Dough's legal team. Give him mergers and acquisitions, contracts, or projects that would take him to the court room. His father practiced tax law, a specialty that put Brock to sleep. And it wasn't that he never gave tax law a shot. His first internship was with The Pearson Group. Though his family's firm, he stuck out like a strawberry in a pint of blueberries.

Brock's head pounded anytime he thought about taxes, the IRS, or anything even remotely close to either of them. His father was disappointed to learn he would be starting his career elsewhere, but Derrick Pearson would never stand in his son's way. He taught him to be a man who stayed true to his own convictions, which was easy to do with his career. A lot more difficult with his personal life.

Brock selected and purchased his promotion-ready tie, retraced his steps through the mall, and slowed to a stop when he neared Ginger's pastry shop again. What-ifs plowed through his mind.

What if he and Ginger started over?

What if they were meant to be together?

What if she broke his heart again?

Brock pushed those thoughts aside and strutted out of the mall. Now that he knew where to find her, he'd need the strength of Goliath to stay away. But he could do so. Years have passed since they've seen each other. There was no need to change that now.

Back in his office, Brock threw his attention into acquisition documents for a merger he'd spearheaded—a project he'd use as an example tomorrow to demonstrate why he was the perfect candidate for his mentor's position. After thirty minutes passed and he realized he'd been rereading the same paragraph over and over again, with zero understanding of what he read, he pushed the document aside.

He stood and stretched. Glancing down at the document on his screen, Brock surrendered to the truth. There was no way he would get more tasks accomplished that evening. Any other day, Brock would be excited about his work, but today, Ginger consumed his thoughts.

That one encounter should not bother him. And he was frustrated with himself because he allowed her to somehow sneak back into his thoughts in a matter of minutes. Brock gathered his laptop and stuffed it into his briefcase. Instead of going home, he drove to the gym to play a game of basketball. He always kept a fresh pair of clothes in his gym bag for days when he needed to work off his frustration. Exercise was his number one go-to when he needed to clear his thoughts.

Inside the locker room, he changed and headed to the rec court.

"What's up, B?" his friend, Jayden Reynolds, called to him. Although he and Jayden were both from the Houston metro area, they didn't meet until college. Outside of the occasional happy hour, their meet-ups were typically inside the gym. Like him, Jayden worked long, crazy hours at the accounting firm.

Brock gave him a one-hand clasp and pat on the back. "What's up, man?"

"Nothing but work, per usual."

Brock nodded. "I feel you. As much as you work, I'll be expecting to hear news of you making partner any time now."

Jayden grabbed a ball and dribbled. "You'd think so, but I feel like I'm on a hamster wheel, man. Hard work leading to nowhere, but I don't want to talk about that right now. Everything all good at the bread company?"

"Ask me that the next time you see me."

Brock and Jayden strolled up to a group of four guys entering the court.

"Down for three on three?" Jayden asked.

The group agreed to the game rules and shuffled to center court to play their game. For the next hour and a half, Brock exerted energy up and down the basketball court, blocking, assisting, and scoring points for his team. Today, he probably put in more effort than he normally did because of the incessant thoughts of Ginger.

Even after the game ended, the depth of her eyes hadn't been washed away from his mind. In the locker room, Brock toweled the sweat off his forehead and face.

Jayden tagged him with his towel. "Man, you were a beast out there today. Do you have something you need to get off your chest?"

Brock chuckled. "What are you talking about? I'm always a beast on the court."

Jayden cocked his head to the side. "So, in other words, you've got woman problems?"

Brock laughed off Jayden's comment. Ginger was no longer a problem for him. Hadn't been for years. But apparently his heart hadn't gotten the message. He shook his head. "Never that."

Jayden lifted an eyebrow as if he could sense there was something more, but didn't press the issue. They'd known each other long enough now that they knew when to back off. Now was one of those times. Besides, Brock couldn't explain the situation to anyone else because he couldn't make sense of why Ginger's eyes, half-smile, and softness in his arms kept attacking his mind either.

He said his good-byes and strolled out of the gym. While the game was good exercise, his thoughts about Ginger were still out of control. He climbed inside his car and slammed the door. This ended now. He made a choice to forget about her.

Again.

Brock shifted his car into gear, driving out thoughts of Ginger and their past. They were over and there was no going back. His career was the only thing he cared about and about the only thing in life he could control. Ginger had been his first lesson in choosing oneself over everyone else. She taught him that falling in love and relationships were for fools, and a fool, he was not.

Chapter Three

Throwback nineties R&B love songs played through Ginger's Bluetooth speaker while she hummed around her home kitchen and put the finishing touches on her cakes. Images of Brock flashed through Ginger's mind—images that made her heart race and her stomach clench. Chills came over her, though the kitchen was warm from the oven. Usually, baking helped her relax and clear her mind, but tonight, she could not be soothed. Wandering thoughts about Brock ran rampant.

What were the chances of running into him after all this time? Would he still love her baked treats? Had he grown to care about anything or anyone more than himself? She dusted her hands against her apron a little too roughly to dismiss Brock-centered thoughts and focused her attention on her ingredients and recipes she'd transform into her soon-to-be-prize-winning cake.

Since moving back in with her father after college to care for him, the one thing he could count on was Ginger transforming his kitchen into a home bakery. Tonight was more of the same, with the addition of her camera positioned on the tripod, recording her baking demonstration for the *O Taste and See* competition entry.

She recorded herself preparing two cakes, videos she'd also repurpose later to use on her social media channels. The first was a triple-layered chocolate caramel cake made with both coconut and almond flour, with the caramel layer in the middle, covered in whipped buttercream chocolate icing she made from scratch. The second cake was a triple-layered chocolate cake made with coconut flour, a recipe she and her mom created together, but never perfected. Once she got it right, she'd add it to Ginger Goodies' growing list of offerings. She topped it with a layer of pink fondant and added fun music symbol cutouts.

She scrubbed her hands along the pink custom-made apron her dad gave to her when she opened her bakery. Her mom made it for her but never got the chance to see her open Ginger's Goodies. She removed her cell phone from the tripod, snapped a few pictures and attached them to a text message to her best friend, Lisa.

G: What do you think?

L: I'm on my way. Give me about twenty minutes.

Ginger chuckled. Lisa always wanted first dibs on anything she came up with if she could help it.

"Whatcha got for me?" Ginger's father, Kenneth Evans, emerged from the living room into the kitchen eyeballing Ginger's creations. He clapped his hands, closed his eyes, and inhaled until she could see his chest expand. "Smells good in here."

Ginger's face lit up like a child on Christmas Day, and her smile widened. Her father's approving eyes were all the motivation she needed on many days. Her cheerleader. Her taste tester. The first person she convinced gluten-free and keto desserts could be as tasty as desserts prepared with wheat flour, or regular flour, as he liked to call it.

"Thanks, Dad."

She flipped her wrist to note the time on her smart watch.

"About ready to submit my entry for the baking contest I told you about earlier. I have an hour left." She chewed the right corner of her bottom lip and squeezed her fists at her sides to still the shaking.

He rounded the golden granite kitchen island, checking out both cakes. As her father, he wouldn't judge her as harshly as a stranger would, no matter how many times she asked him to.

"This one speaks to me." He stopped in front of the fondant-covered cake, turned the cake plate in a circle, and nodded with his approval.

Ginger sang, "Actually, I planned to submit this one." She gestured with jittery fingers like a game show model toward the chocolate caramel cake. "I'm still trying to perfect the recipe in the fondant covered cake."

"This one looks more professional. Everyone will be submitting cakes that look like that one. This one makes you stand out and speaks to your skill. Isn't that what you want?"

"Well, yeah, but…"

"You have time to work on the recipe. First round is judged on your video, right?"

"Right."

"And did you record yourself making the fondant cake?"

"Yes, Dad. I did a demo for both cakes." Something she hadn't initially planned to do, but needed to keep busy to steer her mind clear of Brock.

He slid onto a barstool in front of the cakes. "Then show this to the judges. In the meantime, grab a knife and I'll let you know what you need to adjust."

She chuckled and squeezed his shoulder. "I know I can count on your taste buds."

Ginger's head snapped up at the sound of the doorbell chime. "Oh, that must be Lisa. I sent pics of the cakes to her, and she said she was on her way. I'll get the door. And don't cut the cake yet, Dad, I want to take a few more pictures and make sure the lighting is good," she tossed over her shoulder on her way to the door.

"Hey, honey. Point me to the cake," Lisa exclaimed when Ginger opened the door.

"No, hello, how are you? Don't you wanna warm me up first?" Ginger teased.

"You know I love you." Lisa blew an air kiss.

"C'mon in here, Lisa. I'm about ready to dive in." Kenneth's voice rang through the house.

"Coming, Mr. Evans."

Lisa danced through the living room and into the kitchen. Her eyes widened with delight when she laid eyes on Ginger's cakes.

"The fondant cake looks even more stunning in person. I love it. I like them both, but this fondant cake is next level."

Kenneth nodded his head. "Told you."

Lisa looked from Ginger to Kenneth.

"Dad agrees with you. This isn't supposed to be the competition cake. I made it for fun, and to work on the recipe." And because the preparation required extra focus which was supposed to help keep her thoughts away from the way Brock looked at her earlier that day.

"Honey, please." Lisa dismissed Ginger's comments with a wave of her hand. "Don't be submitting a regular cake for something like this. You want to win, so you need to be different."

Kenneth leaned his head to the side and raised an eyebrow with the *I-told-you-so* look.

"You guys don't know if everyone will be using fondant, either."

"While that may be true, it's clear from the looks of this cake that you're a pro, and the judges need to see it. And not everyone can use fondant. You know how hard it is to mold that stuff to fit perfectly over a cake. The YouTube videos made it look so easy, but that wasn't my experience. I gave up long ago." Lisa chuckled. "Now, where's the knife?"

Ginger reached in front of Lisa and blocked movement with her arm. "Hey. Settle down. I need to take a couple more pictures first. Give me a few minutes."

She snapped a few more pictures, then turned her back to her father and Lisa, who were both quiet with their eyes glued on her and elbows poised on the countertop like they were at a starting line waiting for the referee to blow the whistle. These were the people who loved her most, so their presence should have brought her comfort but it didn't. Ginger shakily tapped, typed, and swiped, but hesitated before sending her video submission. Perspiration formed under her arms and on her forehead. Why was she so nervous? Oh yeah, twenty-five thousand dollars and potentially the difference between her operating out of the mall for who-knows-how-much-longer or purchasing the building she'd been eyeing for her new location—reaching the fullness of her dreams.

She silently prayed, *Lord, I love you, and I know you love me. Above all else, you know what I need. Help me to trust in your plan, even if this isn't it. Strengthen me and prepare my heart for what's next. In Jesus' name. Amen.*

Send.

Ginger released a pent-up breath and spun around to face them. "Alright, it's done. You may cut the cake now."

Lisa cheered and pumped her fist in the air. "Yes! Congratulations, Ginger."

"I haven't won yet."

"You've taken the first step, and that matters. Your mother would be so proud of you," Kenneth said. "I'm proud. From the beginning, you've taken leaps of faith to make your dreams come true. Such a strong young woman. Come here." He pulled her into his arms and squeezed.

Lily Evans had passed away in her sleep during Ginger's senior year in college. No warning. No health problems. God saw fit to call her home, and neither Ginger nor Kenneth could argue with that. When Ginger graduated, she moved back home, settled into her old room, and became a helicopter daughter. While he didn't need her help, she ensured her father went to all of his doctor's appointments and took his medicine daily to manage his hypertension. She couldn't risk losing him, too.

"Thanks, Dad. Mom knows she left me in good hands."

Ginger's love for baking had started in her mom's kitchen when she was four years old. Lily Evans would often call her into the kitchen, drape a pink-and-white striped apron over her body and allow her to stand on a stool to add chocolate chips to cookie dough or assist in adding icing to cookies or cakes. Ginger had a longing to make her proud, too. She'd give anything for her mom to taste one of the cookie recipes she'd created over the last couple of years. She wiped a stray tear from her eye, clasped her hands together, and blew a stream of air from her deflated chest.

"Alright. Dig in and let me know what you think."

She lifted her palms, backed away, wrung her fingers together, and waited for the verdict.

First, her dad cut a slice of the fondant-covered chocolate cake for himself and Lisa. Lisa cut slices of the chocolate caramel cake for herself and Ginger's dad. Lisa took the seat next to Kenneth, grabbed a forkful of chocolate fondant cake and chewed. Her eyebrows shot up, and she took another bite. She chewed thoughtfully. Eyebrows raised, head turned to the side, and chin lifted. Ginger glanced to her father whose expression looked like Lisa's.

Good? Terrible? Throw it away? What?

Well, they aren't spitting it out.

"So?"

"So what? Aren't you going to have any? Want me to cut you a slice?" Lisa answered.

Ginger squinted and folded her arms across her chest.

Lisa chuckled. "Just messing with you. Girl, you've outdone yourself. This is delicious, right?" She turned to Kenneth who continued to shove cake into his mouth.

"Ummm." His finger pecked the air over the cake. "Once again, baby girl, I'm proud to say my daughter made this."

"You guys really like it? You don't think the balance of coconut flour is off? Is it moist?" She grabbed a piece of cake from her dad's plate, and he swatted her hand.

"You have that big ol' cake in front of you, and you over here messin' with mine. Cut that out."

They shared a laugh.

Her apology was muffled with cake, which melted in her mouth, and a moan escaped her lips. She knew the chocolate caramel cake would be good because she baked with almond and rice flour regularly, so she didn't try that one at first. She was amazed at the moistness of the fondant cake she baked with coconut flour. She'd done it—finally perfected the coconut flour cake recipe she and her mom created together—balancing moisture, consistency, and flavor. Her confidence resurged, and her eyes misted. The competition title and the scripture Psalm thirty-four verse eight, from which it was inspired rushed to her mind. *Oh, taste and see that the Lord is good; Blessed is the man who trusts in Him.*

I hear you, Lord. I don't know what's going to come of this, but I trust You.

Lisa reached into her purse and removed two Tupperware bowls. "I'll take a slice of each for myself and Jayden and be on my way. You know he'll be saying I never think about him if I don't grab a piece for him." She winked and drove the knife down the center of the fondant-covered cake, then repeated her efforts with the chocolate caramel cake. Snapping on the lids, she eased the Tupperware back into her purse.

"Always thinking about Jayden, I see," Ginger teased.

"Don't you start."

"What? I'm only pointing out the obvious—something you and Jayden haven't seemed to pick up on yet."

"You know I'm not going to sit here and take this, right?" Lisa chuckled, stood, and kissed Ginger and Kenneth on the cheek, and said her goodbyes.

Ginger walked her outside and stood on the porch with her arms folded across her chest.

Lisa continued down the steps then turned to face her. "Don't think I haven't noticed that something is off with you, but unlike you, I wasn't going to call you out in front of your dad."

Ginger's eyebrows dipped, feigning innocence. "I don't know what you're talking about unless this has to do with the baking competition."

"Oh, no ma'am, that look on your face is different. Something else is on your mind. And since I'm still here, we may as well talk about it now."

"Nothing to talk about, really. Besides, talking about the situation will only make it linger and I just want the thoughts to go away."

Lisa's lips curled into her I-know-something-juicy smile. "If I didn't know any better, I'd think whatever is going on with you is about a guy, but we both know you're in a relationship with your business."

Ginger kept a straight face. That was Lisa's way of testing her and tonight Ginger would pass. She couldn't utter Brock's name because that would be equivalent to summonsing him up.

Lisa and Ginger engaged in a stare down before Lisa finally gave up, spun on her heels and walked to her car. After sitting her purse on the passenger's seat, she turned to Ginger. "It's late, so you get a pass tonight. Not sure why you won't make this easy on yourself and just tell me, but I suppose we can deal with the situation tomorrow.

Ginger smiled and huffed. If she had it her way, she wouldn't even remember Brock's name tomorrow, let alone want to talk about him and the effect those few minutes were having on her.

"Drive safe and text me when you make it home."

Lisa wiggled her fingers in the air and waltzed around to the driver's side of the car. "I will."

Ginger stood on the porch and watched until Lisa's taillights faded in the distance.

Back inside the house, Ginger wished her father good night.

"God's got you covered. Get some rest." Kenneth retreated to the master bedroom, leaving Ginger in the kitchen with her thoughts about the competition and Brock.

How soon would they announce the first-round winners?

What were the chances she'd run into Brock again? She shook the thought out of her head. Who cared if he had the most gorgeous eyes she'd ever seen? The last time she gave him her heart, he crumpled it up like a crunchy cookie and tossed it back to her.

Too bad she didn't have the right words or enough nerve twenty years ago to express her pain. And up until a few hours ago, she'd convinced herself she'd gotten past the hurt he caused her. Yet, a tiny part of her wanted closure. But closure was a fallacy, a lie made up by someone who didn't know any better. And Ginger knew better.

If she didn't see him for another twenty years, life would be doing her a favor. But no matter how much she wanted and needed that to be true, her heart screamed, *lie*. Seeing Brock again today, stirred feelings within her she buried when their relationship died.

To suppress her Brock-centered-thoughts, Ginger pulled out a fresh round of ingredients to test potential cookie recipes for her growing menu: oatmeal cranberry walnut, triple chocolate chip, strawberry cheesecake, and sugar cookies mixed with chopped Snickers.

Ginger's Goodies was now the love of her life.

Chapter Four

Steam filled the small space, and the familiar scent of Irish Spring permeated the air. The warm water relaxed Brock and slowed his racing heart. He rehearsed his pitch to the CEO, Ace Steele, which he'd give during this morning's meeting. This could be his only opportunity to ask for the Corporate Mergers lead attorney position before they replaced Andrew. He and Ace had a cordial relationship, though Brock didn't know him as well as some of his counterparts did. However, Brock believed the work he'd done over the years spoke on his behalf.

Brock spotted the expensive wool Italian suit he set aside for today and smiled confidently. Toweling off and splashing his favorite Dior cologne on his neck and wrists he took more care in getting dressed today. He breathed deeply, the ball of nerves returning. His phone beeped with a text message, but he didn't stop to answer it. Accessorizing with his Apple smart watch and monogrammed cufflinks, he grabbed his wallet, phone, and keys, and made a pit stop in the kitchen where the aroma of freshly brewed coffee called to him, thanks to the preset timer.

He poured the contents into a personalized travel mug his sister-in-law, Tina, purchased for him last Christmas, careful not to splash any on his tailored suit. No breakfast for him this morning. Skipping breakfast when he had a big event ahead of him had become practice. Coffee had to do. Besides, he wasn't hungry, physically anyway.

Brock slid behind the wheel of his Beamer coupe outside of his first-floor apartment, double-checked his briefcase in the passenger seat for his presentation, revved the engine, and backed out of the parking space. His phone rang displaying his mother's name across the illuminated screen.

"How are you feeling? Ready for your big day?"

"Mom, you know I got this. I am *the* Brock Pearson. How are you?"

"Be confident, not cocky, Brock."

Brock could practically feel the stern look that matched her voice. Brock corrected himself. "I'm ready, Mom. I have a good feeling about this."

"Well, I'll be praying for you."

Brock ignored her comment. She, of all people, knew how he felt about prayer, God, church, and anything else that had to do with religion. He cleared his throat. He could kick himself for not calling her first to wish her happy birthday.

"Happy Birthday, Mom! You know the rule is for me to call you first."

"Thank you, but you know I don't care anything about your made-up rules." He could hear the smile in her voice. "I'm trying to figure what your father has up his sleeves for this evening."

"And you called me thinking I'd tell you because Bryce hasn't spilled the beans."

She chuckled. "I called you first. Plus, I don't need to talk to Bryce, his wife will tell me everything I need to know."

Brock laughed because she wasn't wrong. Ever since his brother introduced Tina to their family, their mom and Tina took an instant liking to each other.

"But never mind that, I called to wish you well. I'll be praying and thinking of you throughout the day. I love you. See you later."

"Thanks, Mom. I love you, too."

Ten minutes later, his brother, Bryce called.

"'Sup, dude?" Brock answered.

"Hey, bro, checking in on you. Today's the big day, huh? How are you feeling?"

While Brock loved his family and appreciated their support, he almost wished he hadn't said anything about his work intentions until he'd sealed the deal. "Yeah, yeah, I'm good."

"I'm proud of you. You're a Pearson man. Law is circulating through your blood, but I don't want to see you turning into one of those bloodsucking lawyers racing to the top." Bryce, like their father, was also a tax attorney who worked for The Pearson Group. Slightly disappointed Brock wouldn't be joining their family firm, he'd gotten over it and was glad he at least decided to practice law.

"Thanks for slick calling me a snake, but you know that's not me. No games played here."

"I hear ya. I'm only saying folks racing to the top usually get involved in some shady business. I don't want that to be you." Bryce paused a beat. "Hey, don't forget about Mom's surprise birthday party tonight."

"You know I wouldn't forget about her party. Maybe yours, but not hers."

Bryce laughed. "Whatever, man. You ordered the cake, right?"

Brock slapped his forehead. He'd been so caught up in his own world, he completely forgotten about ordering a specialty cake.

Greeted by silence, Bryce pressed, "Don't tell me you forgot about Mom's birthday cake."

"Oh, no, no I didn't. Got it all taken care of." Brock gritted his teeth. His mind raced back and forth trying to figure out when he even agreed to get the cake or if he was assigned the task, either way it didn't matter at this point.

"Alright then. Just checking. Have a good day, bro. See you tonight."

Now, this was not how his day should be starting. He hadn't even made it to work yet and had a fire to put out. *Think Brock, think.* Two of the specialty bakeries he'd heard his mom mention in prior conversations crossed his mind. Shelly's Sweets and Conscious Confections. Would they even be willing to bake a cake on such short notice?

He straightened in his seat, pulled into the parking garage, and glanced at the clock on his dashboard. Twenty minutes early. Under ordinary circumstances, he'd sit in the car for another ten minutes and prepare his mind for work, but he now had a second mission.

With purposeful strides, he went inside the twenty-five-story building where the Decadent Dough company logo graced the front in oversized white script letters. Inside the elevator bank, he pressed the up arrow and waited for the next door to open.

Inside the elevator, he glanced down at his watch: fifteen minutes left before the start of his workday. And while he didn't have an official start time, Brock preferred to begin work at eight. He casually stepped off the elevator, his cool relaxed demeanor opposite of the jumble of nerves gyrating in his belly. He entered the double glass-paneled doors and his eyes darted to the receptionist. A warm, friendly smile spread across her face.

In a sing-song voice, Ms. Janet greeted him and handed him a brown folder with his name in script. "Brock, good morning." Janet Gordon, who Brock affectionately called Ms. Janet, was the mother figure of the office. Though she insisted he drop the formality, he couldn't bring himself to address her by her first name despite the fact they were in a professional environment. She had to be his mother's age or older, doing so felt wrong.

Brock accepted the folder with a crooked smile. "Good morning, Ms. Janet."

"You'll be in the large conference room today. Would you like bottled water? We'll have breakfast coming in about thirty minutes."

Lightbulb.

He raised his insulated travel mug. "No, I'm fine thanks. I'll drink my coffee for now. However, I need a huge favor—like really huge—and I hate to even ask this of you." Until now, Brock had made a point of keeping personal matters separate from work.

"How can I help?" She leaned forward, gripped her elbows, and rested them on the desk, her chin jutted in his direction with the eagerness of a soldier reporting for duty.

Brock glanced around the reception area and stepped closer to the oversized desk positioned to the right of the entrance. She could see every angle of the area from where she sat. The large conference room to her right was shielded behind glass panels with a horizontal frosted privacy stripe. The sitting area for guests boasted a white leather sofa and two matching white leather chairs. A coffee table decorated with a small indistinct plant and law magazines gave the area a homey feel.

"I need to order a birthday cake, preferably from somewhere nearby." Brock rattled off the names of the bakeries he knew of that could get him what he needed.

Ms. Janet grabbed her chest. "Oh, both of those bakeries have shut down."

Brock frowned. "I need a birthday cake today, Ms. Janet, preferably prepared by five this evening. Think you can check around and find a bakery available on such a short notice?"

"Let me check around and see what I can find."

"Thank you so much. I owe you, big."

"My pleasure." Ms. Janet waved her hand. "Enjoy your day and stop by to see me around the lunch hour."

At the start of his morning meeting with the executives, corporate mergers legal team, and his mentor, Andrew Hutchinson, Brock opened the folder he'd received from Ms. Janet and passed out copies of the letter of intent and acquisition agreement he'd prepared on Decadent Dough's behalf in their latest acquisition of Breads and Bagels. Brock spearheaded the negotiations and due diligence through their merger deal. He smoothed his hand along his red silk tie and updated the team on the progress of the merger deal with Breads and Bagels.

"With the negotiations settled, we're ready to close. Ace, the final agreement is in your inbox awaiting your signature."

"The folks at Breads and Bagels have had nothing but good things to say about you, Brock. Thank you for representing

Decadent Dough well," Ace complimented. "Your hard work is not going unnoticed."

Brock nodded. "Thank you, sir." His chest doubly swelled at Ace's praise.

After Brock finished his case discussion, he and Andrew reviewed the status of Andrew's current projects. The entire time, Ace's eyes remained glued on Brock. He couldn't be certain if he had a case of paranoia because of his intentions or if Ace had an agenda of his own that involved him.

After they'd gone through Andrew's major projects, Brock took his shot.

"So." Brock leaned forward in his seat, clasped his hands together, and rested them on the oversized mahogany conference table. "Any thought on who will take lead on the merger team when Andrew leaves?"

Ace leaned back in his seat and rubbed the gray hairs covering his chin, seemingly surprised by Brock's interest. He raised his salt-and-pepper eyebrows and tilted his head toward Brock to encourage him to continue speaking without answering his question.

"Look, Ace, I've been working beside Andrew since I started here eleven years ago. As the current senior attorney on all of his projects, I'm ready to take the lead on the corporate mergers legal team." Brock passed around copies of his resume and highlighted his most recent accomplishments to Ace, Andrew, and the rest of the team.

Ace chuckled, and a smug smirk rested on the corners of his lips. "Listen, Brock, I do like you, but you're not ready. You need more experience."

Brock's chest deflated, but he rebounded and masked his disappointment with a toothless smile. "And what kind of experience is that? Give it to me."

Andrew shifted in his seat and turned to Brock. "I think what Ace is trying to say is you've done an excellent job so far, but you need something that sets you apart. There are at least two other candidates with the same level of experience."

"I like you, Brock, and I've said as much to Andrew when we discussed your potential." Ace leaned forward and looked him squarely in the eye. "So, here's what we'll do. Andrew retires in thirty days." Ace pointed a finger in his direction. "I'll give you the opportunity to prove you have guts. Dawn and Shawna have their eyes peeled for a unique Mom & Pop business to acquire and operate as a subsidiary of Decadent Dough. If you can come to the table with a viable acquisition target in that time, the job is yours."

Andrew slapped him on the back. "Brock can handle that. He's been waist deep in merger deals for five years."

Though Brock had the legal knowledge of mergers and acquisitions, it was not in his line of work to find targets to acquire. But if it meant he'd get a corner office, double the pay, and the power and prestige, he was all for it.

"You can count on it." Brock flashed one of his I-got-this kind of smiles, rose from his seat, and confirmed his agreement to Ace's terms with a firm handshake. Although this promotion came with stipulations, as far as Brock was concerned, he'd already sealed the deal.

When his meeting ended, it was time for lunch, so Brock made a beeline out of the conference room toward Ms. Janet. He tugged at his shirt collar.

"Do we have anything?" His question was a half plea.

"There is a bakery across the street located inside the mall. Great reviews."

Ginger's image came to mind and without having to confirm, he knew in his soul her bakery was the one Ms. Janet found. They weren't necessarily at a point where she'd do him any favors. As far as he was concerned, he'd ruined his mother's birthday party.

Dang it.

He smoothed a palm over his face.

Ms. Janet's voice snapped him out of his spiraling thoughts. "I can order it for you." She handed him a notepad. "Write down the details: Flavor. Icing. Wording. Pickup or delivery. I'll need the address if you choose delivery."

"She'll deliver?" Brock caught himself. "I meant are you sure they'll deliver?" His eyes widened and his mouth was agape for several seconds. Maybe she'll do so if she didn't know it was for him. Ms. Janet placing the order was for the best and would increase his chances of Ginger helping him out. Besides, if she delivered the cake, he probably wouldn't have to run into her again.

"Not sure yet, but we can always ask."

"That would be a lifesaver." He scribbled his mother's preferences on the notepad, added the address, and handed Ms. Janet his credit card. If Ginger delivered the cake, he would have a few extra minutes to weave through traffic, and at least arrive at his parents' house on time, possibly after she'd already done her business there.

Brock slid the notepad over to Ms. Janet, and she chuckled slightly at his description. Chocolate cake and chocolate icing. She shook her head and flashed that smile mothers gave when their child was wrong, and they didn't want to hurt their feelings. "I'll take care of everything."

Brock lifted prayer hands to his chest. "Thank you."

Chapter Five

Ginger pressed the answer button on her Bluetooth headset.

"Ginger's Goodies. How may I serve you today?"

Ms. Janet introduced herself. "Listen, I've read wonderful reviews about your bakery, and a friend of mine is in a bind. I know it's last minute, but is there any way at all you could make the birthday cake for his mother today? It's her sixtieth birthday," she added.

She'd missed the cutoff for same-day cake orders, but Ginger hated to turn down new customers.

"I'm sure he'd be willing to pay extra for the last-minute order," Ms. Janet pleaded with Ginger.

Ginger mentally ran through her remaining tasks for the day. She already had frozen cookie dough she could bake if she needed to refill her warmer. She'd still have time to prepare dough for tomorrow as well. There was nothing stopping her from preparing the cake other than the fact that she didn't like to rush. "Okay. If it isn't too fancy, I can take care of it for you."

"And by any chance, do you deliver?"

Ginger smiled. "I will for you, Ms. Janet."

"You, my dear, are a lifesaver." Ms. Janet called out the details of the order, including the address.

Ginger scribbled down the order information, ended the call, and went to work. She hadn't delivered before, but Ms. Janet had been so kind. *Maybe delivery is something to consider in the near future,* she thought as she measured, mixed, and poured the batter. She should hire help because running back and forth between the small commercial kitchen and the counter to serve the lunch crowd was running her ragged.

Ginger took a deep breath, audibly exhaled, and sat on her stool in front of the counter when her customer line dwindled. The timer cut through her short-lived break and Ginger disappeared into the kitchen to remove the cake pans from the oven. She placed them on a cooling rack and returned to find Lisa waiting at the counter.

"Hey, lady. What's up?"

"Came for my after-lunch snack. You didn't stay up too late last night, did you?" Lisa leaned forward and rested her elbows on the countertop.

"No, not really," she lied. She stayed awake baking until she could hardly keep her eyes open. Keeping busy was the only way to keep Brock out of her mind.

"Good." Lisa paused a beat. "So, are you ready to tell me what was bothering you last night?"

"No, but check this. I'm baking that three-layer chocolate cake again. Got an order a while ago."

"Yes. And they will love it as much as we all did. I just got off the phone with Jayden. He told me to tell you that cake was amazing."

"Give him my thanks."

Lisa jerked into a standing position. "Okay, but something is still bothering you. What is it?"

"Nothing," Ginger answered and shrugged, scooping Lisa's regular order into a bag, telling a half-truth.

Lisa reached across the counter and placed her hands firmly on Ginger's shoulders. "What's going on? I hate it when you make me beg for information."

Ginger bit down on her bottom lip and squinted, trying to decide if she should share her Brock-thoughts with Lisa. Maybe talking about her feelings would help her make sense of them.

Lisa leaned in and raised an impatient eyebrow.

"Just a little bothered, but I know I shouldn't be. I ran into Brock Pearson yesterday, which is so strange because I haven't seen him in about twenty years. I haven't been able to stop thinking about him since. And what's even crazier is the cake I'm baking reminds me of him for some strange reason." Ginger ended her ramble, sucked in a breath and braced herself for Lisa's commentary.

"Shut up! Love-of-your-life Brock Pearson? The one you sulked over freshman year in college?"

"Okay, now that was too much." Ginger held up her hand.

"I kinda want to meet him." Lisa popped a piece of cookie into her mouth.

"No, you don't. You're not missing anything. Trust me."

"*Hmmm.* Well, okay then." One of those yeah-right-I-don't-believe-you smirks tilted the corners of Lisa's lips. "But that's not what your face says. Clearly there are some feelings bubbling beneath the surface, otherwise you wouldn't have that look on your face."

"What look?"

"The look that says you ran into the love of your life yesterday and neglected to call your best friend immediately with deets."

Ginger threw her head back and laughed. "I shouldn't have expected anything else from you."

"What? Honesty?"

Ginger shook her head.

"Why don't you call him?"

"I don't have his number. Plus, I don't have much to say to him."

"You'll find the words. Trust me. And secondly, most people keep the same number for years. Shoot, he probably kept his number hoping that you'd one day call him."

Ginger huffed and squinted. "I know you're needed back at the bookstore."

Lisa laughed. "Probably. But you don't have to push me away." She backed away with her palms in surrender. "I know when I'm not wanted, but you're not off the hook. We'll finish the conversation later."

Ginger waved her off and released a heavy sigh when she could no longer see her friend. What was Lisa thinking, anyway? She couldn't call Brock after all this time. And say what? She had to let that encounter go. She wished she could just thrust him out of her mind or work hard and make thoughts of him disappear. But based on the last twenty-four hours, that was not her story.

She reviewed the order slip. While she waited for the cake to cool, she made the icing and busied herself preparing cookie dough for the next day. After placing her first batch of triple chocolate chip cookies in the refrigerator, she pulled out her phone and looked over the baking competition details again. The one thing she could look forward to and concentrate on other than seeing Brock yesterday. Her stomach knotted. *Please, God. I need this.*

Two hours left before delivery.

Ginger iced, decorated, and boxed the cake. She keyed the address into her phone's GPS, closed her shop thirty minutes early, and headed to her car.

Ginger pulled up to a stone Mediterranean-style home and entered the semi-circled driveway.

Why did the home feel familiar?

Her belly dipped. She knew precisely why familiarity drenched her.

Please don't let me see him.

She glanced down at her pink customized Ginger's Goodies apron. No uniform, but she wanted to represent her business. Though she was only delivering a cake, she felt under dressed pulling up to the fancy home. She got out of the car and walked around to the passenger-side door, rubbing her perspiring hands on her apron before picking up the cake box.

Shakily, she lifted the box out of the car and closed the door with her hip. The creases of her elbow perspired coupled with the beads of sweat popping up along her hairline. *Get it together, girl. You're delivering a cake.* Preparing to balance the cake in one hand to ring the doorbell, she paused at the sound of footsteps pounding the brick pavement behind her.

"I'll get that," a familiar baritone voice called. She froze like the dried concrete beneath her feet. And not just her movement, but her heart as well. If her heart stilled another moment, she'd need a defibrillator.

You have no reason to be nervous.

She turned to thank him and fumbled with the cake box. *Thank God, I didn't drop it.* Ginger locked eyes with Brock. Her arms and legs tingled, and the tiny hairs on the back of her neck stood up. Her throat was suddenly dry again. The familiar pounding in her chest returned. Booming. Thumping. Thudding.

A nervous chuckle escaped Ginger's lips. "Almost knocked you over again. Sorry about that."

"No, I think you saved me today." His voice was as smooth as the whipped icing on his mother's birthday cake.

She swallowed to moisten her drying throat. She shouldn't be acting like this. Brock Pearson stood before her. Not some random handsome guy she didn't know. Brock broke her heart, so every fiber of her being should not be betraying her right now. Ginger pasted on a smile. The sooner she could disappear from his presence, the better off they'd be.

After a moment of awkward silence, he added, "It's nice to see you're doing well." He extended his hand toward her, holding the cake in the other hand. "It's really good to see you again, Gin."

Ginger accepted his hand, which was awkward considering he hugged her yesterday. However, the handshake was probably safer. She didn't want or need to be in his arms again. They were too familiar.

Too comforting.

Too much like right.

They shook slowly, lingering a bit longer than needed. A tingling sensation sliced up her arm and made its way to her heart, kneading it like a mound of dough.

"I hope your mom enjoys the cake." she said softly, her hand still in his. She should have pulled away, but she couldn't and besides, he hadn't let go.

"If she loves it, you've earned yourself a customer for life. She's always hosting something." He chatted with her as if they hadn't had a twenty-year lapse in communication. As crazy as it sounded, she wanted to be upset with him for how things ended.

She wanted him to be equally as frazzled about seeing her again.

And she wanted him to accept blame for their break-up and be just as unsettled about how their relationship ended, too.

"Well, that's good to know. I'm located in the food court inside of Katy Mills' mall for now."

"I saw."

"Oh, well all of my info is on the card attached to the box." She pointed. "And thanks for your business. Enjoy the cake and the party."

She slid her hand out of his grasp and retraced her steps back to her two-door coupe. Inside she drew in a long breath. He still smelled good and looked even more handsome than yesterday. She could kick herself for noticing. But honestly, what woman wouldn't? And what were the odds of seeing him again today? And bake a cake for his mom?

Ginger drove away and inwardly chastised herself. Hopefully, Brock didn't take that handshake the wrong way. Allowing him to hold her hand a moment too long. So unprofessional. She shook her head. That interaction could've gone a lot better than it did. Instead, she nearly melted at his touch. And after years of not seeing him, she couldn't understand why he still had any kind of effect on her.

She couldn't forget the Brock he had been, and there was no indication the Brock that stood in front of her today was any different. Ginger had to get over him. Again. Though she hoped to make a repeat customer out of his mother, it was best for her and Brock to remain as they were. That meant no more hugs, handshakes and pretending they weren't once dreaming of a future together.

Or thinking about him.

Or having anything to do with him at all.

It had only been twenty-four hours since she'd run into him the first time, and he was already making her crazy again.

Chapter Six

Ginger's presence lingered with him, though Ginger didn't seem fazed by their encounter. And that was just as well because he had more pressing things on his mind—like how he'd get this new position. Besides, his ego hadn't quite healed from the last time he and Ginger were together more than twenty years ago.

"Bro, what's up?" Bryce threw his hands in the air like a referee signaling a touchdown. "You got the cake, I see." Dressed in khakis and a short-sleeved Henley shirt, he walked into the living room, hugged Brock, and slapped him on the back. "C'mon man. Mom should be here soon. She's leaving the hair salon now." Bryce ushered him out of the area.

Bryce's intrusion snapped Brock out of his Ginger thoughts. He followed Bryce through the foyer into the kitchen where their dad stood at the oversized chef island, stuffing lobster tails, extra-large gulf shrimp, and sausage into an oven bag for a seafood bake.

Brock tapped his chest with his fist, coughed and cleared his throat. "Dad, you sure you have enough spice in there?"

"I got this. Your mom likes it spicy. You wait." Derrick puffed his chest.

Derrick Pearson wanted to make this birthday more meaningful by doing everything himself, except the cake, he left that to the professionals.

"Do we have some sort of backup plan?" Brock whispered to Bryce when Derrick turned his back to place the pan in the oven.

Bryce shook his head, arms folded, eyebrows raised, expressing the same concern as his younger brother.

"Where's my sister-in-law?"

"Playing chauffeur. She and Mom did the whole spa day thing. Massages, manicures, and pedicures. Last stop was the hair salon. Should be here in about fifteen more minutes." Bryce hit the side button on his cell to wake the screen.

"Okay. Anything else I can do, Pops?" Brock asked. "Decorations? Balloons? Maybe clean up a bit in here."

"Decorations have been taken care of," Bryce interjected. "Dining room is ready for the festivities, but first let's check out the cake." Bryce tugged at the flaps but hesitated after reading the pink stickered logo on top and slowly turned to look at Brock. His eyes widened, then he raised questioning eyebrows, but Brock only shrugged a shoulder.

Brock kept his voice low. "Long story, and I don't want to talk about it." Seeing Ginger again brought about uncomfortable feelings and talking about them meant acknowledging how he felt. And he didn't want to do that.

His brother cocked his head to the side, his tone even with Brock's. "Man, you can't expect any of us not to have questions."

"Later. Okay?" Brock had no intentions of talking about Ginger, but he had to nip the conversation before his father got involved.

Bryce placed the cake on the island and lifted the top off the cake box. Brock shifted from one foot to the other, sucked in his breath, and waited for a reaction from his father and brother.

His dad nodded his approval. "Looks good."

Brock relaxed and stretched his neck around to look at the cake. But at this point, it wouldn't have mattered if the cake was busted, he couldn't come to the party without one. He would've had to apologize and make it up later.

"Think Mom will like it?" Brock asked.

The three men stood checking out the cake, both Bryce and Brock the spitting image of their father, something Brock heard his entire life. Similar muscular build, same height, give or take an inch, but different hair. Derrick was now bald. Bryce sported short braids with a fade, and Brock preferred a low fade.

"Nice, son," Derrick patted him on the back. "Bryce thought you'd walk in here with a grocery store cake straight from the shelf." He chuckled. "Looks good, but I think the true test is how it tastes. She cares more about that than how it looks, though that won't stop her from taking pictures to post to Instagram."

Brock's chest rose and fell in relief while he shot warning eyes at Bryce, daring him to bring attention to Ginger's logo sticker atop the cake box. Thankfully, his father hadn't noticed, or at least chose not to mention the logo.

Bryce slapped his shoulder. "Come help me get something from my car."

Brock followed him outside, certain there was nothing he needed other than to get in his business.

Bryce popped the trunk.

"There's nothing in here." In fact, the only purpose the trunk door served was to block the Texas sun.

"Yet you knew that already and you came out here anyway."

They stood in a similar stance with their arms folded across their chests.

"I thought you and Ginger were over a long time ago."

Brock blew a stream of air. "And that means I can't patronize her business?"

Bryce squinted. "Seems like this came out of nowhere. When did you start seeing her again?"

"I'm not. We're not even friends." If he said anything more, he'd let on to the truth that he hadn't ordered the cake until today.

"Do you really want to stand here and act like this? It's hot and mom and Tina will show up any minute. I'm sure they'd love to hear this story."

The last thing Brock wanted was for his nosey, or caring family, depending on the viewpoint, to get involved. "Why are you so concerned?"

"Honestly, I wasn't concerned at first. The look on your face when her logo caught my attention is what made me think you need help."

Brock laughed. "Help? Man, stop."

Bryce laughed, too, but then his expression turned serious. "It's okay if you still have some sort of feelings for her, man. Sometimes it's like that and you can't control who you love."

"I never said I still love Gin."

Bryce closed the trunk. "I'm your brother. You didn't have to. But whatever you do, find a way to deal with whatever is going on inside." Bryce pressed a fist to Brock's chest.

"So, you're a relationship expert, now, too?"

Bryce slapped him on the back and led him back to the front door. He pointed at the camera. "No, I saw the two of you on camera."

Brock had no argument there. Good thing Bryce didn't push the issue because Brock remembered how his heart betrayed him on the porch.

"Plus, you obviously haven't loved anyone the same way you loved her. When's the last time you brought a woman over here to meet us?"

"You know I don't like to get anyone's hopes up." Brock ended every relationship when the woman got serious. He hadn't met anyone's family and had no intention of bringing any one around his own family. Casual relationships worked best for him.

"Exactly. Never."

They strolled back inside the house to the kitchen.

Derrick threw the kitchen hand towel over his shoulder and leaned against the counter with his arms folded across his chest. Brock braced himself and hoped his dad wouldn't ask Ginger related questions. "So, what's the verdict? You gettin' the promotion?"

Brock relaxed and shrugged. Though he didn't have the precise answer he wanted about his career at Decadent Dough, he'd much rather talk about work than Ginger. "They've got me jumping through hoops. I have to find a mom-and-pop bakery that would be interested in an acquisition agreement to operate as one of Decadent Dough's subsidiaries."

"You sure you want to do that, son? Sounds a little out of your line of work."

Brock hiked his shoulders again. "I won't get involved in anything shady, Pop. I know when to take a step back." But did he really? That promotion looked pretty darn shiny, and he didn't mind getting his hands a little dirty to get it. But he couldn't admit that. Derrick Pearson would go off on a tangent about how he'd been raised better, and probably remind him that he wouldn't have to do any of that at Pearson Group—the legacy he built for his sons.

"Well—" Bryce slapped his shoulder— "this is the life you wanted. You're hard-headed enough to prove you can do it."

"Looks like you know me so well." Brock shrugged out of his suit jacket, went to hang it in the coat closet, rolled his sleeves, took the kitchen cleaner spray, and busied himself spraying down the countertop.

Bryce took two steps out of the kitchen and turned his ear toward the front entry door. "I think I hear Mom and Tina outside. Dad, this is your show. Want me to blindfold her? Or keep her outside until you can get the seafood bake out of the oven and plated?"

Brock paused wiping down the countertops and joined Bryce in awaiting instructions.

"I don't think she'd like the idea of a blindfold with her hair done. Leading her straight to the dining room will be fine. I haven't checked so however it's decorated is on you." Derrick tilted his head and pointed to Bryce.

"As long as it's pink and green, it's fine," Bryce said.

"I don't know. You know how she's always saying she likes to do stuff in 'A-class, deluxe fashion.'"

Bryce nodded. "Yeah, her fancy way of saying she wants it done in excellence."

"I hope you kept that in mind," Derrick mumbled, shook his head, and opened the oven door to check on the seafood bake. "As long as it's pink and green, tuh! Y'all not about to mess up my wife's day by doing the job halfway."

Seafood bake was ready. Brock grabbed the Swiffer and cleaned the floor before Tina and Mom made it inside.

"Happy Birthday, Mom." Bryce greeted her first with a hug and kiss to her cheek. "I love your hair."

"Thanks." She twirled around to show off her layered haircut.

Bryce shifted his attention to his wife, Tina, and Brock moved in to greet his mother.

"Happy Birthday, beautiful." Brock lifted his mother off her feet and squeezed her in his arms.

She tilted her chin and looked up at him with sparkling eyes. "How did it go?"

"Fine, but we can talk about it later. Today's your day." They followed Tina and Brock into the dining room filled with pink and green foiled balloons. Stringed Happy Birthday lettering stretched from wall to wall. Foil balloons in the number sixty were tied to a green vase filled with pink roses. A fruit tray and vegetable tray sat on either end of the eight-foot rectangular table draped in a pink tablecloth. An empty silver platter was the centerpiece. Bryce laid out the square floral China plates adorned with pink and green roses. Stevie Wonder's rendition of the "Happy Birthday" song was on repeat. Two large pink confetti birthday giftbags sat on a small table, covered in a green tablecloth in the corner of the room.

Della's smile reached her eyes. "Nice."

Bryce pulled out a chair for her at the head of the table. Tina placed a pink sixtieth birthday sash over her shoulder and a tiara on top of her head. Brock saw the gift bags and remembered he'd left his gift in the car. He excused himself to retrieve it, returning to see his dad entering the dining room with the large seafood platter. Brock followed him inside.

"*Ooh,* you've outdone yourself, honey!" She lifted her head and puckered her lips. Derrick happily obliged.

"Anything for you, my love," he murmured against her lips. "My only hope is it meets your expectations. Happy birthday, darling."

Brock brought a tray of wineglasses along with a bottle of Chardonnay, placing a glass at each place setting. He didn't drink, so he brought a bottle of water for himself.

Brock stood at his mother's side. "May I pour?"

Della's smile never left her face, and she glanced around the room, seemingly appreciating their effort. "Please, do."

Brock filled his mother's glass first, then moved to his father, who had taken the seat to her right. After filling Bryce's glass, Tina covered her glass with her hand and gently shook her head. Brock took no thought to it, but Bryce noticed.

"Wait, does that mean…?" Bryce's words trailed off, and Tina's smile grew wide. She nodded. "Yes," he screamed and jumped out of his seat. Everyone's attention was now on the two of them.

"What is it?" Della's head whipped in their direction. She'd been engrossed in a side conversation with Derrick.

Brock took the seat next to his dad and across from Bryce and Tina. He also waited for an explanation.

Tina smiled shyly, tugged at Bryce's arm, and pulled him back into the seat next to her, raising her eyebrows in warning.

"*Ummm,* nothing that can't wait." She reached for a wheat dinner roll.

"I think I'd like to know what has Bryce jumping out of his seat. Sounds like something we'd all want to know," Della pressed, glancing between the two of them, Bryce with a goofy grin plastered across his face.

"Momma Pearson, I don't want to take away from your d—"

"We're having a baby," Bryce interrupted. He jumped out of his seat again.

Della squealed. She pulled her hands into her chest and stomped her feet. "I'm gonna be a grandma. Now *that's* a birthday present." She jumped out of her seat and ran to hug Tina and Bryce. "I'm so happy for y'all. Blessings, blessings. Yes, Lord. I've been waiting on this moment for five years." She lifted her hands toward heaven and jogged in place until she was breathless.

"Congratulations, Bryce and Tina," Derrick lifted his glass toward the two of them before he sipped.

"Congratulations, guys." Brock lifted his bottled water in salute.

"Okay, okay. I'm ready to eat now," Della announced between breaths.

She returned to her seat. Derrick served her first. Afterward, everyone served themselves.

Derrick blessed the food. After the first bite, Della closed her eyes and hummed. "Honey, you've outdone yourself. I love it, seasoning and all."

Derrick kissed her cheek and thanked the rest of the group who chimed in with their praise.

Bryce added, "I'm sorry I doubted you, Dad. Looks like Google and YouTube came through."

Laughter filled the air and Derrick retorted, "Alright now, don't forget who signs your checks Mr. I've-got-jokes."

Dinnertime talk was filled with all things baby, none of which Brock could relate to. He smiled and nodded, adding comments about being a proud uncle. He wasn't anywhere close to marriage or babies—unless his career counted.

"Mom, are you ready for cake?" Brock pushed away from the table. "I can go get it." He was proud of his contribution to the evening, though nothing could top the news of a baby.

"Bring it on."

Brock retrieved the cake from the kitchen, along with two numbered candles he picked up on the way over. He added the six and zero candles while his father took her place setting. He removed the cake from the box, lit the candles, and carried it into the dining room, leading the family in singing "Happy Birthday." He placed the cake in front of her.

"Gorgeous." She beamed while they continued to sing.

"Make a wish," they shouted in unison.

"I don't think there's anything else I can wish for. I have everything I need and want right here." She removed the lit candles from the cake – something she'd done as long as Brock could remember because she had a thing about people blowing their breath over a cake. For her, that was unsanitary.

She paused to glance at Brock. "On second thought, I do have one wish." She closed her eyes and blew out the candles.

Della cut the cake and handed everyone a slice. Brock held his breath until she took her first bite. *I hope you came through for me, Ginger.*

She chewed and a smile lit her face. Her eyes grew wide, and she took another forkful into her mouth, covering her chest with her free hand. Brock exhaled.

"Which one of you is trying to ruin my diet? I can't stop eating it."

"Mom, it's keto," Brock said, remembering the tagline beneath the logo on the cake box.

"Nothing I've had compares to this." She put another forkful in her mouth, closing her eyes and savoring the taste. "I need a cake for my women's Bible study group next week. They'll never believe this is low carb. Think you can get another one for me?"

Maybe this was a sign. A sign he should see Ginger again. Or a sign that Ginger's Goodies was just what he needed to get what he wanted—that promotion.

He was so close, he could taste it.

Brock's lips curled upward. "Let me know when you need it, and I've got you."

Chapter Seven

Brock strolled through the food court with expectancy. Today marked three days in a row he'd lay eyes on Ginger. Though this visit was for business reasons, his heart didn't know the difference. The small organ flipped and dipped with excitement. And good thing no one could see the thrashing in his chest cavity because he couldn't explain why his emotions would respond to her in such a way after all this time.

After the heartbreak.

After the disappointment of their separation.

At his mom's birthday party, he'd had an epiphany of sorts. Ginger owned a bakery much like what the owners of Decadent Dough were looking for in their acquisition. Being the attorney for the company, Brock could ensure the terms were favorable to Ginger, giving her the exposure she needed. An acquisition agreement between Ginger's Goodies and Decadent Dough could be a win-win-win for everyone involved. Brock would get his coveted promotion. Decadent Dough would acquire a new business and product line. And Ginger would get exposure beyond her wildest dreams, plus she'd have Brock to thank for that. Perhaps the new business venture could be the start of a new chapter for him and Ginger.

The start they needed to repair what had been broken for twenty years.

However, his anticipation was short lived. When he walked up to Ginger's Goodies' white and pink striped counter with overhead neon signage, his chest deflated.

"Hi. Excuse me," Brock interrupted the woman at the counter who sat with her face engrossed in an e-reader. "I'd like to place an order for another cake." He smiled to hide his disappointment at not seeing Ginger.

The woman gave him a quick once over and if he didn't know any better, he'd swear recognition filled her eyes, like she knew him. Or could it be wishful thinking that Ginger had talked to her friend about him?

"Oh, hi, I'm Lisa, a friend of Ginger's," She stammered a bit. "Ginger stepped away. Do you mind waiting a few minutes so that she can take your order?" She crooked her head over the counter. Brock's eyes followed hers.

"No, I don't mind. I'm in no rush." He glanced at his watch before he stuffed his hands inside his pockets and paced in front of the pastry warmer display.

"Did you say *another* cake?"

"Yes, she made a birthday cake for my mom, and she loved it. Well, we all did."

"I see," Lisa half-sang. Her eyes widened.

At this point, he was certain recognition filled her eyes.

"Would you like to try a cookie, scone, or croissant? You can't go wrong with either choice."

"Oh, no, I'm fine really. I'm here to order a cake." *And see Ginger once again.*

"You won't regret it." Lisa fished a cookie out of the display case with a napkin. "Here, try it." Lisa leaned over the counter, rested her chin in her palms and hiked her eyebrows.

Curiosity got the best of him. *How much more had she perfected her recipes since they dated in high school?* He recalled the succulence of his mom's birthday cake. The cookies had to be good. Brock bit the cookie, closed his eyes as he chewed. A low hum escaped his lips as he finished off the treat. "This is good."

His mom's request for another cake gave him the excuse he needed to check out Ginger's business. Based on the taste of the cake and cookie he'd just had, Ginger's Goodies would be the perfect subsidiary for Decadent Dough.

"You still have feelings for her, don't you?"

Lisa's question, spoken like a matter-of-fact-statement, caught him off guard and caused the remaining cookie crumbles to slide down his throat the wrong way. Brock nearly choked. He coughed and slapped his chest several times with his fist.

"What?" he managed through his coughs.

"You should tell her." Lisa nodded toward Ginger who approached him from behind.

"Tell me what?"

Brock coughed a few more times, pressing and rubbing his fist against his chest. Ginger rushed into the kitchen, returning with a small cup of water. "Here you go."

Lisa glanced between Brock and Ginger. "He still loves," her eyes lingered on Brock and somewhat of a wicked, teasing smile touched her lips, "your chocolate chip cookies," she finally finished her sentence.

While he didn't know Lisa, he didn't like the feeling that washed over him when her eyes locked with his, as if she knew him like a page from a book she'd read several times and knew by heart. Or perhaps this was one of those situations where his mind was playing tricks on him as a manifestation of what he was trying to hide—his suppressed feelings for Ginger.

He worked to clear his throat in between gulps of water. "I…uh…that chocolate chip cookie is probably the best one I've ever had. I'd like a dozen of them, please. And about six of the gluten-free oatmeal cookies as well." He'd gift them to Ms. Janet.

There were so many things he wanted to say and ask. He'd pursed his lips to ask more about her business, what inspired her to take the leap, what happened with school, and simply what else she'd been up to since they parted ways, but now didn't feel like the right time. His eyes wouldn't take the signals from his brain to look away, so it was a good thing she avoided eye contact with him while she prepared his order, though the pain in his heart was similar to that of accidentally touching a hot pan without an oven mitt because of Ginger's lack of warmth.

∞

Ginger moved robotically, packaging Brock's cookies in a pink Ginger's Goodies logo printed box. *What is wrong with me?* Ginger's hands trembled. She always made small talk about baking when she waited on customers, but not today. She glanced at Brock, who watched her intently and adjusted his tie at the base, which didn't need adjusting at all.

"Oh, my mom loved your cake. She couldn't stop talking about it."

"Well, that's great. I appreciate your business."

"Yeah, that's why stopped by. I need to order another one for her Bible study group next week."

"Oh, I see," Lisa sang, raising a curious eyebrow and looking between the two of them. "Gin, I'll catch up with you later." She tapped her shoulder and stepped from behind the counter into the open space next to Brock.

"Lisa, you don't have to leave." Could Lisa see the plea in her eyes and hear the near begging in her voice? Being alone with Brock, though they were in the mall's food court, was not part of her plan. Ever. Seeing him regurgitated memories of the emotional bond they once shared. Though she shouldn't turn away any customer, Brock was one that need not return. It was only a matter of time before their past interlocked with their present. So many things were left unsaid when they parted ways. Words she didn't have for him then, but she could certainly find now.

"Yes, I do. You have a customer, and I don't want to get in the way. Plus, I have to help my mom with that thing at the bookstore." Lisa's eyebrows danced before she sauntered off.

"Thanks for your help again, Lisa." *More like, thanks for nothing.* When had Lisa stopped reading her signals? Ginger returned her attention to Brock. "That's good to know. I'll ring up your cookies first, then I'll take your cake order." Ginger swiped his card, returned it, and handed the box of cookies to him. His hands slightly brushed hers, sending a tingle up her arms. She released a slow, even breath.

I can get through this moment. It's just Brock.

Ginger reached for the order slip behind her and grabbed a pen. He watched her every move, and she did everything she could to avoid eye contact while remaining professional.

Her attention focused on the Ginger's Goodies logoed notepad and pen in hand. "I'm ready. Tell me what you'd like."

"Actually, a repeat of everything you did last time will work, without the Happy Birthday message. She wants to prove to her group that a keto cake can be good." Brock chuckled and rocked back on his heels. She glanced at him to catch the smile framing his face. One that reminded her of the first time she baked a batch of cookies for him. He'd been out of school for a week with the flu. She fought back a smile at the memory. *Not going there.*

"Got it. When do you need it?"

"Next Tuesday after work. I can swing by and pick it up. Better yet, can we make it Monday? I don't know how my day will go, and I'd much rather her have it a day early as opposed to running the risk of missing you—I mean, you closing before I can make it over."

Miss me? Her heart galloped. *You've done this before. Not doing it again.*

She scribbled on her pad and tucked it inside of her apron. Another slow, heavy sigh eased from her mouth. "Anything else?" She smiled then gnawed her bottom lip.

"That's it. Thank you." He picked up the box of cookies, but hesitated before moving away from the counter. She knew him well enough to know there was more he wanted to say, so why didn't he? "I guess I'll see you, then." His eyes lingered.

"Your mom loved the cake, but what did you think of it?" *Did his thoughts matter?*

"The best cake I've ever tasted." He winked and turned on his heels toward the food court exit.

With every step he took away from her counter, her heart meditated on his words, on repeat in her mind. *The best cake he'd ever tasted.*

She almost hated that he said things like that because his words caused her heart and mind to conjure up the what-ifs. And they couldn't go down that road again. Just because he showed up in her life unexpectedly didn't have to mean that she should consider dating him again.

But what if a relationship could work between them this time around?

∞∞∞

Ginger worked late that evening to upgrade her display. Placing the bell on the counter for guests to ring in case someone stopped by while she was in the kitchen, she went to work, tearing through the large brown box with a boxcutter.

"This looks like one of my cakes," she gushed, unwrapping the custom fake cake. "I'd try to cut it if I didn't know any better." She had ordered several realistic looking cakes for her new display. Her business was more than cookies, croissants, and scones. She grinned proudly as if it was a creation of her own.

She busied herself placing the cakes at the bottom of the clear countertop display to leave room for freshly baked cookies she'd have ready for the next day. She rounded the counter and stood in the corridor, just in front of the display, arms folded, chest puffed. *Just what I needed.*

"My very secretive master cake baking friend," Lisa walked up behind her and whispered in her ear. Ginger jumped and squealed, holding her chest to steady her heartbeat.

"What are you talking about, and why are you sneaking up on me? You scared the heebie-jeebies out of me." Ginger's mouth hung open while Lisa circled her suspiciously, eyeing her up and down. "Why are you acting so weird?"

"I could ask you the same thing."

"What?" Frown and confusion filled her eyes.

Lisa pointed at Ginger and wiggled her finger up and down repeatedly, an I-know-you're-holding-something-back-from-me smile covered her face. "Don't think I didn't notice that little thing happening between you and Mr. Handsome earlier today. What was that about?"

"I don't have the slightest clue what you're talking about." Ginger walked behind the counter and into the kitchen with Lisa following close behind, pausing at the swinging kitchen door.

"Liar." Lisa jabbed a finger in Ginger's direction. "You should see your face."

"That was just Brock. I've mentioned him plenty over the years. Plus, this isn't news to you. I just told you about the non-situation yesterday."

"*Just* Brock? After all this time, he's still holding a torch for you. I know you can tell, right? I picked up on it within sixty seconds of him standing at your counter wanting to order a cake." Lisa used air quotes with her fingers when she said cake.

Ginger countered, "Like the torch Jayden is holding for you? Besides, I don't know why you're acting like that. He did order a cake."

"I've known Jayden since we were in diapers. We are friends, plus, this isn't about Jayden. Brock didn't come up here just to order a cake. He could have called and placed the order."

"*Hmmm.* Well, it doesn't matter how Brock feels. He's part of my past." Ginger busied herself gathering ingredients to prepare cookie dough.

"I don't know. He is clearly making himself part of your future, too. You both are fighting the feeling." Lisa shifted her attention to her freshly manicured nails, flexing her fingers in and out of her palm.

Ginger burst into laughter. "You're funny. There's no feeling. Just business. I'd take the order whether it was him or anyone else. He's not receiving any special treatment from me." Ginger shrugged. She rolled moist circles of cookie dough between her palms to refrigerate for tomorrow.

"So that's how you want to play this? All nonchalant like? Okay, I see how things are between us. I thought we were better than that." Lisa pretended to pout.

"I'm not sure what you want me to say."

"Admit that he's gorgeous and that the idea of dating him has crossed your mind. Or maybe that if things were different, you'd go out with him."

Ginger huffed and shook her head.

When Lisa didn't respond, but eyed her as if she had some kind of powers to make Ginger say what she wanted to hear, Ginger said, "Lay off the romance novels, friend."

"I mean, it has been twenty years. You're both much more mature now. You're single. And from the looks of his left hand, he isn't married. Okay, let me stop playing. I looked him up online. There is nothing that indicates he's married."

Ginger rolled her eyes. "Seriously, I'm going to hijack your Kindle."

Lisa laughed.

"I'll tell you what. If you go on a real date with Jayden, I'll consider talking to Brock."

"You play too much. Jayden and I are just friends."

"Exactly what I thought." Ginger put the cookie dough in the refrigerator and removed her buzzing phone from her apron. She opened the e-mail app and read the congratulatory message welcoming her to the second round of *the O Taste and See* baking competition. Her breath caught in her chest while she read through the e-mail. The message also contained a list of ten students enrolled in the culinary program at the Art Institute of Houston and their profiles, for her to choose as a baking assistant to help on the day of the competition.

Ginger jogged in place. "Yes! Thank you, Lord! Yes!" She jumped and punched the air.

"What is it? What is it?"

Ginger ran to Lisa and held the phone in front of her face to read the e-mail. Lisa threw her arms around Ginger and lifted her off the floor in a tight embrace. "Congratulations! I'm so proud of you! How are we going to celebrate?"

"I don't know. Let me make it to the finals first, and then we can celebrate."

"Girl, *pssh*! That's as good as done. Maybe we can go out for dinner. My treat. Tomorrow night after work."

"Deal." Ginger and Lisa squealed in unison, their fingers linked.

She had two weeks to get ready for the local competition. Ecstatic, she couldn't wait to tell her dad he and Lisa were right about that cake. It opened two doors for her: the competition and

Brock's mom, who had become a repeat customer. She inched a step closer to winning twenty-five thousand dollars to scoop up that vacant building in Katy for Ginger's Goodies' new location. Slowly but surely, things were coming together for her. *Thank you, Lord, for bringing me this far.*

Turning off the lights and locking the kitchen doors, she rounded the counter and gave her food court storefront unit a once-over. Warmth and satisfaction washed over her. Another step closer to her dreams coming true.

Arm in arm, Ginger and Lisa left the area to the nearest exit.

"Gin, this is so exciting. When I tell Jayden and my mom, they'll want to celebrate with you, too. Do you mind if they come to the dinner? Shoot, my mom will probably want to cook for you."

Ginger chuckled. "I already know where this is going to lead." Lisa's mom, who Ginger affectionately referred to as Aunt Debbie, would want to create an entire event. Then, she'd invite Jayden's mom, who they all referred to as Aunt Wanda. While Ginger didn't care to have everyone fussing over her when she hadn't won yet, she could use the distraction.

Lisa joined her with her own soft chuckle. "Yeah, she'll do the most, but it'll be fun."

"Let's go for it." Anything that would help keep her mind off Brock Pearson was a win in her book.

She and Lisa bid their goodbyes when they made it to the parking lot. Inside her car, Ginger chose to live in the moment. Soak up the now and the unfolding of God's plans, which were much greater than hers and she could hardly wait to see what was next.

Chapter Eight

Due diligence.

Brock spent a couple of hours researching Ginger's Goodies. Gluten-free. Keto. Paleo. Her business, though small, was everything Decadent Dough wasn't. With the right resources, she could do extremely well. Decadent Dough could circulate her goods all over the U.S., as opposed to the local business she did now.

In Brock's mind, this could be a win for everyone involved: him, Decadent Dough, and Ginger.

After he'd done his research, Brock found himself stuck on the home page of Ginger's website. A smiling image of her in the pink and white logo apron she wore to deliver his mom's cake stared back at him. Her captivating eyes told stories of their past love. Brock shook his head to rid himself of Ginger's smiling face and slammed the laptop closed. This mission wasn't at all personal, strictly business, and it seemed that Ginger had everything he needed to get that promotion.

Brock yanked his suit jacket off the chair and trotted out of his office through the double glass entry doors to the elevator bank. Instead of driving, Brock walked across the street to the food court, grabbed a coffee, and sat within view of Ginger's Goodies. He watched her, feeling more like a stalker than an investigator or lawyer.

Her smile was brighter than the lights that illuminated the food court as she greeted every customer warmly. Small talk. Smiles. An invitation to visit again. He couldn't hear her, but he imagined that's what she said.

Brock's thoughts trailed back to when all of this was a dream for Ginger. A dream she'd gush over when they took their Sunday evening walks way back when. And now her small frame moved behind the pink-and-white striped counter with ease, living the life she'd always wanted.

Except they were supposed to be living life together.

Brock almost choked on his coffee when the thought pushed through the forefront of his mind. He massaged his chest and shook his head to dismiss the notion. He couldn't get caught up in their past when he had an idea that could change their lives.

From his memories of Ginger, the chances of her agreeing to acquisition terms with Decadent Dough were slim, but still, he had to try, because this could be an opportunity for both of them.

When the crowd disappeared, Brock locked eyes with her, and she fidgeted under his gaze, now less comfortable than she had been thirty minutes ago. Brock approached the counter.

"Back for more cookies?" Ginger's smile spread across her lips.

"I'll take some in a minute. But listen, *ummm,* can we talk? Mind having a seat with me?" Brock gestured toward the nearest table for two within thirty feet of her storefront. "Please." He added and pressed prayer hands to his chest. "It'll only take a few minutes, and I'll let you get back to work."

Her shoulders dropped, and she tilted her head. She peered up at him from behind her large frames. He couldn't read her until she finally smiled. "Five minutes."

Ginger followed Brock to the empty table that he'd occupied during the lunch hour. Brock pulled out her chair and sat across from her.

"So, what's this about?" Ginger sat with her legs crossed at the ankles and her arms folded across her chest.

"Ginger, I—" One look into her eyes and he couldn't do what he'd set out to do when he walked over to the mall. He should be securing his promotion. But all he wanted to do was spend more time in her presence. "I've been thinking. We've run into each other too many times over the last couple of weeks not to catch up. Are you free for dinner or coffee this week?"

For the life of him, he didn't know why he'd put himself out there again and especially with her, but he couldn't help himself. He just hoped asking her to hang out with him didn't backfire and he'd end up wishing he'd taken the chance to bring up the business deal.

Her eyes softened and smiled before her lips did. The tightness in his chest eased.

"I'd like that. It's been a long time and I'd love to hear how life's been going for you." She reached across the table and rubbed a thumb over his jacket lapel. "Although by the looks of it, I can see it's treating you well."

He smiled and bit his bottom lip then gestured toward her pastry counter. "And we can clearly see how things are going for you. I'm proud of you, Gin."

Her lips seemed to have grown wider or maybe that was all in his head. But the twinkle in her eyes was unmistakable. "Thank you, Brock. I appreciate that." Her voice was now lighter and as sweet as the chocolate chip cookie he'd had the other day. And the way his name still rolled off her lips squeezed his heart with the compression of a blood pressure cuff. A simple one syllable name, yet no one said it like Ginger.

"You're welcome. I can make myself available whenever you are."

"Minuti Coffee is about two minutes away. Meet me there in the morning at seven."

"I'll be there."

Ginger jutted her thumb toward her shop. "I need to get back to work. I'll see you in the morning."

"Until then."

Brock walked her back to her counter where he said goodbye with promises to see her first thing in the morning. The anticipation of having coffee with Ginger carried him through the rest of his work day. No, he hadn't accomplished what he set out to do, but in a weird turn of events, his heart was happy.

∞

She should cancel.

What good would it do for her to have coffee with Brock? She'd convinced herself that coffee with him was an opportunity for them both to get the closure they needed and deserved. But closer shouldn't have had her changing her outfit three times. Besides, she was headed to work where she was likely to get flour or dough on her clothes. Although she wore an apron, most days she always found dough stains on her shirt on jeans.

She settled on a pair of skinny jeans and a pink V-neck shirt. Casual clothes she'd also be comfortable in while working.

Ginger arrived at Minuti Coffee at seven sharp. When she walked inside, fresh coffee beans greeted her. The aroma was like a good morning kiss. She spotted Brock standing at the counter perusing the menu. He turned to her and smiled when she walked through the door. They were the only two customers inside. Everyone else was in the drive thru line.

He wore one of those I-didn't-think-you-would-actually-show-up smiles. "Good morning."

She joined him near the counter. "Good morning."

Brock caught her off guard when he wrapped his arms around her and squeezed. While a quick hug, she was still surprised by the gesture.

"What are you planning to order? You look like you've been standing here a while."

Brock chuckled. "No, I came in about two minutes before you. Didn't want to be late."

She brushed his shoulder with her own. "I can appreciate that. I'll have the vanilla latte. It's so good."

"I think I'll take that, too."

Brock approached the counter, ordered, and paid for their drinks. He didn't say much while they waited. Once the barista prepared their drinks, Brock grabbed both of them and led them to an open table.

"I have to say that I'm surprised you showed up. I thought you'd stand me up."

Ginger chuckled. "Can't say I didn't think about it."

Brock laughed. "Well, I'm glad the odds were in my favor." He sipped his latte. "So, tell me what you've been up to. It's been about twenty years. Are you married with kids?"

Ginger gave him a side eye. "Do you think if I were married with children I'd be sitting here talking to you? My husband probably wouldn't like that very much."

"I guess you're right. If it were me, I wouldn't."

Her heart skipped a beat or two. Before the thought could form, Ginger put a stop to it. She wouldn't go there during this outing. Whatever they were once planning to be in each other's lives didn't matter.

"I know it's been forever, but I have to ask. How did everything work out for you at UT?" It seemed insane trying to cram twenty years into about an hour of coffee time, but that was all they had.

Something flashed in his eyes, but she couldn't read the emotion. "The first year was hard, actually. I had a difficult time getting over things not working out the way I thought they would. But once I pulled myself together, life at UT was great. I had my share of fun, pledged a fraternity, enjoyed college life, and still graduated at the top of my class, then went to law school right after. My life is pretty much consumed with work nowadays."

And by things not working out the way he thought they would, he meant their relationship. Ginger had never known him to sugarcoat anything. There was no reason to skate around the issue now.

"I'm happy to hear everything went well for you, despite our relationship not working. My first year at UH was tough, too. And looking back, I wouldn't change my decision to stay. Staying gave me the opportunity to spend more time with my mom. Had I gone away, I wouldn't have had that time with her before she passed during my senior year."

While she hadn't meant for her statement to be emotionally harmful to Brock, she could see the change in his eyes and the way his jaw now sagged. "I'm sorry to hear about your mom, Gin."

"Thanks. Grief doesn't get any easier, I've just learned how to cope, I guess. But I don't want to dwell on that right now. How's your family?"

"They're good. Bryce and my dad are at the Pearson Group and my mom retired. And I'm sure she'd be happy to see you."

"She knows I made her cakes, right?"

Brock shook his head. "Nope. I ripped your logo sticker off the box to avoid questions."

Ginger burst into laughter. "You did not."

"Did, too. You know what kind of questions I'd have to endure? Bryce already hemmed me up when he spotted your name on the box. I couldn't take the questions from Mom."

Ginger sipped her latte and leaned forward in her seat. "Did he? And what did he say?"

"Call him and ask him."

Ginger threw her head back and laughed. Conversation between them was easy, reminding her of old times. Before she'd fallen in love with Brock, he was her friend. She'd spent many occasions with him and his family, too. Church. Dinners. And even the occasional weekend trips to their beach house in Galveston.

At eight, they left the coffee shop with Brock suggesting they hang out again. Ginger agreed, but they didn't set a date or exchange phone numbers. However, he knew where to find her when he was ready. And she didn't know how to feel about that. They were supposed to drink coffee, reminisce, possibly apologize for past hurts, and move on. Not make plans to *do this again.*

Chapter Nine

Brock stood before the bathroom mirror and smoothed his hand along his red tie after adjusting the Windsor knot. He released several long puffs of air from his chest, but the heavy breaths did nothing to fight off the nerves. Three days passed since he had coffee with Ginger. And since that morning, all he could think about was her. His mind played tricks on him because he'd somehow fallen under her spell. Again.

Her brown soul stirring eyes.

Her spirit lifting laugh.

The comfort of her presence.

But he couldn't allow his shamble of emotions to interfere with this opportunity.

Brock washed his hands and marched out of the mall restroom. He didn't stop until he stood in front of Ginger's Goodies' counter. He'd timed his visit for the end of the lunch hour. Brock stood back while Ginger served her last two customers.

"Hey, what can I do for you this afternoon?" A wide and genuine smile spread across Ginger's lips when they stood face-to-face. Their last encounter must have left a lasting impression on her as well.

"Can we talk when you're free? I'll just grab a seat in the sitting area."

Ginger surveyed the area. "Sure, I have a few minutes now."

Brock led her to the same table they sat at a few days ago when he asked her to join him for coffee. He pulled out Ginger's chair and waited for her to sit before taking the seat across from her.

"So, what's up?" Her smile and eyes were still bright and receptive. He'd almost asked her out again, but he had to focus so that he'd know whether he needed to look somewhere else for Decadent Dough. Time wasn't on his side if he wanted to secure his mentor, Andrew's position when he retired.

"We didn't talk much about my work at Decadent Dough, but I'd like to run something by you to get your thoughts."

Her eyebrows dipped and her smile weakened. She looked as if she wanted to help him if she could. *Was that guilt because of how she ended their relationship?*

"Okay, what's that?"

"I work on the mergers and acquisitions team, and I have a proposition for you."

"The softness in her eyes vanished and her face sagged. Her disappointment was evident. "The answer is no."

"You didn't even hear what I had to say."

"You've said enough. The answer is no. I know enough about Decadent Dough to know I'm not interested. Is that all?" The sides of her lips turned down and her eyebrows crinkled.

"Decadent Dough is looking for businesses to partner with to expand their product offerings."

Ginger threw her head back and chuckled. "You're kidding, right? You cannot be serious." She huffed and blinked and threw her hands in the air. "Is that what this is all about? I thought…well, never mind what I thought. You're still the same person I thought you were. And as far as Decadent Dough, you and I both know they're only concerned with themselves and their bottom line. They'll take my recipes, and I'll be out on my behind. Nothing about this—" she used air quotes— "'deal' works for me, so thanks for thinking of me, Brock, but that'll be a hard no. Now if you'll excuse me, I have to get back to running *my* business."

Ginger stormed away, murmuring something he couldn't quite understand. He watched her retreating frame, and remained seated until he'd finished off his cup of coffee, thinking of ways he could've gone about it differently. Maybe her answer would've been different had she trusted him. After all, he could pretty much guess what she thought about him given the way their relationship ended years ago. Brock crushed the cup, tossed it in the nearest trash bin, and walked to her counter.

"How may I help you?" Ginger avoided eye contact, kept her focus on the Squareup touchpad on the countertop.

"Ginger, it was not my intent to offend you. In fact, it's a compliment. It was my thought that a company like Decadent Dough could help grow your business beyond what you ever thought possible."

Ginger scoffed, shook her head, and shot him a narrow-eyed warning glare.

Brock swallowed his pride and the lump in his throat and tried once more to appease her. "Let's start over. Can I take you to lunch? Buy you a coffee?"

"We've done that already and you clearly have an ulterior motive. I guess next time you'll try to woo me out of my baking secrets. I'll pass."

"Can I buy up all the cookies in this case here to make it up to you?"

Ginger folded her arms across her chest, planted her feet firmly, and blew out an exasperated breath. "Why?" Her neck rolled, and he knew he was in trouble. "In case I haven't made it clear, the answer is no to anything you're offering. Please find someone else to harass. This space is for paying customers." Ginger waved him off.

Brock fished his wallet from his back pocket, removed a hundred-dollar bill and slapped it on the counter. "I am a paying customer. I want as much as this can buy me."

"Brock, please leave. I don't want anything from you." Ginger slid the bill back across the counter.

"I'm one of those paying customers you just mentioned. I'll take as many cookies as this will buy me." Brock slid the bill back across the counter to Ginger.

Ginger huffed and engaged him in a stare down for several seconds. She cocked her head to the side and narrowed her eyes. The energy between them was not working in his favor. She twisted her lips, seemingly deciding if she'd serve him or not, but his thoughts shifted away from cookies and business to wondering if her lips were as soft as he remembered. *Stop it.*

Ginger snapped him out of his thoughts when she snatched the bill off the counter and moved to box cookies.

"Look, Gin, I'm being sincere here. It was not my intent to offend you. Can we just start over? Allow me to take you out for lunch?" Brock held his palms up in surrender. "No hidden agenda. We don't even have to talk about business."

Her glare could've burned a hole through his skull. Brock turned on his heel and momentarily shifted his attention to the few stragglers in the food court seating area. He inhaled sharply to collect his thoughts and turned back to face Ginger.

She boxed and slid four dozen assorted gluten-free and keto chocolate chip, snickerdoodle, cinnamon, double chocolate chip, peanut butter, and oatmeal cookies across the counter. "Thank you, sir."

Brock reached for the boxes and accidentally grazed her hands.

Ginger snatched her hands away and stuffed them in the back pockets of her jeans. Her glare said everything but please come again as she often told other customers.

"Sir? I think we're way past formalities." *You used to tell me you loved me.*

"May I help you with anything else, sir?" Her expression remained blank.

"You could say yes to going out with me."

Ginger sighed heavily and tapped her foot. "Then, I guess that's all. Have a nice day." A smile that said everything but mirrored the sentiment covered her face.

"I'll see you soon."

Brock grabbed the cookie boxes from the counter and retraced his steps back to the office. He hadn't intended to spend a hundred dollars on cookies; he didn't even eat cookies often enough to spend that kind of money on them, but desperation crept in. Way back when, Ginger had this way of making him crazy and it seemed she still had that effect on him.

He refused to buy that she felt nothing when their eyes connected. For him, their souls were entangled and though his mind wanted to let go and go back to life as it were before he laid eyes on her days ago, his heart wouldn't agree.

If Ginger wouldn't accept the business deal, fine, he could find another small business that would make Ace and the folks at Decadent Dough happy, but this just got personal.

They had unfinished business.

Chapter Ten

"I feel like I just walked into an episode of a Food Network baking show. I'm impressed." Ginger walked wide-eyed into the designated competition room inside of the George R. Brown Convention Center with her father and Lisa by her side.

Five baking stations were set up, complete with ovens, sinks, and ample counter space. Shelves and refrigerators lined the back of the room stocked with what seemed like an unlimited supply of sugars, flours, syrups, nuts, fondant, and every other ingredient any baker could dream of. An *O Taste and See* sign was strung from wall to wall. Ginger's emotions were all over the place—from excitement to wondering if she was in the wrong room. A hint of intimidation crept in when she compared herself to the other bakers who appeared much older and experienced.

Ginger's feet were like lead, and the chatter around her faded after she'd taken ten steps inside the swinging double-door entrance. She forced herself to breathe normally, but her erratically pulsing heart wouldn't cooperate. Suddenly, the sixty-five-degree temperature and two thousand square feet of space sparked beads of sweat and an onset of claustrophobia.

Ginger strutted to her baking station while her father and Lisa took their seats in the audience. Her eyes were drawn to the man behind them–Brock. She figured he came because he worked for the competition sponsor, Decadent Dough, or he was on the prowl to convince someone else to take the deal she turned down. Whatever the case, she didn't care, but a tiny part of her hoped he'd come to show his support for her.

Never mind the fact she wasn't happy with him right now. And she felt silly allowing herself to be optimistic about the two of them, even for a second. She thought he took her out for coffee to reconnect with her but the only thing on his mind was closing a business deal—a deal where she didn't believe she'd come out on the winning end.

Ginger intentionally avoided eye contact with Brock, though she could feel his eyes searing through her skull like a baker and his butane torch preparing crème brulee. She imagined he wore that same forget-me-not smile on his face he had when he bought the cookies from her a few days ago, and again when he returned to pick up another cake for his mother. That stupid smirk she'd been trying to forget haunted her.

She took her place behind her assigned table and turned to introduce herself to the other bakers. Three of the four were welcoming and receptive. One, not so much.

Ginger glanced toward the judges who were having a conversation amongst themselves, which happened to be closest to her working area. She took several calming breaths to relax her mind. She had this. All she had to do was what she did every day—bake—and she'd be alright. This was her happy place. Her zone. Her purpose. Her place of creativity. Her place of freedom.

With a pink apron and high ponytail, her assistant joined her side, jutted her hand forward, and introduced herself. "Hi, I'm Jessie. So nice to meet you in person. This is so exciting." Her wide hazel eyes sparkled just as much as her toothpaste commercial smile, probably perfected by years of braces. After reading Jessie's resume and career aspirations in the e-mail and talking to her on the phone, Ginger thought her to be the best fit.

"Nice to meet you in person, Jessie. Mr. Rizer has nothing but great things to say about you."

"Thanks, Miss Ginger, but I'm even more excited to learn something from you today."

Ginger's chest swelled at the thought of someone learning from her. She offered Jessie a wink and toothy smile, but her chest constricted when she caught sight of the host.

"Welcome to the second round of the *O Taste and See* competition where today's bakers will demonstrate their skills live right here on our stage," the host announced, quieting the room, sashaying to the front, a video camera following. Ginger's heart plummeted and then pumped rapidly. She recognized the host, Cinnamon, from the popular Netflix baking show, *Baking Bundts & Breads*.

Jessie recognized her, too, because she squeezed Ginger's hand hard enough to pain her knuckles.

"Let's learn more about our competitors." Cinnamon went from table to table, holding the microphone for the contestants to introduce themselves.

Ginger inhaled and put on her best smile. "I'm Ginger Evans, the owner of Ginger's Goodies, located inside Katy Mills Mall, where I specialize in keto, gluten-free, and paleo based treats. I'm so excited to be here today." She tried her best to introduce herself and her business in one stream of air to keep her voice from sounding shaky.

"Welcome, Miss Ginger. We're excited to have you."

Although Ginger didn't know Cinnamon, her sentiments felt genuine. When Cinnamon moved on to the next baker, she eyed her father, who winked, and Lisa, who waved and thrust two thumbs up.

"Alright, we have a surprise for our bakers this morning," Cinnamon announced, just as lively as she was on the TV screen, stretched her arms wide, and emphasized her every word. Pointing to the audience, she asked, her voice rising several octaves, "Who loves cho-co-late?"

The audience cheered, and she continued, "This morning our bakers will prepare for our judges…" She paused for dramatic effect before finishing her announcement, "succulent chocolate cupcakes. And who doesn't like tea or coffee with their cupcakes? Our bakers must wow our judges with this." She flashed a photo of a teakettle to the audience and then to the bakers.

The crowd gasped then cheered.

"That's right bakers. Add your special flair and show us your teakettles."

"You got this, Ginger," Her father and Lisa cheered.

"Let's start the timer. Bakers, are you ready?" Cinnamon turned her back to the audience, now facing the bakers. "You have two hours to complete your creations. You will be judged on appearance and deliciousness." She shimmied her shoulders. "And your time starts now." She threw her arms down like a referee at a car race.

Ginger thought of her mom, their recipe she recently perfected, and knew she had to bake that cake today. To honor her mom and win the competition. That cake was created for this moment. She filled her chest with air, whispered a prayer, and released her breath. Peace transcended her and no matter the outcome, at the moment, she believed everything would work out alright.

Thank you.

She and Jessie took a few minutes to sketch their design of the teakettle. Images of Mrs. Potts from the hit Disney movie, *Beauty and the Beast,* flooded her mind, and that's what she went with as inspiration for her teakettle. She drew the image as best as she could and began calling out a list of ingredients for Jessie to gather.

Jessie ran to and from the pantry while Ginger prepared the cupcake mixture.

Ginger started two mixtures at once – one for the cupcakes and the other for the cake she'd use to create the teakettle. Jessie followed her instructions and imitated her every move to create the second batch. With the batter in the oven, Ginger and Jessie made the decorations for the teakettle out of fondant.

Thirty minutes passed.

Ginger moved steadily with Jessie by her side, in sync, their symmetry sizzling.

One hour left. Cupcakes cooled and decorated with pink icing.

Time for the teakettle shaped cake.

The part that could make or break them today.

She used gum paste to create the spout, inserting toothpicks to support the weight of the cake on the spout. She added buttercream to each of the three cake layers. Ginger cut and inserted four straws into the cake to help support the cake plate she inserted on top of the first layer, then added the next layer. After she repeated this step for the top layer, she carved the cake, shaved off pieces to cut into a teakettle shape, and inserted one long straw through the middle to keep the cake from falling to pieces.

Covering the cake with fondant, she and Jessie worked together to smooth it to prevent lumps.

The teakettle decorations were added right before the buzzer.

Utensils down.

Hands up.

When she watched baking shows on TV, this part always gave her goosebumps. Sometimes, it was hard to watch the outcome. She glanced in Lisa's direction. Thumbs up. Smiles. Photos. Brock sat a few seats away from Lisa, his presence hard to ignore. Her eyes darted to his. Surprised, his smile was more one of adoration, and it took everything within her to reel her heart and mind from reversing twenty years and basking in his admiration. She'd almost fallen for his tricks in the coffee shop.

Not today.

"Miss Ginger, you did good. The cake and cupcakes look so nice. I loved making this with you."

"I couldn't have done it without you."

Jessie waved off her comment. "Of course, you could've, but thanks for saying that. I'm happy to help whenever I can. Just look at this."

"Alright, Miss Ginger," Cinnamon sauntered to her table. "Let's look at what we have here." She turned to the audience. "What do you think folks?" In response, the audience cheered.

She returned her attention back to Ginger. "Do you know the Scripture that inspired this competition?"

"O taste and see that the Lord is good. Blessed is the one who takes refuge in Him. Psalm 34, verse 8."

"Look at our Bible scholar here, folks. Alright, so we know the Lord is good, but are these cupcakes? You may now take the plated cupcakes and teakettle cake over to our judges, Miss Ginger."

Cinnamon moved on to the rest of the bakers, but Ginger didn't hear anything Cinnamon said. She lifted her cake teakettle creation, set it on a portable table along with a cupcake plated for each of the three judges, and wheeled it in front of them. She fought hard to steady her hands, which trembled in sync with her nerves.

Ginger watched each judge bite into their cupcake. Raised eyebrows. Smiles. Confusion.

Trepidation tore through her.

"My, Ginger, I have to say when I saw you go for the coconut flour, I thought you were out of your mind. I don't know a lot of bakers who can ensure moistness when using it, which is why so many of us shy away from it. So good," judge number one said and took another bite.

Judge number two dabbed the pink icing away from her lips with a cloth napkin and flipped her blond hair over her shoulder. "I agree. Not too sweet either. Perfect balance. Thank you." She gave Ginger a thumbs-up signal.

An older white-haired gentleman leaned forward, his eyebrows crinkled, and his lips formed a straight line. Ginger couldn't read him. "I don't know how I feel about this cupcake. It's good, but unlike anything I've had before. I know something is different, which is the coconut flour, but you've done an amazing job with the texture and taste." Finally, a smile formed on his lips, and the knot in her stomach loosened. "And that teakettle you're standing next to is phenomenal. How long have you been baking?"

"Thank you, sir. I started baking as a child helping my mother, but my business is two years old."

Judge number three nodded and smiled. "Your experience is evident. Thank you, Ginger. Please leave your cake there." He pointed in the direction for her to move the cake out of the way of the next contestant, but still within view.

Ginger returned to Jessie's side at her baking station. It was all she could muster to keep her legs from giving out. She braced herself against the counter and listened intently while the judges critiqued the other contestants.

Moments later, the winner was announced: Ginger's Goodies.

"They loved it, Ginger. You won this round. I'm so glad I got to be a part of this with you."

Ginger and Jessie linked fingers and cheered. Kenneth and Lisa stood in the crowd, joining them in celebration. She won the second round with her chocolate chip cookies dipped in chocolate, securing her spot in the final competition to be held in Austin, Texas, in four weeks.

Weeks that would bring her one step closer to building the business she'd always dreamed about.

Chapter Eleven

Brock stayed behind after the competition ended and most of the other spectators left. He told himself it was only right to congratulate Ginger, hopefully clear the air between them. She'd glanced in his direction a few times but hadn't given him an inch of indication she was no longer upset with him about the Decadent Dough proposal. After seeing her in action, his confidence that the deal would be beneficial for her increased, but he wouldn't dare mention the proposed deal again since she didn't want that for her business. His concern was for her, but demonstrating that would be difficult at this point.

But he had to try.

"Brock Pearson." Ace Steele, CEO at Decadent Dough, and the man who held the cards to his promotion at the company, slapped his shoulder and took the seat behind him. His presence snapped him out of his Ginger induced thoughts.

"Oh, hi, Ace. I didn't think I'd see you here today."

"Last minute decision since my granddaughter, Jessie, was on stage assisting the competition winner." Ace's gaze rested on Ginger, her father, Lisa, and Jessie, with a scowl etched in his features. "Any headway on prospects for Decadent Dough?" Ace never shifted his attention away from the group.

"I'm working on it. Figured I'd come out here today to support the competition since we're sponsoring it and also scout a few prospects. Each of the competitors have their own bakeries."

Ace's frown deepened while he watched Ginger and her family. Brock was ninety-nine percent certain Ace hadn't heard his response. "Know anything about Ginger's Goodies?"

"Actually, I've talked with her already and she isn't interested in any business arrangements with Decadent Dough." Brock quickly added, "but don't worry, I know that Dawn is itching for a new bakery line—something fresh as she likes to put it. I'll take care of it."

"I don't have to remind you what'll happen or not happen, in your case, if you don't."

Brock nodded. He hated the fact Ace dangled the promotion in front of him like a carrot. He also couldn't help but wonder what he'd have to do when he wanted another promotion? Would he constantly have to chase a moving goal post? This wasn't what he signed up for, but he couldn't shy away from doing his part to advance in his career. "I understand."

Ace gave a curt nod. "But please excuse me. I need to have a little chat with my granddaughter." Ace patted his shoulder, stood, and strode over to Ginger, Kenneth, Lisa, and Jessie's huddle.

Why was this promotion important to him again? To prove to his dad and Bryce he could get to the top on his own merit. All his life, all he'd ever heard was how much like his dad and Bryce he was. Three peas in a pod. Looked alike. Acted alike. Studied law. It was time he ducked out of their shadow and forged his own path. He'd been doing a good job of that so far—until Ace threw the proverbial monkey wrench in his plans.

∞

Ginger gushed over her advancement to the final competition and Jessie's assistance to her father and Lisa until she was interrupted by a middle-aged man in a nice suit, dressed way more formal than anyone else at the event. He extended a congratulatory hand to her.

"Great job up there today."

"Thank you, sir." Ginger accepted his firm handshake.

Jessie hugged the man. "Grandad, I didn't think you'd make it to the competition."

"Glad I could stop by to see you in action."

Jessie beamed.

"Nice to see you again, Ace." Kenneth shook Ace's hand while they engaged in a stare down, a move that made Ginger's skin crawl and doubt the sincerity of her father's greeting.

"Likewise." Ace squinted, nodded in Ginger's direction, but kept his gaze zeroed in on Kenneth. "Is she your daughter? I take it she didn't get her skills from you."

"Beautiful just like Lily, isn't she?"

Whatever her father and that man had going on, Ginger wanted no parts of it. She cut through the awkwardness between her father and Ace. "We made a great team up there."

The only other person she baked with was her mother. To combat the emotion threatening to overtake her, Ginger shifted her attention to her assistant. "Jessie here is a natural. Shoot, I probably need to hire her." Ginger offered a weak chuckle.

Jessie's eyes and smile grew equally wide. "Are you serious? That would be great because I just started looking for a job."

Ace released his grip on Kenneth's hand and draped an arm over Jessie's shoulder. His eyes beamed, hopeful even, as he glanced from Ginger to Jessie. "Sounds like the perfect idea to me."

"I really could use your help, Jessie, if you have time for it."

Jessie squat jumped; her hands flew to her lips. "Count me in. I'd love to learn from you, Miss Ginger."

"You just got yourself an intern." Ace shook her hand like he'd closed a deal.

"Thank you, sir." Ginger paused; her eyebrows knitted together. "I'm sorry, what's your name, again?"

"Ace Steele, a proud grandfather."

"Well, thank you Mr. Steele. And Jessie, I'll give you a call Monday morning to talk specifics."

Ginger made a mental note to ask her dad about Ace later. She looped an arm through her father's and Lisa's and strutted past Brock who'd been sitting in the same seat he'd occupied during the competition. He jumped up, met her in the aisle, and fell in stride with the trio.

"Congratulations, Gin."

"Thank you, Brock." Ginger didn't turn to look at him, but her father halted their tracks.

"Brock Pearson. It's good to see you. How've you been?" Kenneth greeted Brock warmly, which was beyond Ginger since he knew very well how and why things ended between her and Brock. He was supposed to be on her side, but he smiled and shook Brock's hand like they were long-lost friends.

"I'm good, sir. Glad to see you're doing well. Mind if I steal Ginger away for a second?"

Kenneth looked to Ginger for approval. "I'll catch up with you at home, Dad, go get your rest. It's been a long day."

"I love you and am so very proud of you, my dear. See you in a bit."

"Love you, too. Thanks, Dad."

Kenneth kissed her cheek, said his goodbyes to Lisa and Brock, and strolled out of the room.

Brock eyed his retreating frame, and as soon as Kenneth was out of earshot, he said, "Why are you being so cold? I'm trying to make nice here."

Right outside of the room's exit, Ginger stopped and jammed a fist into her hip. "Why? So, you can warm me up and steal my business?"

"You said no, and that's the end of it. I've moved on. You should, too."

"Are you kidding me?" She dropped Lisa's arm and inched forward, closed the distance between the two of them, jutted her chin up, and glared. "If you've moved on, why are you here?" Ginger shoved a finger toward her feet.

Brock folded his arms across his chest. "I work for Decadent Dough, remember? And this competition is sponsored by us, so it seems only right that I come to support."

"Yeah, right. You're searching for someone else's business to rip from under them so you guys can stay on top." She jabbed a finger into his chest. Even in her frustration, that single touch sent a ripple effect up her arm that landed in her heart pushing her pulse to a higher rate. "Don't they have enough? They're in all the grocery stores. All over the country. Commercials blasting on the TV screen every day." Ginger flailed her hands in the air. "They're obviously the biggest, most successful bakery retailer in the industry. Why are you sniffing around here for them?"

Brock crossed his arms over his chest. His eyes piercing hers. "I don't think this is about Decadent Dough at all. This is about us, about your feelings for me."

He had a point, but she'd never admit as much to him. Part of her agitation had to do with the emotion he reawakened in her only to show that the feelings weren't mutual.

Ugh.

"Always about you, isn't it? Bye, Brock." Ginger pivoted and reached for the comfort of Lisa's arm, but not before Brock clutched her hand.

"Don't do this, Gin. Let's talk this through."

His touch shouldn't have caused her entire body to ache, but it did, and the only reaction she had was to pull away. Every time he touched her, it was as if he took a piece of her heart with him. And she couldn't engage him in the way he hoped right now. Not only had he awakened her emotions for him, but also her wounds. She wasn't ready.

"Not here, Brock. And not today."

She reclaimed the comfort of Lisa's arm and left him standing there.

"You can't keep running away. I thought we were long past that."

Ginger paused but didn't turn around. Brock's words echoed and jabbed her heart. The reference to their break-up was out of bounds. Besides, his selfishness ended their relationship, not her running away.

She could stay and defend herself, but they'd end up in a fight. She closed her eyes, squeezed tighter to Lisa's arm, and took a deep breath. "I'm not doing this with Brock today," she whispered to Lisa. *Leave the past in the past.*

She tossed a hand in the air and strutted away.

∞

"Ginger, what was that back there? The fireworks between you and Brock are something serious." Lisa rested her elbow against the windowsill with her penetrating gaze assessing Ginger behind the steering wheel. She hadn't said anything before now, and for that, Ginger was thankful. She needed a moment to decompress from her encounter with Brock. After all this time, he shouldn't make her crazy.

Ginger shifted in her seat. "Who does he think he is? I mean, didn't you see him standing there with his arms folded across his chest like he was Pharaoh or somebody?"

Lisa picked at her nails. *"Hmmm."*

"I mean seriously, did he have to be there? And what was that crap about trying to make nice. And let's not forget…" Ginger turned the sides of her lips downward and mimicked his voice, "'This is about your feelings for me.' I swear he's purposefully trying to get under my skin. Why can't he just leave me alone?"

Lisa looked at her like she'd grown a third eye. "Because you don't want him to."

Ginger leaned against the driver's side door, her chin pressed down, and her eyes doubled in size.

"Don't give me that look. I've figured it out. The reason this bothers you so much is because somewhere deep down inside, you still have a thing for that chestnut six-foot Adonis."

Ginger tapped the unlock button on the door. "You're about to walk home."

Lisa chuckled. "It's okay to admit it." She looked around the car. "Just me and you in here. No one's gonna know. And how could you not? The man's picture is probably in the dictionary next to the word *fine.* Besides—" Lisa casually continued to pick her nails— "he's in the same boat, looking at you like the glass of milk he needs to wash down his cookie."

Ginger started the car. "Let me take you home so you can get a shower and wash away your delusions."

"Okay, fine, but let's go on record right now saying I called it."

Ginger shook her head. "I can't believe you. I thought you were my friend."

"Oh, I am, and that's why I'm telling you the truth. The worst kind of deception is lying to yourself. You can fool others—except me—but you can't fool you. Besides, it's not the worst thing in the world to admit. Like I said, he's easy on the eyes."

"Maybe, but let's not forget I've been on the Brock rollercoaster before."

"He's obviously still on the roller coaster and wants you to be his riding buddy. He did try to make nice with you." Lisa chuckled.

"That was more about himself and less about me. He's trying to control what I think of him. I can see past his award-winning smile and dreamy eyes. I know him."

"Award-winning? Dreamy?" Lisa poked Ginger's arm. "See, I knew there was something there."

"I can agree. He's handsome, but he's just the type of guy that any woman with good sense needs to stay away from." Ginger gripped the steering wheel tighter.

"Convinced yet?"

"Why are you like this?"

Ginger and Lisa laughed.

"I'm your friend. If I don't hold up the mirror for you, then who will?"

Ginger sighed and shrugged.

"In all seriousness, since he bothers you so much, the best thing to do is to sit down and talk with him. Get all of your thoughts and feelings about him off your chest. Don't hold anything inside because you'll make yourself sick. Literally. He wants you. You want him. It's been twenty years and both of you are single. What's the harm in giving it another shot?"

Lisa's advice made sense, but Ginger's grudge against him was twenty years old. And grudges didn't just go away overnight, did they?

"Brock is too self-centered. Another *shot* wouldn't work."

It took every ounce of willpower within her to believe everything she'd said about Brock. How could she even trust him after he presented that *deal*?

An insult to the dream she promised her mother she'd pursue?

An insult to her slowly-but-surely-growing entrepreneurial skills.

And an insult to her mother's memory.

Perhaps it was high time she and Brock had a talk so they could properly package their past and move forward without being in each other's lives.

Chapter Twelve

Ginger's business picked up in a week's time. Though she hadn't seen Brock, she assumed she had him to thank for the now standing orders of assorted cookie and pastry trays for both Hawkins Law Partners and the Pearson Group's weekly partner meetings. If nothing else, for sure the Pearson Group since the firm was owned by his family. Specialty cake orders were up one hundred percent. Before this week, she received cake orders sparingly, but the orders poured in daily since the competition. Not only was hiring Jessie a smart move, but her assistance couldn't have come at a better time. She took care of Gingers' Goodies deliveries which gave Ginger more time to manage the baking and counter inside the mall.

Jessie bubbled into the kitchen. Her eyes sparkled and before she uttered a word, Ginger sensed her energy. "Ooh! Miss Ginger, I just had the perfect idea. Why don't you start weekly live sessions on social media and give baking tips? You were perfection at the competition, and I can totally see that working for your business."

"I post videos about four days a week." Ginger rolled the cool mounds of cookie dough between her palms, an activity that soothed her on many days.

Jessie shook her head, a huge smile formed on her lips. One of those *oh, you poor thing* pity kind of smiles. "No ma'am. You have to do more than that. I can help you with your social media.

Kick it up a few notches. Go live. Folks love that stuff. We could do a test video first, then tap that live button. And you'll have to be certain you mention the same-day delivery as a warm-goodie-on-demand sort of thing."

She almost wanted to be offended, but knew her social media platforms could use a boost and more eyes. "I deliver now."

"Well, yea, but you don't necessarily advertise that you'll deliver. Let me take care of updating your social media accounts because you're missing out on an entire market. I'll also create a widget for your website and get back to you by the end of the week."

She hadn't even touched Ginger's social media yet and already had her chest puffed out like she'd done something transformative to Ginger's pages. And while that was true, her confident energy excited Ginger. Her heart pulse ticked up at the possible outcome of what updated socials could do for her business.

"Thanks, Jessie. I can't wait to see what you come up with."

Jessie had been the fresh pair of eyes she needed. Her heart raced and danced at the possibility of her business excelling with this social media thing and by advertising as a pastry-delivery-on-demand service. Maybe she'd eventually purchase a car or two plastered with her company's logo to be her treat delivery vehicles. And open her own storefront. Maybe even operate in the mall and the storefront. Was that dream too big?

∞

Brock pulled into the Katy Mills parking lot and followed signs to go through Entrance 7. His stride matched his confidence, like that of a lawyer in the courtroom who knew the law like he knew his own name. He had to figure something out when it came to finding a company for Decadent Dough to acquire as a subsidiary, and he was back at square one. Brock came up short twice when he approached two of the bakers from the baking competition about the possibility of partnering with Decadent Dough. But who was he kidding? Decadent Dough wasn't interested in partnering with anyone, but taking over another company, masquerading like they wanted a partnership. Could he not sell the idea because he didn't fully believe in it? He believed in that promotion though.

A promotion he desired to prove to himself and his family that he could climb the corporate ladder without them.

A promotion he worked toward for the last ten years of his career.

A promotion that would prove that his choice to work outside his family's firm had been worth the headaches, long nights, and slow social life.

But first, he had to smooth things over with Ginger. As much as staying away from her for the past week pained him, he gave her the time and space he believed she needed. However, he couldn't leave things as they were between them. He still cared about her, and he didn't doubt that she still cared about him, otherwise, she wouldn't be as upset as she was with him, right? At least that's the story he repeated to pacify himself.

Inside Katy Mills Mall food court, Brock took a few sure steps to Ginger's Goodies pink and white counter. Ginger's head was down, her attention focused on the notepad in front of her. When she looked up, he flashed his most charming smile and searched for some sign of a truce when their eyes met.

He stuffed his hands in his pockets. "Good morning, Gin."

"Good morning, Brock." Ginger flashed an I'm-going-be-nice-to-you-today-even-though-I'd-rather-not smile.

Well, she isn't running me out of the mall today, so that's a good sign.

"How have things been since the baking competition?"

"Actually, very good." She folded her arms across her chest and shifted her weight to one foot. "I guess I have you to thank for some of it. I now have weekly standing orders from The Pearson Group and Hawkins Law Partners, so, thank you." She nodded, and a warmer smile covered her lips.

Did she bat her eyelashes? Intentionally?

Brock took another step forward and maintained eye contact like a vulture going in for the kill.

"You're welcome. It was the least I could do to make it up to you. I came at you wrong. My way of saying I'm sorry. You're obviously passionate about your business, and partnering with anyone is out of the question. I just want you to know I respect that."

Ginger's chest rose and fell, and she parted her lips like she was about to say something sassy, but she restrained herself for some reason. He couldn't tell if there was a hint of sadness that had flashed across her eyes or something else. That plastered-fake-pleasantry smile spread across her face and he took a step back.

Brock held her gaze, her light brown eyes illuminated in the overhead lighting. "Do you accept my apology?"

"It's only right that I do." Ginger picked up the notepad she'd been focused on and placed it inside her apron pocket. "Is there anything else I can help you with this morning?"

What had he said that had her now avoiding eye contact again?

"Go out with me." With the rollercoaster they'd endured since being reacquainted over the past couple of weeks, he should probably stay away from her, but he couldn't help himself because he experienced this pull whenever they were in the same vicinity. He held his breath.

Ginger tossed her head back and chuckled, the length of her high ponytail swinging behind her head. That wasn't a good sign, but he liked it.

"You're kidding, right? After we had coffee, things didn't work out so well. Not the best idea to go through that again, don't you think?"

"I wouldn't have asked if I didn't think so."

"If you have another proposition, you don't have to waste our time. Get on with it now so I can tell you no."

"Tell me you don't think there's anything left between us."

She froze and stared wide-eyed at him. There was a truth he knew Ginger wouldn't admit. Not now. After several silent seconds, she jammed a fist into her hip. "Give me one good reason why I should even consider going on a date with a man who thinks the world revolves around him."

"Sounds like you have me all figured out."

"Yes, Brock Pearson, I do. You haven't changed one bit. Everything has always been about you." Ginger braced her hands against the counter.

She obviously hadn't forgiven him like she said. Honestly, he had been thinking more about himself when he first presented the business deal between Gingers' Goodies and Decadent Dough, but every time he got a chance to look into her eyes again, old memories and feelings crept in, opening the window to *what-if*.

Brock stepped to the counter and rested his thigh against it. "Really, the only way to know if you're wrong or right about me is to let me take you on a date. I think we owe it to ourselves seeing as though life has found a way for us to meet again after all this time. It'd make my day if you'd say yes." The corners of his lips turned upward as memories of the good times they shared flooded his mind.

"Brock, why would I be interested in *making your day*?"

He held up crossed fingers.

"Does this—" she wagged her finger at him— "little thing work for you often?"

Brock chuckled. "What thing?"

"This charm you're trying to use to get your way."

"Is that a yes or no?"

Ginger pressed her hands into the counter and leaned in toward Brock. "Which answer will make you go away faster?"

Brock matched her stance, his eyes drawn to her lips. "Which answer do you want to give? And it's only one date. Besides, I recall you being a woman who likes to be right about everything. Are you afraid I'll prove you wrong?"

"You've already proven my point standing here the last ten minutes. But," she paused and grinned, "I'll only go out with you under two conditions."

"And those are?"

Ginger leaned forward on the counter. "One, bring me two more customer referrals. Two, I'll only meet you for breakfast."

Brock's hand flew to his chest, and a hearty chuckle erupted from his throat.

"You say those two conditions like they're impossible. Woman, I'll get you three more referrals, and I'll see you in the morning for breakfast at the Snooze Cinco Ranch location. Seven sharp."

"I didn't say I'll go out with you tomorrow." Ginger raised an eyebrow and folded her arms across her chest like a defiant child who refused to come in from outside after being called by her mother. "But, I will if you can make good on your end of the bargain, which means I'll need those orders placed before the day's end." She smirked as if she knew he wouldn't come through.

"Consider it done. I'll see you first thing in the morning." Brock tapped the countertop and backed away. He winked, turned on his heels, and with his mission-accomplished stride, made his way back to his car. Though he wasn't sure why what she thought of him mattered after all this time, he had every intention of proving her wrong.

Calling in favors and seeking out businesses for her was not part of his plan.

His sole intent was to ensure she was no longer upset with him and to show he'd made an honest effort to start over and possibly start the process to restore what they once had. Somehow, he'd gotten caught up in the canvas of her eyes—eyes that tugged on the better parts of him. Eyes that now had him promising to help build her business when the goal was to rebuild them.

∞

Ginger fought back a smile that threatened to curl her lips when Brock walked away. With every step farther away from her counter, her heartbeat slowed to a normal pace. She disappeared through the double doors of her commercial kitchen so she wouldn't have to war within herself to watch or not watch him disappear out of the food court. Ginger released a long, slow breath and gave herself a much-needed pep talk. Brock would not get under her skin.

Why didn't she just ignore him—accept his truce and move along? Instead, she fed into his ego. Gave him more attention than she should have. Flirted with him a little. Bartered with him to bring her more business before she'd go out with him. The way she saw it, he owed her more business than she asked for to make up for trying to steal her dream.

Agreeing to go on another date with him was the last thing she should do, especially after his last stunt—his big idea for her to allow Decadent Dough to buy out Ginger's Goodies. While the additional exposure would be great, she couldn't see how she'd ultimately win in that situation.

And agreeing to go on another date with Brock?

Going out with him again wasn't the worst thing in the world. And it was just one date. Plus, he was easy on the eyes, and they had a past which should have made it easier for her to read him. Maybe more time alone with Brock would help her figure out his angle. He had to be up to something. Now that he'd presented that Decadent Dough *deal,* she'd didn't think his intentions were pure. While in the deep recesses of her heart, she wanted any time with him to be solely about them reconnecting, she didn't trust that notion. Or Brock. Wasn't there a saying that went along the lines of keeping your enemies closer than your friends? Brock was certainly one she needed to keep an eye out for, she reasoned, which is why she had to go out with him.

Ginger preheated the oven and removed the chilled dough to make blueberry scones from the refrigerator. She gave Brock enough of her time that morning. Normally, the warming display case would already be filled with croissants, muffins, blueberry scones, and the occasional cinnamon rolls, but seeing Brock sidetracked her. When the first batch of pastries were ready, she carried the tray of morning pastries to the counter to fill the warmer, strategically organized by customer favorites, scones lining the top shelf. They were always the first to go. Cinnamon rolls, croissants, and muffins lined the rows in the warmer after.

"That one's mine," Lisa called out to Ginger, the tongs raised midway to the warmer.

"Anything for you. What's up?" Ginger bagged a scone and handed it to Lisa.

"Opening the bookstore for my mom this morning and stopped by to get my morning breakfast." Lisa dug through her crossbody purse for cash and handed the money to Ginger but didn't let it go when Ginger tugged the bill. "And what's up with you? You seem different."

Ginger pulled the cash out of Lisa's hand and frowned. "How so? Just the normal busyness in the morning."

"No, no. Look at me." Lisa lifted Ginger's chin and looked from one eye to the other like a doctor assessing her ill patient. Her eyebrows dipped and she squinted. "Something is definitely off. Are you sick?"

Ginger swatted Lisa's hand away. "I'm good, girl. What makes you think something is wrong with me?"

Lisa giggled and shook her head. "Nothing." She popped a piece of scone into her mouth and engaged Ginger in a stare-down.

"Maybe I should ask what Jayden has done. You're acting weird. Not me." Ginger returned to the kitchen and the oven timer rang. She removed pastries from the oven and returned to the counter to place them in the warmer. Lisa hadn't moved from her spot.

"I thought you were in a rush to open the bookstore."

"I didn't say that, but you seem to be in a rush to move me along this morning. Why don't you just go ahead and tell me what your problem is so I can go to work?" Lisa rested her elbows on the counter, chin in palm, a goofy smirk on her face.

Ginger shook her head in slow motion. "Everybody's got a thing for me this morning, I see."

"Now we're getting somewhere. Closer to confession time." Lisa rubbed her palms together and grinned like she already knew what Ginger would share. "Tell me exactly who else had a thing for you this morning."

"From the looks of you, seems like you already have the answer to your own question. And I thought we agreed not to ask questions we already knew the answer to."

Lisa stood from the counter and dramatically clutched her chest. "Oh, but I don't. Please tell me whose bothering my dear friend. Is it that mean old lawyer?" She puckered her lips.

Ginger shot Lisa a knowing glance, but didn't answer her question.

"Why is this so hard for you?" Lisa chuckled. "I know it was Brock. Saw him in the parking lot on my way in." She popped the last piece of scone in her mouth and wiggled her eyebrows in a dancing motion.

Like a teenager back in high school, Ginger wondered if Brock said anything to Lisa about her, but she dared not ask. Besides, there was no way Lisa wouldn't pounce on the opportunity to tell her. Ginger twisted her lips, shifted her weight on one hip and folded her arms across her chest. "So, if you knew it was him, why the charade?"

Lisa counted off on her fingertips. "For one, you have that same look on your face you had in the car after the competition. Two, I wanted to see how long it would take you to say something— or if you'd even say anything at all. And three, you're fun to tease."

Ginger smirked and shooed Lisa away. "Go to work."

"Not until you tell me what he did this time."

Ginger huffed. "He thinks the world revolves around him."

"And?"

"And what?"

"You're not giving me enough information. How does he think the world revolves around him? What did he *do?*"

"And he asked me to go on a date with him."

Lisa leaned forward on the counter again. "And you said no?"

Ginger shrugged, left Lisa at the counter, and returned to her kitchen. Lisa followed her and stood at the swinging door entrance. "You agreed?" Lisa's mouth hung open wide and long enough to give flies passage.

"I didn't outright agree. I agreed with conditions. And before you say anything, it's not a real date, only breakfast."

"Is that what you told yourself?"

"Yes, because that's the truth."

Lisa shifted her weight against the swinging door to hold it open. "Please do define a real date."

Ginger cocked her head to the side and pursed her lips. "Don't go there. You know exactly what I mean. This thing isn't going anywhere with Brock." Ginger held up her palm to keep Lisa from interrupting. "I only agreed to this breakfast so that I can figure out what he's up to."

Lisa chuckled and backed out of the door. "Just know that it'll probably take more than—" Lisa used air quotes— "'one non-date' to figure out what he's up to."

The whooshing of the swinging doors signaled Lisa's departure.

It wasn't as if Ginger hadn't considered that she'd want to go out with him again, but she didn't think it necessary to concern herself about future dates with Brock. He'd already shown his hand, which pushed her to accept a new one of her own. She'd use his connections to further her business. Her heart didn't get a vote in the matter and would have to take the back seat to what her business needed.

Chapter Thirteen

Though Brock had overpromised Ginger when it came to sending her three additional clients, he delivered—and on the same day. But that was his last favor to her. He'd more than made up for his offenses. He couldn't allow her to hold this over his head forever. They had to move on.

And hopefully their upcoming breakfast date meant they were off to a fresh start or at least had moved past their rocky reconnection.

Brock dressed in his normal suit and tie for his breakfast date with Ginger, but opted for a different cologne, something he hoped she'd like. Creed Aventus. He loved the way the scent mixed with his body's natural scent to create a powerful cologne that turned most women's heads. However, the only woman's attention he desired this morning was Ginger. Why did he care so much about what she thought of him after all this time? The last time she'd been a priority in his life, it didn't end well and the part of his brain that housed his common sense warned him not to go down this path again with Ginger, but he couldn't help himself.

He needed all the help he could get when it came to her.

He'd been ready to propose to Ginger after high school graduation. His parents warned him to slow down because he and Ginger were too young to take such a serious step, but Brock was convinced their relationship could sustain anything, until Ginger decided The University of Texas at Austin wasn't right for her. That part he could understand, but they'd made plans together for a year beforehand and she never gave any inclination that any other school was on her radar. The plan had been to go to the same university, graduate, and get married. But one day, she came to him with a tear-stained face accusing him of being selfish and only thinking about his future. UT was not the school for her, and she refused to attend and follow him around.

Ginger blindsided him.

Brock still recalled the crippling hurt he experienced from their breakup. And while twenty years had passed and he should be over the situation, in the deep recesses of his heart, he clung to that pain and used it as a buffer not to develop true intimacy in any relationship he'd been involved in since Ginger.

While sad, that was still his life's story.

And maybe their past is what he needed to reconcile to move on—to put this thing with Ginger behind him.

Because of Ginger, his heart was out of service when it came to love and anything remotely close to it. He'd finally embarked on the moment to change that.

∞∞∞∞

Brock arrived at Snooze about ten minutes before seven. He'd thought of stopping by the supermarket to bring her flowers but decided against it. She'd probably remind him this was sort of a business arrangement, that she wasn't really interested in him.

115

Except he knew that was a lie she told herself. One look in her eyes revealed she still cared.

Brock stood near the entrance, looking around the parking lot, waiting for her to arrive. He recognized her car from the cake delivery to his parents' house. When she pulled into the parking space near him, he waved and walked over to open the door for her after she cut the engine. Ginger stepped out onto the pavement with her ballet flat-clad foot, revealing a black pencil skirt and a cowl-neck orchid blouse. Brock mumbled, "Wow" as the high-ponytail, jean-wearing serious baker Ginger had been replaced with soft-curls-flowing-loosely-around-her-face, skirt-wearing, could-have-been-a-model-despite-the-fact-she-didn't-have-the-stature Ginger.

"Good morning." A smile as bright as the morning sun lit her face.

"Good morning." Brock instinctively drew her into his arms for an embrace. Ginger didn't pull away although she stiffened for a second before relaxing into his arms. An overwhelming sense of home engulfed him.

Brock stepped away and closed the door behind her. "Glad you were able to make it."

"Well, you did hold up your end of the bargain. I have three new customers because of you, so this is me holding up my end."

Maybe he could find her a few more if she'd show up looking like this again, not that she wasn't always attractive, but today felt like she'd dressed up for him. Whether it was true or not, he'd lean toward the fact she'd done so for him.

He extended his hand toward the door, but had the urge to take her hand in his or extend his arm for her to take hold.

He shouldn't be doing this to himself—hanging out with her, regardless of the reasons. All this situation did was stir up emotions and cause confusion for him.

Brock reached around her to open the door and held it open for her to pass.

"Good morning. Welcome to Snooze A.M. Eatery. Party of two?" The young brunette greeted them with a warm and friendly smile, likely induced by extra milligrams of caffeine. Chipper. She escorted them to a nearby booth and handed them menus. "Stephanie, your waitress, will be right with you."

"Thanks," they said in unison.

"Do you come here often?" Ginger asked after they were seated.

"Actually, this is my first time. I've heard a lot about it though. Been wanting to try it for a while. You?"

"First time as well. If I have breakfast at all, it's usually on the go." Ginger perused the menu. "I think I'll try this hash brown scramble."

"Me, too, and maybe even a pancake."

Their waitress neared their booth to take their orders. Her eyes and demeanor were equally as bright as the hostess and her orange restaurant logoed uniform shirt. Her blond hair dangled in a ponytail as she approached. "Good morning and welcome to Snooze. I'm Stephanie and I'll be taking care of you two this morning. Can I get you started with something to drink?"

Brock and Ginger both ordered a caramel macchiato and a cup of water. Stephanie scribbled their drink requests on the notepad.

"May I interest you in our pancake of the day? It's a cinnamon roll pancake drizzled with homemade cinnamon syrup and topped with almonds."

"Sure. What about you, Ginger?"

"Yeah, I'll try it."

She quirked an eyebrow and looked from one to the other. "Have you two been here before?"

"First timers," Brock answered.

She flipped her ponytail over her shoulder, and tapped the writing pad in her hand. "Well, I have to warn you that our pancakes are huge. You two may want to consider sharing. I can always bring another if you'd like."

Ginger's eyes glowed like a deer caught in headlights. Brock chuckled. Clearly, the thought of sharing anything with him was too much for her, and he'd take it.

"Yes, that'll be fine. I'm sure Ginger here wouldn't mind sharing a pancake with me."

"Actually, I do mind, but as long as I can get my share first, it's a deal."

Stephanie looked at Brock for approval.

"Deal." His eyes locked on Ginger's. "Thanks, Stephanie."

Stephanie reached for their menus, but Brock gestured for her to leave them on the table in case they decided to order more food. She nodded and spun away from the table.

Although he and Ginger had history, his heart hijacked his nerves, pounding in his chest like a judge banging his gavel. Sitting across from Ginger felt like a first date and he had to ask a question she'd be comfortable answering to *break the ice.*

"What do you plan to do with the $25,000 grand prize when you win the baking competition?" Brock had no way of knowing she'd win, but he had to show Ginger his level of confidence in her skills.

Before Ginger could respond, Stephanie had already returned with their waters and caramel macchiatos. "Here you go," she sang. "Enjoy. I'll have that pancake out for you two in a moment."

Ginger sipped her specialty coffee drink and her eyes lit up, though not from the jolt of caffeine, Brock imagined. Ginger's Goodies was her baby, and he knew she didn't mind talking about her business. "I've had my eye on this old house that I plan to transform into my own bakery. The house sticks out like an orange in a bag of apples in this area in old Katy that is now mostly businesses. It'd be perfect for Ginger's Goodies. The competition prize money will be my downpayment." Ginger grinned like she had already won. She hid her contagious smile with a sip from her water glass and folded her hands in her lap.

"I love your energy, Gin, and despite everything that's happened between us, I want the best for you and your business. You'll have to show me the house sometime."

She quirked an eyebrow. "You really want to see it?"

"Of course. Have you had any contact with the owner to get their asking price?"

She nodded. "I have. The current owner was willed the house from her grandfather. She's been approached many times to sell, but after meeting me and hearing about what I want to do with the place, she wants to sell to me, knowing that I won't completely tear the house down."

"And has she given you a timeline to purchase?"

"No, she hasn't. From my understanding and my lengthy prayers, she isn't in a rush to sell, but I don't know how long she'll sit on it before someone else comes along."

"While anything could happen, I get the feeling you won't have to worry about losing out on this building."

Ginger sipped her macchiato, peering at him over the rim of the antique looking mug. "So, The Pearson Group? Why not work with the family's firm? I thought for sure you'd go there once you finished law school. Wasn't that always the plan for you and Bryce?"

"Yeah, that was the plan until I'd done my internship at my dad's firm." Brock leaned his head back against the booth cushion and shook his head. "That summer was the worst."

Ginger chuckled.

"I'm serious. While I appreciated the opportunity, I want to be as far away from taxes as I can. And since my family practices corporate tax law, I didn't see a future for myself at The Pearson Group. Tax is pretty much their brand, so it worked out for my brother, just not for me."

"But can't you practice whatever kind of law you want? I mean they can do the tax stuff while you practice whatever it is that excites you."

He should have considered Ginger's idea before now, but the thought had never occurred to him. All he knew was that he couldn't work at The Pearson Group, so he made it his mission to strike out on his own and create his own path. If he didn't find a suitable option for Decadent Dough, he might be practicing law with his family after all.

"You may be on to something." He tilted his coffee mug toward her. "Perhaps one day I'll present the idea to my dad to see what his thoughts are, but not now." He shook his head.

"You never know. God's plan is often much greater than ours, something I've had to learn and remind myself of over the last few weeks."

Brock nodded, but didn't comment. He and God weren't on speaking terms, at least he wasn't speaking to God. Hadn't done so in quite some time. Religion just hadn't been something he thought he needed. Sure, he believed that God existed, but his beliefs didn't go further than that. Ginger knew that about him, but it never stopped her from bringing Him up in conversation.

She continued, "And from what I remember about your dad, he'd love for you to come work with him."

"I'll be sure to throw in the fact that this was your plan when I mention this arrangement to him."

Ginger chuckled, then winked. "You do that, and you may be going home." She clasped her hands together. "Okay, while I'm enjoying our time together, I have to know something. What's your angle, Mr. Pearson? What is it you really want, and what do I have to do with it?"

Brock took another sip of coffee then rested his linked fingers on the table and glared with an intensity that could've burned a hole through her soul. There was the Ginger he knew.

Direct.

"There is no angle. Why do you think there has to be an angle?"

"I don't believe you." Ginger laced her arms across her chest.

"And why's that?"

"A couple of weeks ago, you waltz up to my counter with this grand idea of being a part of Decadent Dough. I got the feeling you had some sort of stake in it. I find it hard to believe you would just walk away from that. That's why."

"Why would you find that hard to believe? I get the feeling you're intent on believing the worst about me. Why is that? Even if I told you I was past it, that I'd moved on to find another bakery, or that I planned to go in an entirely different direction, you wouldn't believe me. If I told you that I asked you out simply because I wanted to get to know you again and be in your company, that you're the most beautiful woman I've ever seen, you wouldn't believe me."

She fought the pout of her lips turning into a smile. Why was she fighting so hard against their attraction? There was no way she didn't feel what he felt, especially when he hugged her. There had to be something there.

Stephanie interrupted their conversation with their pancake, placing it on the table. "Sorry that took so long. I'll be nearby so let me know if you'd like to order anything else."

"I like to pray and give thanks before I eat. Would you like to join me?"

He didn't, but again, he didn't want her to think he was an even bigger jerk than she had conjured up in her mind. And it wasn't like he didn't believe in God, just that he could do without the extras.

"Sure."

She extended her hands to his and bowed her head. Though they weren't quite seeing eye-to-eye just yet, the warmth of her hands and the sincerity of her prayer did something to him. What, he wasn't sure.

After closing the prayer, Brock held on to her hands a moment longer. She squirmed in her seat under his gaze. He should've pulled away, but every nerve in his body wanted to remain there. He could see in her eyes she wrestled with the idea, too. Ginger cleared her throat and pulled away, wiping her hand on her napkin. She still had feelings for him, and there was no way she could hide it.

And he shouldn't care because he couldn't help but recall how things ended between the two of them when they were younger. But that's just it – his gut reminded him that they were older with more life experiences and a relationship could work this time around.

However, right there, with his heart soaking in Ginger's eyes like a wet sponge, he promised himself that he wouldn't get caught up in her, lose focus, and end up sitting on his parents' front porch dumbfounded, confused, and heartbroken like eighteen-year-old-him again.

Chapter Fourteen

After an early breakfast with Brock, Ginger strolled into her bakery on cloud nine, unsure of what happened. Her primary reason for agreeing to the date was so she could find out his ulterior motive. She was supposed to be strong enough to will her emotions back into a perfectly sealed box. She failed on the former because he'd cut through the toughest tape. She'd tried her hardest to keep an emotional distance, but he'd found his way back into her heart again, a forbidden space, yet she had no control over her heart when it came to him.

She knew that to be true without any doubt. And now that she'd relinquished her power to him, how could she get it back? Though the unspoken truth, there lied a tiny piece of her that relished in the way his eyes softened when he looked at her, the smoothness of his baritone voice, and even the way her heart craved to be enveloped in his arms.

Inside her commercial kitchen, she found Jessie rolling dough, which pulled her out of the euphoric daze. Protective of her business and recipes, Ginger's heart dipped. True, she hired Jessie to help, but she restrained herself from tackling the young woman and thrusting her out of the kitchen.

She kept her voice even while she walked over to greet Jessie. "Good morning. Thanks for getting things started for me." Ginger peered into the mixing bowl Jessie scooped lumps of dough out of and whirled it around. "What ingredients did you use? How did you find the recipe?" *Please don't let her mess up my recipes and everything I've worked so hard for.*

"I've learned your recipes from watching you. I've been mentally taking notes and paying attention to your social media tips. Don't worry. Everything is gluten-free and keto. I've practiced at home a few times and kinda wanted to surprise you. And you have more orders coming in from your website, so figured I'd help get a jump start on them. I hope it's okay." Jessie paused mid-scoop. The look in her eyes reminded Ginger of a younger sibling seeking approval. Ginger reassured Jessie with a lopsided smile.

"Actually, I'm impressed by your initiative. Can't wait to taste them."

"Thanks. Oh, and I also have two batches in the oven that I pulled from the refrigerator to be ready for your morning deliveries."

"You're all over it this morning. Thank you!" Ginger's pulse returned to normal as a sense of calm washed over her. Jessie had been the kind of help she needed all along. She had to pull herself together. Jessie was the reason she had the opportunity to spend an extended amount of time with Brock that morning for breakfast.

"You're welcome. I'm learning from the best. You look very pretty this morning, by the way. Anything special happening today?"

Ginger glanced down at her blouse and skirt. "Thank you. Nothing special. Just had breakfast with an old friend, that's all." Ginger donned her apron and tied it around her waist.

"You must really like this friend because you are gorgeous. You're pretty every day, it's just obvious you did a little extra. Does he know he's just a friend? Because if not, you might have given him the wrong impression." Jessie wriggled her eyebrows and smirked.

"No worries. He knows where we stand." And so did she. The trouble was that her heart hadn't gotten the memo. The timer dinged and Ginger removed the cookies from the oven. She grabbed the batch Jessie prepared. "Jessie, why don't you go man the counter while I box up the morning deliveries? I'll put these in the oven."

Jessie nodded and retreated through the swinging metal doors. Ginger released a heavy breath as she picked up where Jessie left off—mixing and rolling dough into cookie balls—her happy place. She prepared muffin mixture and scones and placed them in the oven, giving the cookies time to cool.

Jessie's absence gave Ginger time to process everything happening. Brock. Jessie working in her kitchen—alone. Was she as amazing as she seemed to be? Ginger wanted to believe so, but an uneasy feeling set up shop in the pit of her stomach like burnt cupcakes sticking to a pan. Did the doubt arise because of Brock's initial proposition? Ginger shook her head to get rid of the thoughts. She boxed three sets of two dozen cookies for this morning's delivery and met Jessie at the customer counter.

"Your deliveries are all ready for you."

"Got it covered. See you in a bit."

Ginger waved her off. With Jessie gone, her thoughts shifted back to Brock.

She could still feel the imprint of his hand in hers. Like it was supposed to be there. When she saw Jessie mixing dough her kitchen twenty minutes ago, it distracted her from thoughts of him.

Thoughts of the way his eyes pierced hers bringing about images of how things used to be between them.

Thoughts of the way her heart had begun a rhythm of its own the moment their fingers touched.

And thoughts of the way she had to will her palm steady against the current of electricity that slithered up her arm.

She shook her right hand as if that would make the feeling go away or destroy the memory. Though it had been a couple of hours since *the touch,* she still remembered what his felt like: secure, stronger, and smoother than she remembered. Her heart's flutter tickled her chest.

The oven timer rang, jolting thoughts of Brock out of her mind, which was much needed. She transferred the pastries to a rack and returned to the counter to place the pastries in the warmer.

"So, this is the new Ginger," Lisa said, seemingly appearing out of thin air.

Ginger hadn't seen her coming and jumped when alerted to her presence. She'd almost dropped her pastries. "Geez, girl, you scared me."

"*Umm hmm.* What is really going on?" Lisa asked, leaning against the wall with her arms folded across her chest. She squinted and sized her up. That woman could smell any kind of relationship activity in her life.

Although Ginger appreciated Lisa stopping by to support her almost daily, she almost wished Lisa skipped today because Lisa had this way of pulling information out of her and she'd rather not revisit the Brock situation.

Not yet.

Especially when confusion still had a tight grip on her.

"What do you mean? The same thing is going on today as it is every day. I'm baking."

"Baking what? A batch of love?"

A soft chuckle escaped Ginger's lips. "You think you're funny, don't you?" She placed the pastries in the warmer, avoiding eye contact with Lisa.

"Don't make this about me. Look at you all dressed up. Lip gloss poppin', hair shining, fancy skirt, thirty teeth," Lisa assessed, vacating her space from the wall, pacing the floor, pointing out the changes she noticed in her friend.

"Lisa, I'm not that dressed up. I always wear lip gloss. My hair is like this every day. As for the teeth comment, I'm always smiling," Ginger counted off on her fingers. Ginger had taken extra care with her appearance that morning since she had a breakfast date with Brock. No matter what she thought about him, she wasn't going to show up to their little meeting looking any kind of way. He needed to see what he'd missed out on all these years.

"No, no, something is definitely different about you today. I've never known you to wear a skirt to work." Lisa's voice had been a crossover between singing and teasing. "You're not concerned with getting flour on your nice clothes?"

"Yeah, but it'll be okay. I had breakfast with Brock this morning," Ginger mumbled, rubbing her hand across her mouth to mask her words, yet Lisa heard her clearly.

Lisa twisted her lips. "Really? Is that all you have to say? You know I love a good second-chance love story. So, give me the good stuff."

"No story to tell." Ginger motioned a baseball referee's strike motion.

"So how was it? And so soon? Did you get all the information you needed to—" Lisa used air quotes and mimicked Ginger's voice— "find out what he's up to?"

Ginger shrugged and continued her task of adding the final pastries to the warmer.

"So, do you need to go out with him again to figure it out or what? Give me something to work with," Lisa pushed. "I'll take my usual."

Ginger bagged a blueberry scone for Lisa and rung up her order.

"Brock is the last thing on my mind. The final round of the baking competition is about all I need to be concerned with now, okay?"

"You're becoming a pro at avoiding questions. Are you going out with him again or not?"

"I haven't decided yet."

Lisa paid for her order. "But did he ask?"

"Yeah, he did." Ginger spun on her heels and marched into the kitchen. Oh, how she loved Lisa, but she could be exhausting, pressing her to consider things she didn't want to think about— mainly Brock and the spark that reignited between them when their hands connected at breakfast. Wouldn't he have let go if he hadn't felt it too?

Lisa was like a mirror. She wouldn't go away, and her words reflected Ginger's thoughts. There was no hiding from either. But that had to be expected given they'd known each other for more than fifteen years.

"Still here, huh? Thought you would've returned to the bookstore by now."

"See, that's the beauty of working at your family's bookstore. My mom doesn't complain because I pull my weight around there. Plus, she does the same thing with Aunt Wanda. And besides, we—" Lisa waved her finger between the two of them—"have unfinished business."

Ginger sucked a breath in between her teeth, her chest puffing up. "I believe you're overthinking this, Lisa. Don't give Brock too much headspace. I'm not quite sure he deserves it."

"My dearest friend, I'm only trying to help get that puzzled look off your face. Your head is about to explode because you're trying to figure this thing out. But I'm here to help."

Ginger cocked an eyebrow. "Is that right?"

Lisa gave her a slow nod. A smirk formed on one corner of her lips. "It's simple really. Either you like him, or you don't."

Ginger huffed and gripped the countertop and recited the lines she'd repeated to herself on her drive to work from her breakfast date with Brock. "There are so many reasons why this isn't as simple as you, me, or Brock want it to be. Had he been some guy I've never dated who wasn't initially trying to take my business, then that would make this a little easier. But I can't pretend that didn't happen nor can't I pretend we don't have history. For all I know about him now, he's just some slickety-slick lawyer trying to run game on me. I don't know who he's become in the last twenty years. He'll have to do a lot more than buy breakfast and send customers my way to prove his intentions are pure."

"Like what?"

Ginger threaded her arms across her chest and thought for a moment. She frowned and twisted her lips. "You know what? I don't know."

"Well, if you don't know the answer to that, you've already set him up to fail. There's nothing he can do to prove he's not shady, so stop talking to him. Send him packing and get on with your life."

That wasn't easy either.

"It's funny how you have all this advice for me, but when it comes to Jayden, you're deaf."

"Different situation. Plus, this isn't about me." Lisa double tapped the countertop, flicked both pointer fingers toward Ginger, and backed away. Of course, she'd walk away when Ginger brought up the subject of Jayden.

However, Lisa's advice about Brock was rational given Ginger wasn't sure she could trust him. And because of that fact, she was secretly compelled to see how things would play out. To prove Brock hadn't changed and was everything she presumed him to be.

But what if he wasn't?

Chapter Fifteen

If anyone had told him two months ago that he'd be setting his alarm clock to wake him before sunrise so that he could meet Ginger for breakfast every day, he'd have thought they'd lost their minds. To go from not hearing from her for more than twenty years to looking forward to seeing her every morning was everything he didn't know he needed in his morning routine. He sat across from her at The Toasted Yolk. They'd both ordered the restaurant's most popular omelettes, sampling the one the other one ordered.

They'd slowly fallen into a comfortable rhythm. Most days he felt like they picked up where they left off after a twenty year fight. Crazy, but true.

She'd taken a bite of his omelette, closing her eyes to give herself a moment to concentrate on the flavors. "This is so good. Now I'm wishing I'd ordered the Big Ben."

Brock chuckled. "Don't be coveting my omelette. You're the one who wanted all vegetables in yours, which is good, but I need meat in mine."

Ginger fake pouted. "You wouldn't trade with me?"

That woman had no idea that he'd give her the world if she asked. And it sucked for him that she had his heart wrapped around her finger again, yet, she didn't know it. And Brock still couldn't be certain if she even cared to know.

He pushed his plate toward hers. "If this is what you want, then yes."

She tilted her head to one side, seemingly deciding if he was serious. Ginger smiled. "Since mine is good, I wouldn't ask that of you, but I do have one question."

Brock placed his fork on his plate, linked his fingers on the table, and leaned forward. "What's that?"

"Remember, Jayden?"

He nodded. "Yeah. We play ball at the gym together from time to time. What's up?"

"He's having a game night at his place with some of the partners in his firm. Lisa invited me and said it was okay for me to bring someone. Would you like to come with me?"

Brock's heart dribbled. Her asking him out answered his question of whether she cared or rather how much she cared. The Ginger he knew could have asked anyone, yet she wanted him to go. He gripped his chest. "I'd love nothing more than to be your plus one."

Ginger chuckled and waved him off. "No need to be dramatic. I'll send you all the details through text later. Are you sure work won't prevent you from coming?"

"I'll make time to be there for you."

His sentiment made her blush. And in turn, his heart wanted to jump out of his chest and hug her knowing he still had that effect on her.

They lingered around The Toasted Yolk for another forty-five minutes after they'd finished their breakfast. Brock appreciated the fact that Ginger became more relaxed with him, allowed herself to laugh at his jokes, and shared more about how she started her business. He loved the way her eyes twinkled like the evening stars and words rushed from her lips like champagne bursting from a newly opened bottle when she talked about Ginger's Goodies.

How could he ever believe she'd give it up for a deal with Decadent Dough?

Other small business owners probably felt the same as Ginger.

Brock rationalized that Decadent Dough provided an opportunity for small businesses to expand their brand and reach a wider customer base. Couldn't they work with them for a few years, then branch off to do their own thing? By that time, they'd have more experience in how the larger businesses did things and could apply that knowledge to make their business more successful, right?

He tested his theory later that morning when he walked into Hasty Pastry, a local bakery that dominated the University of Houston area. At first, Brock drove along Scott Street taking in the neighborhood with Wheeler Avenue Baptist Church on his right and Hasty Pastry's Pepto-Bismol building directly across the street, in the same parking lot as the popular Frenchy's, a fast food chicken joint. Excellent location—within walking distance of the university and one of the largest Baptist churches in Houston.

Brock parked and entered the pastry shop. The aroma of doughnuts, muffins, pies, and cookies filled the air. It was like a Saturday afternoon at his grandmother's house growing up. Sugar mixed with love as she called it. Amid the chatter, eighties music wafted through the old speaker system, yet the young crowd didn't seem to mind the out-of-date tunes or the rickety sound system.

Hasty Pastry was littered with college students, their books and tablets strewn on the old-fashioned metal tables that reminded him of the ones in a seventies ice cream parlor. Coffee and their choice of pastry on the table. Their faces plastered with the best-time-of-their-lives smiles. They were living the dream, and probably didn't even realize it.

Brock locked eyes with an older, white-bearded man who could've been easily identified as Santa Claus, except he didn't wear glasses and his smooth ageless skin was like coffee. And today he wore a red shirt. His welcoming smile beckoned Brock to the counter.

"Welcome to Hasty Pastry where the goods are sweet, and the company is sweeter. How may I help you today, young man?"

"Hi. I'm Brock Pearson. By any chance, are you the owner?" He should've led with something else. Maybe even ordered something first.

"Yes, sir, I am. How may I help you, Brock Pearson?"

Work on your people skills, Brock.

Brock flashed his most charming smile, the one that worked on everyone but Ginger. And from the looks of it, wasn't working on Mr. Hasty Pastry either.

"Well, I've never been here before, so what do you suggest I try?" Brock glanced at the overhead menu. No gluten-free or specialty items like Ginger's Goodies.

"You look like a cake donut man with black coffee. How does that sound?"

"Sounds good. I'll take it."

Brock paid for his order and accepted the pink paper bag and white Styrofoam cup of coffee.

"Do you mind if we talk for a minute?" Brock gestured to the nearest empty table, and Mr. Hasty Pastry looked over Brock's shoulder to ensure no customers were in line behind him.

"Sure. What's this about?"

"As I said, I'm Brock Pearson. What's your name?" Brock extended his hand this time, and the man accepted.

"Elijah Livingston." He rested his linked hands on the small table, blew out an exasperated breath, and poised himself for Brock's pitch, like he'd heard it a thousand times. He'd already made up his mind about him, of that Brock was certain. He cocked one eyebrow and nodded, giving Brock permission to proceed.

"Mr. Livingston, this is an amazing place you have here. Have you ever considered a partnership to get your pastries mass produced and into all the large retail chain stores?"

"I haven't. That has never been the goal here." Mr. Livingston's eyes flattened. He pulled his lips into a tight line, and Brock could tell he minced words. He had that same look in his eyes his father had when Brock got out of line as a child—the look that said he needed to clean up his act quick, or there'd be trouble.

"Is there a way you'd consider it? Decadent Dough is in the process of seeking out a local bakery to partner with in hopes of expanding their product line. I do believe that this could be a mutually beneficial partnership. More resources. More visibility." Did he still believe that lie he tried to sell? Not necessarily, but he believed in his promotion, the corner office, the additional zeroes in his salary, and the prestige that came along with all of that.

Mr. Livingston held up his palm with the authority of a school crossing guard, and Brock knew the conversation was over. "Let me stop you right there, son. You're not the first person to walk in here within the last twenty years with a better opportunity for us. You see that woman over there standing behind the counter?"

Brock glanced over to see Mrs. Claus accepting orders and nodded.

Mr. Livingston pointed at her. "My sweet Elaine dreamed of owning a small bakery. This is her dream, and there is not a check in hell that would make me sell it. And before you move on to some other bakery with this spiel, I want you to ask yourself something."

"What's that, sir?" Brock hadn't received so many rejections in his life than he had in the last month with trying to get the head of corporate mergers position. He'd take all the advice he could get at this point.

"If your mother owned a bakery, would you encourage her to take this deal you're offering? Is it a good deal for your wife?" Mr. Livingston glanced down to Brock's empty left hand. "Well, if you were married, would you and the Mrs. benefit from this supposed opportunity? If the answer is no, then stop trying to sell false dreams to other folks. No good will come from this, son. You're young—say mid-thirties. You have a lot to learn, but mark my words, they're using you. Whoever you're working for, they're not thinking about you, and whatever they're promising you, whatever carrot they're dangling in front of your face, can and will be snatched away, like that—" Mr. Livingston snapped his fingers— "when they get what they want out of you."

"Yes, sir, I understand." Brock bit into his doughnut. Tasty, but not as tasty as Ginger's Goodies, and he'd just about sampled everything she'd baked.

"But, if this deal is as good as you're trying to make it out to be, God will lead you to the right establishment, but this—" he jammed his finger on the table— "isn't it. Enjoy your coffee and doughnut. Have a nice day, son."

Mr. Livingston left Brock at the table with more to chew on than the doughnut. His heart pulsed stronger and louder in his ears the more Mr. Livingston cut him down to size and sliced through his ego. He swallowed the disappointment. Images of that shiny corner office and hefty pay raise slowly faded. Was he naïve to think he could make this work for him and someone else?

Chapter Sixteen

Ginger should not be stressing over what to wear to a casual game night get-together at Jayden's house, but she was. Charades. Dominoes. Card games. Trivia games. None of those required her to wear the perfect pair of jeans and tee, but she felt the need to look great. Not only was this sort of a date, but possibly an opportunity for her to sell her pastry business services to Jayden's counterparts or their plus ones. Her business wasn't always her first thought, but one had to be prepared for anything, which meant she couldn't show up looking raggedy. She would represent Jayden, Lisa, and her business tonight. Brock, too. What possessed her to invite him as her plus one, anyway?

Duh, you still care for him.

So much for keeping an emotional distance.

She'd just go with the flow, while being on guard.

Ginger finally settled on a pair of dark wash skinny jeans and a black V-neck fitted tee.

Her phone vibrated with a text from Lisa.

L: So glad you're coming and that I won't be alone to schmooze the partners in Jayden's firm.

Heart faced smiley faces followed.

G: No worries. I've got you. Sure you don't need me and Brock to bring anything? We don't mind swinging by the store on the way.

L: I've taken care of all the food. Bring dessert if you wish. Could mean more business. ☺

Ginger chuckled. She could hear Lisa's voice through that text.

G: Got it covered. See you soon. Brock should be here any minute.

L: <3

Ginger gave herself a once over in the mirror. Satisfied with her hair, light makeup, and nude lip gloss, she sauntered into the kitchen to pull a batch of cookies out of the oven. Though probably overkill, she'd take the cake she baked last night as well. She chuckled when she remembered how she had to fight off her dad from taking a slice.

When the cookies cooled, she packaged them in one of her logo boxes. As soon as she tied the pink ribbon, her doorbell rang. Thank goodness her dad was out of the house. She hadn't talked to him about her seeing Brock again. Although she was a grown woman who lived in his house voluntarily, she shared her dating experiences with him. But she and Brock had history and she wasn't ready to share just yet.

Ginger opened the door. Brock stood there with a bouquet of flowers, dressed in a pair of jeans and a crimson short sleeved collared shirt. While he looked great, he smelled even better. A combination of citrus, cedar wood, and him. He smothered her in his arms where she relished the masculine smell of him. She all but melted in his embrace. No matter what she tried. Ginger had no amount of willpower to keep her heart from thumping and her mind from conjuring up thoughts of a future with him. When Brock released her, he handed her the bouquet.

"For you."

Her smile spread wide like a girl receiving flowers for the first time. "Thanks, Brock. Let me put these away and I'll be ready."

Ginger removed a vase from the kitchen cabinet, filled it with water, added the flowers, and set the vase near the kitchen window above the sink. She stacked the cookie box on top of the pink cake box and took them back to the foyer where Brock remained standing. "We're taking these."

"Perfect. I was thinking we should stop and grab a bottle of wine or something."

Ginger smiled. "Lisa said we're good, but no one ever turns down desserts."

Brock winked. "Especially not Ginger's Goodies."

The way the sentiment rolled off his lips made her heart play double dutch. She really should be careful about getting involved with him again, but living in the moment felt good and right.

∞

Ginger and Brock were the first guests to arrive at Jayden's one story, three-bedroom, red brick house in the Katy suburbs. On the drive to their destination, Brock held casual conversation with her, like they were old friends. And they were. It's just that they weren't *only* friends and while they enjoyed each other's company, Ginger couldn't be quite sure what to make of them now.

He cut the engine and turned to her. "As long as I've known Jayden and played ball with him, I've never been to his

141

crib. I almost feel like I'm taking my friendship with him to the next level."

Ginger threw her head back against the headrest and laughed. "Gotta start somewhere I guess."

He held her gaze, obviously wanting to say more, but didn't. The way his eyes bore into hers caused a stirring in every fiber of her being. He had to stop doing that to her. She didn't know how much more she could take until she completely let her guard down and threw caution to the wind, declaring her undying love for him.

Okay, that was silly. Pull it together.

Brock joined her in laughter. "Ready?"

"Let's do this."

He climbed out of the car and shuffled around to the passenger side to open the car door for her, then relieved her of the pastry boxes. "You know I plan to win, right?"

She winked. "Then I have the right partner."

When Ginger climbed out of his coupe, he closed the door with his hip and led them up the concrete path to Jayden's front door. While his lawn was mowed, Jayden didn't put much effort into anything else. No flowerbeds like that of his neighbors or welcome signs or mats on the front porch.

Before Ginger lifted her finger to ring the doorbell, Lisa swung open the front door and threw her arms around Ginger.

"Glad y'all could make it." She then whispered in Ginger's ear. "I guess this means we're keeping him?"

Ginger bubbled in laughter. She recovered and pulled out of Lisa's embrace. "Just living in the moment."

Lisa stepped out of the way and opened the door wider to allow Ginger and Brock inside. She led them through the foyer and into the kitchen where Jayden maneuvered around double checking his food and drink stash.

"Gin and Brock are here," Lisa announced.

Ginger hugged his neck. "Hey, Jayden. Looks nicer than I expected for a game night. I guess you let Lisa run wild with the purple and gold decorations, huh?"

Jayden chuckled and cast gleaming eyes at Lisa. She never seemed to noticed how the man looked at her. Ginger always found that strange considering Lisa could point out chemistry between other couples, yet Jayden was still hovering in the friend zone.

"Lisa has a way of keeping me straight and not allowing me to look bad. Like I've told her many times, I couldn't do this without her."

"Nah, you couldn't," Ginger teased, but neither of them noticed.

Brock placed the pastry boxes on the kitchen island then greeted Jayden. "What's up, bro?"

"Hey man, glad you could make it."

"I appreciate the invite. So, is this you getting one step closer to partner?"

"Something like that. It's an unspoken rule that senior managers and partners host get-togethers." He jutted his thumb toward Lisa. "She suggested we have a game night. Gives everyone a chance to loosen up and have fun without any pressure."

Ginger butted in the conversation. "Hold up, did you say, *we?*"

"Yeah, Lisa is my right hand in all of this. It wouldn't happen without her."

Ginger nodded. "So you keep saying."

But Jayden scrunched his eyebrows. His confusion evident, unless he was playing a role, which is what Ginger believed. Someone needed to help those two.

An awkward silence passed through the room before Lisa snapped everyone out of their trance.

"Gin, come help me finish setting up the snack table, then we can figure out where to put your cake and cookies."

Before she turned to follow Lisa, she caught sight of Brock's lingering gaze. He'd given her one of those you're-so-beautiful-and-I'm-glad-I-get-to-be-here-with-you kind of smiles.

In the dining area, a dark purple tablecloth covered a six-foot table. Tortilla chips, cheese dip, vegetable trays, fruit trays, three different flavors of wings, chicken salad croissant sandwiches, and a do-it-yourself taco bar lined the table.

"Goodness, how many people are you and Jayden expecting?"

"Five more couples. His mentor, Joe, and his wife. Two senior managers and their dates. And two partners and their plus ones."

Ginger looked around. "The food looks taken care of. What did you need me to do?"

"Oh nothing. You just needed to be stopped. Don't think I couldn't see what you were doing."

Ginger burst into laughter. "What? Jayden needs a push."

"No, he doesn't. We're really great friends. Don't ruin it, Gin."

Ginger walked around the table and stood shoulder to shoulder with Lisa. She kept her voice low. "Is that what you're afraid of? That things may not work out and that'll ruin your friendship with him? Where is all of that *take a chance* energy for yourself?"

Lisa's low voice matched Ginger's. "I'm not afraid of anything. Things just work with us. We're good."

Ginger's mouth dropped open. "This is the first time you admitted to liking him."

"Never said that. Now cease and desist."

Ginger giggled. "For tonight. But you have to promise to do the same when it comes to me and Brock."

Lisa jammed both fists into her lips. "Your situation is different, and you know it."

Ginger shrugged and hiked an eyebrow. "So what?"

"Fine. No comments tonight." Lisa clasped her hands. "Okay, so where are we going to put your cookies and cake?"

"I don't think there's any room for the cake, but we can put the cookies here and bring out the cake later."

"That works. Now come with me to the living room and tell me what you think of the setup for games."

Lisa and Jayden had moved the sofas to the side of the room. A group of folding chairs formed a circle in the center of the room. The box of games were stacked on an end table. They'd positioned a white board where everyone could see it for the game of Pictionary. Soft R&B music played through one of the music apps on Jayden's wall-hung flat screen television.

"Personable but are you sure folks will want to sit in a circle like they're part of an AA meeting?"

Lisa chuckled. "This setup forces us to stay in the moment, don't you think? If we're in the circle, I think everyone will be inclined to focus on the games and the people in the room."

"I get it. Plus, everyone knows why they're coming, so this should be fun. Thanks for the invite. I could use something to get my mind off the baking competition."

Lisa rested an arm on Ginger's shoulder. "I'm glad you could make it. I never mind helping Jayden with hosting his parties or being his plus one when he goes to them, but these are Jayden's people. It feels nice to have one of my own here."

"We've got each other's backs. Now—"

The doorbell rang, interrupting their conversation.

Lisa yelled. "I'll get it."

Ginger watched her saunter away, walking through Jayden's home like it was her own. She returned with an older gentleman and his companion. The man stood about six inches taller than Lisa and his date. His smile was framed with a groomed silver speckled mustache and short beard. He dressed in a pair of jeans and light blue short-sleeved collared shirt. Lisa had an arm linked in the crook of the woman's elbow. She was the same height as Lisa and Ginger. And if Ginger didn't know any better, she'd believe the woman was the same age as them. She wore an all black sleeveless jumpsuit with her blond hair pulled back into a ponytail. "Ginger, this is Joe, Jayden's mentor, and his wife, Patricia."

Ginger shook their hands. "Nice to meet you both."

"Gin, will you show them to the appetizers while I go tag Jayden?"

"Sure, thing. Follow me." Ginger led them to the dining room.

Lisa had strategically placed a bottle of hand sanitizer on the end of the table next to the fancy looking dollar store purple clear plastic plates. Not that they needed a rundown of the spread Lisa and Jayden offered, but Ginger did so anyway and stepped out of their way to give them room to self-serve. When they arrived at the dessert section, which was the box of cookies she bought, Ginger took the opportunity to introduce herself.

"You have to try the cookies. I baked them myself."

Patricia added one to her plate. "They look delicious." She flipped the box to see Ginger's logo on the lid. "You own a bakery? Do you have any cards?"

That was one of Ginger's favorite questions. She always kept a few business cards in her purse. "I sure do. I'll get one to you before you leave."

Ginger didn't have an opportunity to continue with small talk because the doorbell rang again, and the rest of the guests arrived at once. Lisa greeted them. The men seemed to separate to meet Jayden, Brock, and Joe in the kitchen. The women went straight for the food table. Afterwards, they gathered in the living room circle to chat.

Lisa handled herself well, but as her friend, Ginger kept an eye out for that *save me* look. The woman didn't need her assistance though. She worked the room like the party was her own. Once she ensured the ladies had their food and drinks, she returned with the men trailing behind with their own plates. She turned the volume down on the television music and moved center circle.

"Okay, folks. You came here for fun and that's what you're going to get. Our first game is Pictionary and I thought it'd be fun to switch up the teams this time into ladies versus gents. However, I don't want to be the reason anybody is sleeping on the sofa tonight."

The group burst into laughter.

Kelly, the companion of one of the partners waved her hand and yelled out. "No worries, you're good. They're big boys. They'll recover from their loss before they get home."

The laughter continued.

Ginger locked eyes with Brock, who sat next to Jayden. She couldn't put into words the kind of smile that framed his lips. The kind that made her squirm in her seat and her heart dip all at once. She mouthed, *You're going down.*

Her phone vibrated. She opened it up to a text from Brock.

B: I play to win.

She glanced across the room to see the grin on his face.

G: Not happening for you tonight. Sorry.

B: I play to win. EVERYTHING.

He meant her heart. Their relationship. And he didn't have to say the words for her to understand. When she looked up at him again, his expression was different. He winked and everything in her responded. A chill spread over her causing her body to shiver. Her heart burst into a chaotic rhythm, too. The possibility of Brock throwing his effort behind winning over her love excited her, but also made her want to run away. Good thing they were in a room filled with people because that meant she didn't have to address his message. Ginger sent a smiley face and tucked her phone away in her back pocket.

"Okay, looks like we're ready for our first game of Pictionary. Ladies versus Gents. And since they're gentleman, I'm sure they don't mind us ladies going first."

Jessica, the companion of one of the senior partners jumped out of her seat. "Since I'm done with my food, I'll go first."

"Alright, have it." Lisa sat next to Ginger.

Jessica sauntered over to the stack of games and opened the Pictionary box. She withdrew a card, created a discard pile, and stood next to the dry erase board. Jayden started the timer. "Go."

As much as Ginger enjoyed a good game night, she'd never played Pictionary. And Jessica was not the best artist, so she was no help to her team in the first round, although the ladies guessed the answer and scored one point.

The first round seemingly set the tone for the duration of the game, because an hour later, the score was seven to three, with the women leading. Ginger looked over to Brock. "I guess not, *everything,* huh?"

Though she spoke directly to him, no one paid attention to the two of them because they were all involved in their own battles, with the men's dates rubbing the win in their faces.

Brock laughed. "We're not done."

Jayden stood. "Okay, what are y'all not good at? That's what we'll play next."

The women laughed.

"Give it up, honey, we're good at everything," Patricia called out. The women echoed her sentiments and high-fived each other.

"I've never been good at Poker," Jessica said.

All the women laughed, except Ginger. Lisa elbowed Ginger and clued her in. "We beat them in poker a few times."

Jayden shook his head from side to side. "Fine. Let's just play trivia. We've got this, guys." He fist-bumped his team.

Lisa had several trivia games stacked in the pile. While she allowed the group to vote on which game they wanted to play, Jayden ensured everyone had enough food and beverages. He and Brock, along with Joe grabbed extra chicken wings, tacos, and drinks.

The group played three rounds of trivia with the ladies winning all but one game.

"Reynolds, this has been fun, but it's time for us to head home. I'd hate to wear out my welcome," Jayden's mentor, Joe said as he stood.

"Never. I appreciate you coming by."

"Anything to support you."

His other guests also made preparations to leave, with everyone saying their good-byes to each other.

Jayden raised his voice above the chatter. "Please take as much food as you want. Less for me to clean up."

A round of laughs came from the group.

"Anymore of those cookies or that cake?" Kelly asked.

Jayden called from the dining area. "No cookies and only two slices of cake left."

She shot out of her seat. "I call dibs."

Ginger's soul beamed as her chest inflated. She took that as her opportunity to promote Ginger's Goodies. "There's more where that came from. Give me a call anytime and I'd be happy to take care of a custom order or stop by to see me inside the Katy Mills food court."

Patricia returned to the living room area. "That reminds me. I need your card."

How could she have forgotten to give the women her contact information?

She had physical cards, but remembered Jessie helped her create digital business cards. Ginger opened up her phone and instructed Patricia to scan her QR code. After going through the motions with her, the remaining ladies also scanned her card.

"Thanks, Ginger. You'll be hearing from me." Patricia hugged her and turned her attention back to Lisa, Jayden, and her husband, Joe.

The remaining couples followed Joe and Patricia out, with Jayden and Lisa escorting them all to the front door. As the perfect duo, they thanked their guests for coming and wished them safe travels home and a good night. Ginger and Brock hung around to help Jayden and Lisa clean and arrange his furniture back in its rightful place.

"We appreciate you all," Lisa said as she and Jayden walked Ginger and Brock to their car.

Brock gave Lisa a side shoulder hug. With Jayden, he clasped his hand, pulled him close and hugged him with the opposite hand. "This was fun. A much-needed break for me. You'll be partner soon, man. It's obvious they want you."

Jayden shrugged. "So they tell me. When it happens, the four of us will get together to celebrate."

"My man." Brock fist-bumped Jayden. "I'm all for it."

"Yeah, this was really nice, guys. You did well," Ginger added.

"And the desserts were fire. I'm sure you've found some new customers."

"I appreciate you looking out for me, Jay."

"It's all good."

Ginger wrapped her arms around Lisa's neck. "See you soon. Don't stay out too late."

"You know I'm going to make sure she gets home safe."

"Don't I know it. Good night, guys."

After their final round of good-byes, Brock escorted Ginger to the passenger side door, opened it for her and waited until she secured her seatbelt before he rounded the car and claimed the driver's seat. During the twenty-minute drive back to her house, she and Brock laughed about the night's events. And although they weren't alone at the party, every moment she spent with him chiseled away at her heart's defenses. He didn't mention that text about him playing to win everything, but the message lingered with her causing that little organ pumping in the left side of her chest to shift into an irregular rhythm.

Ginger didn't bring up the text either, partly because she didn't want to know what he meant by it. Or more like she already knew and didn't want to acknowledge what could be happening between them.

Again.

Chapter Seventeen

Brock hated the war going on inside of him about his feelings for Ginger. The whole should-they-or-shouldn't-they was getting old. They enjoyed each other's company just as they always had, but their past had them in a death grip. He arranged to attend the final round of the baking competition. Though he'd be there as an obligation to Decadent Dough, he was more interested in supporting Ginger. And he hoped that by the time they were in Austin, they would decide whether they would move on or figure this thing out.

He prided himself on being focused. Productive. Certain of his life plan—a life plan that involved getting his career on track.

A life plan that excluded a long-term partner.

A life plan that excluded Ginger, since she'd made it clear long ago she didn't want a life with him. His heart still bled from disappointment.

But maybe life had a different course for him. The possibility that Ginger still loved him and would consider another relationship with him sent chills rippling through his body, but also squeezed the breath out of his chest. Brock wanted to believe the years apart were good for them, grew them up, made them stronger, and better for each other. But he couldn't escape the nagging voice in the back of his mind.

This is a setup for another heartbreak.

He ignored the negative thoughts and navigated his car into a parking space in the City Centre parking garage. Before he climbed out of the car, he brushed his hair and mustache. Satisfied that he looked his best for Ginger, he walked toward Brio Italian Grille to meet Ginger for their date. Her work schedule had them taking separate cars so that they wouldn't miss their reservation.

Brock called her to make sure she'd arrived. She'd just stepped out of her car, so he turned around to meet her outside the parking garage exit. Ginger appeared in her lemon V-neck blouse and skinny jeans that accentuated her small curves. An appreciative smile formed on his lips.

"You look beautiful."

Ginger looked down at her simple ensemble. A smile that was as bright as her shirt lit her face. "Thank you."

Brock took hold of her hand while they walked. It felt like the most natural thing to do so he did, acting off instinct. He assumed Ginger sensed the same because she didn't pull away, she matched his grip.

They rounded the corner and climbed the deep cherry brick stairs to the entrance, passing manicured bushes and the shaded, fenced-in outside patio. Brock opened the door and halfway regretted his restaurant choice. White linen tablecloths. Waiters dressed in crisp, white button-down shirts with black ties. Dim lighting. Soft music.

He hesitated.

"Is this okay for you? If not, we can find something else." He projected his uncertainty, more concerned about what this type of atmosphere may bring out of him. His feelings were in a weird place, unchartered territory, and he'd lost faith in himself to keep them tucked away.

"This is perfect. And it smells so good in here." Ginger closed her eyes briefly and inhaled. "I don't think I realized how hungry I am until now. Are you trying to back out?" Her eyes searched his.

He cleared his throat. "No, we're celebrating your accomplishments in this baking competition. I'm looking at a winner, so just making sure this works for you."

She gave him the same pat on the arm she'd give to console a child. "This is just fine."

The hostess, also dressed in a black tie and skirt with a crisp, white buttoned shirt, greeted them. "Hello, Welcome to Brio Italian Grille!" Her voice cheerful. Friendly. Welcoming. "Do you have a reservation?"

"Yes, Pearson."

She searched the screen before her. "I've got you right here. Please follow me." She grabbed two menus from the hostess station and led them to their seats. Brock pulled out Ginger's chair and waited until she sat comfortably before taking the seat across from her.

"Everything looks so good," Ginger commented, perusing the menu. "That may be because it's been a while since I've eaten."

"No, you're right. I think my eyes may be larger than my stomach, but that means we'll have to come back again to try whatever we don't get to try today," Brock said casually, testing the waters.

"May I interest you in a glass of wine?" A red-haired waitress appeared at their table holding a book of wine offerings.

Brock gestured toward Ginger who shook her head. "No, thanks, I'll have a glass of tea."

"Water for me. And I believe we're ready to order."

She turned to Ginger. "Alright, ma'am, what would you like?"

"I'll take the grilled salmon fresca. Any chance I can get the balsamic glaze on the side?"

"Sure can. And what would you like, sir?"

"Lobster and shrimp fettucine sounds good."

"Alright. I'll put your orders in and return with your drinks shortly." She took their menus, lightly brushing Brock's hand as she reached for his, flashing him a smile and asked, "Is there anything else I can get for you?"

"No, thank you."

"Let me know if you need *anything*."

Her flirting didn't faze him, because he wanted to hear those words only from Ginger. Though the truth would be he wanted her.

"I guess she didn't see me sitting right here." Ginger folded her arms across her chest and hiked one eyebrow.

"Never mind her. I'm where I want to be." Brock slid his chair closer to the table and leaned in, turning his ear toward her. "But is that jealousy I hear? I think I like this Ginger."

"Don't flatter yourself. I'm simply pointing out she was rude. She can hit on you some other time."

"Maybe she's using that intuition you women have and knows that you aren't interested in me."

"She's not crazy."

"Just how interested are you? Up until this point, I thought you half-hated me."

"Doesn't mean I can't still be interested." Ginger winked.

"So, when you're not baking or thinking about me, what are you doing?" They'd spent quite a bit of time together lately, so he had a good idea of what she did in her free time, but that still didn't stop him from asking. He wanted to know her fully.

Ginger threw her head back and gave a laugh that sent ripples through his core. He could listen to that melodious sound all day. He'd been missing out on the joy spread across her face for far too long.

"Reading or watching Hallmark movies, volunteering in the youth ministry at church. I take walks around my neighborhood from time to time." She twisted her lips in thought. "And of course you know I take care of my father."

"What illness does he have?"

"Heart disease caused by untreated hypertension. His medicine works for the most part, and he walks with me when he's up to it. I make sure he keeps his doctor's appointments and takes his medicine. He's a lot better. And with my mom no longer with us, I moved back in with him after college graduation."

"He's lucky to have you for a daughter." Brock circled the back of her hand with his thumb. The waitress returned with their drinks, and they acknowledged her with a nod, Brock not wanting to lose the moment they were having.

"Thank you for that. My life is fairly simple. What about you?"

"Mostly work. When I'm not at work, I'm reading law articles, keeping up with current news. Some—mainly my family—would say I need to get a life. I get in a few workouts a week, and Sundays are set aside for dinner with my family for the most part. That's about it. I must say breakfast has been one of my favorite things to do, lately."

"Same here, and I don't even consider myself a breakfast person."

"Wait. Wasn't breakfast your idea?"

"Well, yeah, but I didn't think you'd go for it. I joked, and you turned up the heat in the oven."

Brock threw his head back in laughter.

"You're a baker. I'd think you'd know not to play around with heat."

Ginger slid her hands out of his and sat up in her seat. "Apparently, I haven't learned my lesson because I'm clearly dancing in the fire. I just hope I don't get burned."

He heard everything she didn't say, giving him the yeah-I'm-talking-about-you look. What he'd been listening for was her to add *again* to the end of her statement.

"Consider me the cool compress or aloe vera you'd use for a home remedy in case of burns. I don't want to do anything to hurt you, in fact, quite the opposite—"

"I have a fettucine and salmon," their server announced, interrupting Brock. "Be careful, these plates are hot," she said, placing them on the table. "Can I get you anything else? Parmesan? More bread?"

"No, thanks. We're good," Ginger answered on their behalf.

She didn't reach for his hands this time, but Ginger prayed over their food before they took the first bite. Their conversation shifted to TV shows, movies, favorite foods, and recreational activities. She enjoyed many of the same activities he remembered, with bowling now added to the list.

"You've been making desserts all day. Think you want any?"

"It's hard for me to go anywhere and not try dessert. We can share something, if that's fine with you."

Things were going his way if Ginger suggested they share.

"Sure. You're the lady of the hour. Your choice."

"Gotta go with the warm chocolate cake."

Brock signaled the waitress and ordered dessert. He and Ginger finished their entrees in hopes their dessert would be ready shortly after.

The waitress returned fifteen minutes later with the check and a warm chocolate cake, anglaise sauce oozing from the middle and melting vanilla gelato. Brock inserted his credit card into the receipt jacket and positioned it for the waitress to pick it up without interrupting them.

"First bite goes to you. Taste it and describe it to me."

"What do you mean?"

"Describe it like you were on live television trying to persuade an audience to try it."

"Okay." Ginger scooped a spoonful of cake, careful to ensure cake, sauce, and ice cream were in the first bite. She moaned and closed her eyes as she chewed. "This is a melt-in-your-mouth-fresh-out-of-the-oven moist chocolate cake." She clutched her chest.

"Perfect blend of chocolatey goodness. Oh, and this sauce is succulent and creamy. *Ummm.* Nothing is too sweet, even with all three combined. It's a celebration in my mouth."

"I think I want to take it home to meet my parents." Brock scooped a piece onto his spoon to try.

Ginger's hand flew to her mouth to cover her grin, which disappeared when the waitress returned with the final receipt and her phone number written across the top, numbers Ginger could see clearly across the table.

She lingered for a moment and rested her hand on the receipt with her back turned to Ginger. "If you ever need anything…" Her eyes traveled down to her number on the receipt before she winked and strutted away.

Ginger's gaze followed Brock's to the receipt.

"Hey." He reached across the table to take her hands in his. "Don't worry about her or her number. I'm not. Let me get her manager."

"No, no. Leave her. She's young. We won't let her ruin our night. Besides, you're handsome, and she couldn't help herself. I hardly can," Ginger admitted.

"Is that right? Tell me more." Brock positioned an elbow on the table and rested his chin in his hand.

Ginger giggled and dismissed him with a wave of her hand. "Stop it."

"Come on, let's get out of here." He ripped the receipt and tossed it in the trashcan on the way out. Instinctively, he linked his hands in hers and led her toward the parking garage. The smile that followed encouraged him to believe that a Brock-and-Ginger-thing was even more possible.

"This was nice. I needed it, so thank you."

"Thank you for letting me be a part of this experience. I admire you for going after what you want and going about it honestly." Brock squeezed her hand.

"You know, Brock, I believe God will grant you the desires of your heart, but you're going to have to trust Him and do things His way." Ginger squeezed his hand. "And you know sometimes, the path we're on may not be the path God meant for us to travel, but because of choices we make, we end up in what I like to call Egypt, being a slave to our own selfish desires."

"Ouch." Brock winced like she'd slugged him in the shoulder. The instant she mentioned God, Brock wanted to tune her out, but he didn't doubt her sincerity, though he doubted that God wanted anything to do with him the way he'd shut Him out after everything that went down between him and Ginger the first time.

"I'm serious. Spend some time praying and asking God for guidance. You'll get where you need to be, and I believe you'll recognize His hand on the situation."

"Thank you. I'll consider that." He couldn't remember the last time he'd prayed. Did he even know how to pray anymore? Brock added, "There are probably a few other things I need Him to help me understand."

He glanced down to see Ginger looking up at him.

Could she see past his smile?

Could she see through his eyes and into his soul?

Could she see beyond everything left unsaid?

Ginger squinted and cocked her head to the side. "What's that?"

Maybe he'd feel better if he got some of the feelings off his chest. "This." He pointed between the two of them. "What are we doing? Because it feels like no time has passed and maybe we can get back what we had before.

Their steps slowed when they made it to her parking space.

They stood in front of Ginger's driver side door with both hands linked.

"I don't know what we're doing," her voice barely above a whisper, "and I wish I could trust this feeling, but I can't say I do."

Brock stepped closer. "I know things ended badly between us, and I admit my fault in that. I guess I thought since I was the one with the full scholarship, it made more sense for you to follow me to UT. I honestly didn't think you'd take my ultimatum seriously. I was young and conceited."

"Yeah, but there's no reason for us to bring that up now."

"I think we should. I can sense you're still holding some of that against me, and I want to apologize. We never got a chance to talk after that fight."

"I'm pretty sure that's because you made yourself clear in saying that I didn't value our relationship because I chose to attend UH. I was choosing a school, Brock, not choosing the school over you. But that's over and done. I've moved on so we can leave it in the past," Ginger said with a wave of her hand.

"Gin, I don't want to leave it in the past when it affects now." Brock exhaled sharply before he continued. She stiffened under his gaze. "If we could just think back to that time, I was all about you. We were talking about marriage and spending the rest of our lives together even though our parents thought we were out of our minds. But I didn't care what anyone had to say because you were my girl and I loved you with everything I had in me. We made plans and part of those plans was to attend the same college and get married right after. I just felt so rejected when you came to me about your plans to attend UH—plans that you made without me. Back then, it felt like you were rejecting me, like you weren't choosing us. I couldn't help but take it personal."

Brock hadn't planned to be as vulnerable as he was now, but once the words poured from his lips, he couldn't stop them. And after revealing his true feelings, he thought he'd feel better, instead, a pain parked in the center of his chest, snaking up to his throat.

Ginger slid one hand out of his, dabbed at the tears hinged in the corner of her eyes, and released her pent-up breath. "I suppose we were both a little full of ourselves because I never really saw it like that, but as you being selfish and making my decision about you."

Brock kissed the back of her hand that wiped away her tears. "And we were both too stubborn to talk about it like adults." His voice cracked. "I apologize for not listening to you and trying to see things from your point of view, but I want to do better. I'd like to think that I'm more rational now. One thing I'm certain of is that I've never stopped loving you and have never been able to love anyone since you."

Her glistening eyes seared through his soul. "It's always been you, Brock."

He lifted her chin and pressed his lips softly against hers, savoring each second, searing the moment in his memory, sending shudders to every limb of his body.

He was afraid to break the kiss.

Afraid for the feeling to end.

Afraid of what would happen next.

Afraid this was only a dream and he'd never get the life he wanted with Ginger.

Chapter Eighteen

It took every ounce of strength Ginger had to tear herself away from Brock's kiss. Had it been that long since she'd been kissed that she'd forgotten what it felt like? To be suspended in time.

To be oblivious to her surroundings?

To be so completely caught up in the moment that nothing else mattered?

And it didn't.

Nothing mattered.

How had she allowed herself to fall for Brock again? She was double-minded when it came to him. The part of her that desired love enjoyed every moment of what was happening between them, but the other part sounded an alarm whenever he was near. An alarm that grew more silent the more time she spent with him. Time spent that was supposed to give her a clearer idea of who he was and his angle. Instead, her heart had other plans.

She drove home on autopilot. She could still feel the impression of his lips against hers. Completely in the zone. The Brock zone. If she wasn't sure about where her feelings stood with Brock before the kiss happened, she knew now.

Could kisses do that?

Ginger could no longer hide behind her quest to grow her business. She still wanted that—a thriving business—but now she also wanted something else. Someone else. Brock Pearson. But she wasn't ready to give in to her emotions.

Logic and reason had to stay in control.

Not her heart.

Ginger shook herself out of her thoughts only to realize she'd missed her exit. She'd driven down Interstate 10 hundreds of times, gotten one kiss from Brock, and forgot her address.

She exited the freeway at the first opportunity, made a U-turn, and set herself on the right path. When she arrived home, her dad sat in his recliner, waiting for her like a teenager who stayed out past curfew. That may not have been what he thought, but that's how she felt.

"Hey, Dad, how are you feeling?" Ginger quickly walked over to him, placed a kiss on top of his head, patted his shoulder, and plopped down on the sofa end nearest him. A wave of calm coursed over her when she saw the empty pill box on the end table. He'd taken his medicine without her reminding him. Her father didn't need her help, but she felt better being able to keep a close watch on him.

"I'm doing all right. I want to hear all about your day."

"Pretty good. Business is steady. And remember the contacts I made at Jayden and Lisa's game night?"

Her father nodded.

"I've already received three cake orders and a recurring weekly order for the staff meetings at Jayden's accounting firm."

His eyes and approving smile burned bright. "That is good news and business is only going to get better." He paused and rubbed his belly. "You know, I was scrolling through the pictures Lisa sent from the competition a few weeks ago. I wouldn't mind having the chocolate-dipped chocolate chip cookies you made. I know they knocked those judges' socks off."

"Thanks, Dad. I can whip us up a batch." Ginger moved to stand, but her dad halted her. He opened the messages app on his cell phone and showed her the pictures Lisa sent to him, a smile covering both their faces. He paused for a moment and shot her a side glance when he got to a picture of her and Brock battling it out at the end of the competition.

Lisa.

She'd shake her if she were within arm's distance.

"What's going on with you two?"

"Dad, Brock and I are just friends."

Friend. Could she even call him that?

Did that kiss prove they'd advanced past the friendship stage or skipped over it?

"You know he was my favorite baseball player back when you guys were in school. I'd bet my money that he was going to play for the 'Stros. But are you okay with seeing him again? I remember how upset you were over the breakup."

"Yes, Dad, I'm fine. We're just catching up, I guess. Nothing serious."

Her heart wouldn't agree with her lips.

"I see. I saw him briefly at the competition, but I'd like to catch up with him, too. Invite him over."

"Really?" Ginger swallowed what felt like pieces of crunchy cookie crumbles.

"Yes, really. Seems things are different with you two. You should see your face. Smile shining brighter than these lights in here. Blinded me the moment you walked through the door."

Ginger laughed heartily.

"I'll set something up. I'm gonna get the cookies in the oven, then hop in the shower. Would you like a cup of tea with your cookies?"

"I'll take a small cup. Sweeten it up a bit, please," he called over his shoulder, picking up the remote and unmuting the TV to catch the ten o'clock news.

Ginger's thoughts whooshed around like cake batter blending on high speed while she prepared the batch of cookies for her and her father to enjoy. Everything she'd felt that day melded together, and now her father wanted Brock over for dinner. What would Brock think about that?

Even after the kiss, were they ready to bring their parents back into their whatever-ship?

With the batch of cookies in the oven, she stepped beneath the shower head. Too bad the warm water couldn't wash away her racing thoughts. She didn't want to give Brock the wrong impression by inviting him over to dinner. The last thing she wanted was familiarity clouding her judgment, although it may already be too late for that. She could just tell her father she wasn't ready to invite him over. They weren't on that level again, just yet. However, they'd been good together once. But they were teenagers then, not much life experience to know if what they had was real.

Could she see a future with him now? Could she trust the moment they experienced a while ago in the parking garage? Her heart believed him, but her mind couldn't get past what he initially wanted.

Ginger's Goodies.

What if he was secretly going after her business? Not only could she not risk losing everything she built, but Ginger also wasn't ready to put herself in a place to lose at love again. Though it was long ago, her heart still remembered the pain.

She fought back the thought. Even Brock wouldn't be that low down and dirty to her. The love they once shared had to count for something.

∞∞∞∞

How did Ginger manage to put such a hold on his heart?

Manage to creep in there and interrupt his plans?

Manage to make him believe love was possible and intricate to living a fulfilled life?

Manage to make him think about a future with her? Again.

Brock sat behind the steering wheel, engine running, tracing the outline of his lips.

Exhilaration and anxiety equally tore through him. Would calling her tonight be too much? She left minutes ago. Brock glanced at the dashboard. Actually, she'd been gone about forty-five minutes, which meant he'd been stuck equally as long. He smoothed a palm over his face. He'd been so sure about everything else he pursued, but he couldn't see his way through this thing with her. Especially with the pressure to secure an acquisition deal for Decadent Dough.

Brock backed out of the parking space and set course for the drive home. He dialed her phone using Bluetooth but hung up before the first ring. They didn't exchange many words after the kiss and if he were to be honest, that left him in a weird place. However, he couldn't be sure what he wanted to hear from her or what would satisfy his emotional turmoil. That she was ready to try again?

Brock merged onto Interstate 10 east toward his apartment, letting the window down so the wind could whip some sense into him.

But it didn't.

Exercise was the next best thing. If it wasn't dark, he'd go for a run, but he settled on pushups. As many as his body would allow. Exercise cleared his mind most of the time and helped make fuzzy situations clear.

Not this time.

Brock showered and climbed into his king-sized bed, opening the *Wall Street Journal* app on his phone as he did most evenings. *Call her.* He glanced at the clock on his nightstand. Ten fifteen. Perhaps she was already in bed.

Maybe a good night text?

Lame.

Why was he trippin'? She wouldn't have allowed him to kiss her if she didn't have some feelings for him, so he texted her.

Did you make it home okay?

He held the phone for a moment, waiting for her response. After ten minutes of nothingness, he figured she was asleep. He tossed the phone on the bed, trading it for the remote control.

Something quickened within him at the phone's vibration.

I did. You?

Yeah, I did. Can you talk?

He tapped the side of the phone waiting for her response.

She responded with a call.

"Brock, how do you feel about dinner with my father?"

"I don't mind. Why do you ask?"

"Lisa sent him a picture of us—one from the competition when we were having our little conversation."

"You mean when you were going off on me?"

They both chuckled at the memory.

"Yeah, that one. He mentioned something about you being one of his favorite baseball players back then and asked if I would invite you over for dinner," she added, "Seems you still have a fan. But it's completely fine if it's too soon for you. I don't want you to feel like I'm rushing you into anything. I told him I'd ask."

"Well, at least I have one fan. I couldn't say no to that. Tell me when you need me, and I'm there." He'd be out of his mind to give up any opportunity to spend time with her, even if that meant being in the room with Kenneth Evans again. The invitation from him was quite the surprise because Brock always got the feeling the man didn't care for him too much, especially when it came to Ginger.

"We can work something out. Maybe dinner next Sunday or so to give you time to make arrangements to be here."

The richness in her voice reminded him of the warm chocolate cake they'd shared earlier that evening. Smooth. Satisfying. Scrumptious.

And he wanted more of both.

Next Sunday was the first one in the month –the one he always had dinner with his family. He never missed, so maybe they wouldn't mind him skipping this time. He wanted to suggest the next day, but he didn't want to put that kind of pressure on her to cook when she wasn't prepared. Three Sundays from now was too far away because she'd be away for the final competition.

"Not much I need to do to be ready. Sunday evenings are usually free, except when I meet my family for dinner."

"Oh, is tomorrow too soon, then?"

"It'd be my pleasure to hang out with my one fan tomorrow." Saved from having to explain to his family he was having dinner with a woman—a woman who had his heart in her pocket again in a matter of weeks, and he didn't know what to do about it—and her father instead of with them as had been their tradition for the last few years. When they realized it was Ginger, they'd have a million questions to which he didn't have the answers. "Would you like me to bring anything?"

"I haven't thought it through yet. I don't even know what I'm going to cook or order. I'll call you after church tomorrow and let you know."

"Sounds good."

"Hopefully, I'll have a pretty good idea about dinner then. Any special requests for dessert?"

Images of the warm chocolate cake they'd shared at Brio Italian Grille filled his mind, followed by every moment after.

Every moment.

A moment he needed to push to the back of his mind.

"That's your specialty, so how about you make whatever you're in the mood for, I'm sure my taste buds won't regret it." Like his lips didn't regret touching hers.

"You're not making it easy for me, Brock."

"And neither are you." She'd completely complicated his life, with his rekindled love for her as close to the top of his list as his career – a career that had always been first.

"Is that right? Tell me more," Ginger crooned.

His Adam's apple bobbed up and down a couple of times. How could he explain it in a way that would make sense?

"I feel like I'm in the courtroom pleading my client's case, but I'm all out of defenses, and the client is me. I lost and there is nothing that'll help me. No law. No regulations. No precedence. Nothing."

"So, you feel like a loser?"

Brock couldn't help himself. He laughed. Hard. He may have snorted once. Ginger joined in.

"I'm sorry. That's the complete opposite of what I meant. Maybe a terrible analogy." Brock started over. "What I mean is that all of this is complicated, and I don't know how to deal with it. You've got me feeling stuff I didn't know I could feel again." Brock put himself out there. All the way out there. "But I'd rather have this conversation face-to-face. We can talk later after tomorrow evening's dinner. Is that cool with you?"

"Yeah… Tomorrow. Good night, Brock." Her voice was the sauce poured over that chocolate cake. Warm. Creamy. The extra layer of sweetness.

"'Night."

Stop the timer and take him out of the oven because he was done.

Brock swiped the screen to end the call and lay back in bed with his hands tucked behind his head, staring up at the spinning ceiling fan whirling around in circles, much like his feelings about Ginger. It was time to stop fighting against his feelings and give in to them. At least if she didn't want a relationship with him, he could move on knowing he tried.

Chapter Nineteen

Brock couldn't show up to dinner empty-handed even though Ginger said he didn't need to bring anything. He called his sister-in-law Tina for ideas—a move he'd probably regret later, but he needed a woman's perspective. If the decision were left up to him, he'd probably go overboard. He wanted his token to indicate that he'd put thought into the gesture but not to the point where she'd think he'd use things to win her over.

Your destination is ahead on the left. Brock switched off his GPS. He pulled into Ginger's driveway behind her car, taking in his surroundings, the landscaping much like he remembered except for the fresh mulch and newly planted flowers. He pinched his nose at the stench. Red brick lined the walking path leading up to the front porch, crowded by the oversized white porch swing.

Brock held a frosted pink vase filled with red and pink roses along with a giftbag from the Chocolate Bar in one hand and rang the doorbell with his free hand. Tina suggested he buy chocolate from the Chocolate Bar. Thoughtful but not overzealous. Apparently known for having the best chocolate in the area, he went out of his way to find it. The first location closed before he arrived, so he had to find the other, which took him in the opposite direction. However, that didn't stop him from being on time.

Brock saw Ginger's silhouette through the double paned glass door. *Deep breath.*

"Hey. Glad you were able to make it. Come on in." She stepped to the side to allow him entry, her cream floral maxi dress flowing effortlessly with every movement.

"I wouldn't have it any other way. Here." He handed the candy and flowers to her. "These are for you."

"Thank you. They're beautiful." She accepted the roses and sniffed "Nice. I'll put these in the kitchen. Follow me." She waved him in.

"Dad!" Her voice rang through the one-story house. "We have company." She turned to Brock. "I'll be finishing up in the kitchen. Dinner should be ready in about fifteen minutes, so make yourself comfortable."

"Can I help? Promise to not burn anything." Brock flashed a heart-stopping smile.

She twisted her lips and hesitated. "I'm sure I can find something for you to do. Come on. Right this way."

Brock followed her into the kitchen, the trail of her lightly floral and fruity scented perfume leading the way. Teasing his nostrils. Tantalizing his senses. Testing his resolve to pull her into his arms.

Ginger reached into the cabinet, removed three plates and three drinking glasses and handed them to him. Setting the table was easy enough. Ginger filled a serving tray with pot roast and steamed potatoes, another with green beans, and a basket with dinner rolls.

When her father walked in, Ginger rested a hand on her dad's shoulder and the other on Brock's when they shook hands. "Dad, you remember my friend, Brock Pearson. Brock, I'm sure you remember my dad, Kenneth Evans."

The F word again.

Was that really all she thought of him?

Would she kiss a friend the way she kissed him or allowed him to kiss her?

"Nice to see you again, sir."

"The man who has my daughter smiling like a kid on Christmas morning."

Ginger gasped and covered her mouth. Her eyes widened with an I-know-you-didn't look. Her cheeks flushed. "Dad!"

Brock flashed her an I-knew-it-smile as pleasure rose within him, knowing he roused something within her. Heart wrenching and soul stirring. There was hope for him after all.

"What? I'm telling it how I see it. So..." Kenneth pulled out his chair and sat at the head of the table. Brock followed suit and took the seat to his left. "Ginger tells me you're a lawyer now. What happened to baseball? No one could tell me you weren't headed for the pros. I followed your career through college."

"Thank you, sir, but it was just a hobby that paid for tuition. Law is my real passion, so it was an easy decision and always the plan."

"You had something in you, I know that much. Tell me about your family. How've they been?"

Ginger busied herself putting food on their plates and pouring tea from the glass carafe while Brock talked about his family.

"Please do us the honor." Kenneth nodded toward Brock and closed his eyes for the blessing of the food after Ginger sat to the right of her father. They all linked hands, and Brock hesitated. When was the last time he'd thanked God for anything, let alone asked Him to bless his food?

And why did Kenneth assume he wanted or even knew how to pray anyway? Is that what he expected of any man who dated his daughter? He hated to shatter those expectations because he and God weren't gelling like that these days.

"Thank you, God, for this food, Ginger, and her father. Amen." There, that should do it.

Brock lifted his fork to take a bite of the pot roast. "This is really good. Tender and juicy. Full of flavor."

"Thanks, Brock."

"Delicious as always. Thanks, sweetheart." Kenneth turned his attention back to Brock. "So, you practice law. What's your area of expertise?"

Brock tugged at his collar before answering and darted his gaze to Ginger, who seemed to be poised for his response. A hint of uncertainty cast a shadow over her features. He'd avoided the topic of his work in conversation, mostly because of the deal presented to her and to prevent casting more doubt in her mind about his intentions with her. And he didn't want to talk much about it now because from the look in her eyes, she still had her reservations about him when it came down to his job. She still didn't fully trust him, and he couldn't blame her.

Did he even trust himself to do the right thing when it came down to it? And what was even the right thing to do in this finding-a-bakery-for-Decadent-Dough-to-acquire-situation? He couldn't just throw his entire career down the drain, but he also wouldn't be able to live with himself knowing that he'd destroyed someone else's business so that he could get one step ahead.

"I'm a senior member of Decadent Dough's corporate mergers and acquisitions legal team, but I'm working to change that. The head of the team is retiring, so I'm holding out hope that I'll be named as his successor." He took another forkful of roast and potatoes. He'd probably said too much, but a small part of him couldn't help showing off his achievements. He'd done so since he was a child, competing with his brother. Though it may have been a solo competition, because Bryce didn't seem to care as much.

"Decadent Dough, huh? The competition sponsor. Isn't that right?"

"Yes, sir."

"So, is the promotion yours and it's just a matter of paperwork? Or is there something else you have to do?"

"It's always a moving goal post. A few years ago, they told me I was too young. Not in those terms, but that's what they meant. This time, I have to find a smaller bakery, for example, like a mom-and-pop business willing to be acquired by Decadent Dough and operate under our name as a subsidiary. And before being tasked with the assignment, I thought it'd be much easier, but finding anyone who would say yes is proving to be more difficult than I thought it'd be."

Kenneth scrunched his eyebrows and looked between him and Ginger. As if he'd had an epiphany, his eyes grew wide. He wagged his finger. "That is why my daughter was upset with you after the competition. You thought she'd operate Ginger's Goodies under Decadent Dough and she said no? Am I right?"

Brock sucked air between his teeth. "That was before I knew better. I've apologized to her and have been trying to make up for all of my mistakes ever since."

Kenneth exchanged a look with Ginger.

"Indeed, he has, but I've forgiven him." She tacked on a smile, but not the kind of smile that convinced him she'd gotten past his faux pau. He didn't doubt she loved him, but he wasn't persuaded that she'd fully let go and allow herself to be with him again. However, his goal was to change her mind and prove that they could be good together.

Again.

"Well, you seem like a smart man. You'll figure it out."

"Thanks. So, Ginger mentioned you're retired. You were an engineer, right?"

"Right, Petroleum engineer in the oil and gas industry for the last forty years."

Brock asked more questions about Kenneth's career because he was genuinely interested, but mostly so he could avoid more questions about his own, which was possibly going down the drain as they spoke. Brock and Kenneth spent the rest of dinner talking about careers and sports, laughing and talking like old friends. Ginger was quiet for the most part, laughing when they told a joke, but mostly assessing the interaction between the two.

Without interrupting their conversation, she took their plates and put them in the dishwasher, returning with an apple pie. She cut slices for the three of them.

Kenneth rubbed his hands together and licked his lips like someone who hadn't seen a pie in years.

"We have ice cream if you want some, Brock. Dad doesn't like ice cream on his pie."

"Nah, that's too fancy for me. I don't need any extras. Just give me a warm pie and a fork, and I'm all set."

Ginger chuckled. She served herself a scoop and added one to Brock's plate as well. "I also have caramel syrup. I like to drizzle a little over mine. So good. Wanna try?"

"Yeah, sure." Brock's mouth watered, and he swallowed. Hard. Thoughts of what happened the last time they had dessert crossed his mind. At least they weren't sharing this go 'round.

He averted his eyes from hers to his plate.

Was she thinking the same thing?

Ginger doctored up their desserts and reclaimed her seat.

"Mmmm." The warm pie and cold ice cream combination was one of Ginger's favorite desserts and growing on him, too. "You are so good, Ginger."

Kenneth shot Brock a look that was a cross between confusion and one ready to reach for his shotgun. Ginger burst into laughter.

"I know what you mean."

"I'm sorry. That came out wrong, didn't it? I mean you've done a good job on everything. Dinner and dessert. All delicious." Brock patted his torso. "Thank you."

"Brock, what are your intentions with my daughter this time around?"

He should've known that question was coming. He hadn't even had that conversation with Ginger yet.

She leaned in close and listened with her eyes and ears. Brock straightened in his seat, squared his shoulders, and looked at her before giving her father eye contact. His fork rested on his plate.

"We're getting to know each other again, but I'm only seeing her, and she's the only woman I'm interested in."

"That's good to know."

"And however this thing between us works out," he paused to look at Ginger. "I want her and you to know my intentions are pure, and I want to be here for her, encourage her to pursue her dreams, cheer her on, and help in any way I can." *I love her.*

"Lawyers." Kenneth shoved a thumb in his direction. "Over here pleading his case like he's on trial." Kenneth stood and patted Brock on the shoulder. "Nice to see you again, young man. You're alright with me. I'm gonna leave you young folks to it and go to my recliner and watch a little TV."

Brock stood and shook Kenneth's hand. "Nice to see you again as well, sir. Thanks for the invitation."

Brock took the dessert plates and loaded the dishwasher. Ginger added the drinking glasses, closed the door, and leaned against the counter. She folded her arms and looked up at him. The corners of her lips turned up in delight.

"I guess I should release you to go home and get ready for work tomorrow."

"Release me? I'm not sure I like the way that sounds." He rubbed his hands up and down her arms. "But I'll go if you promise to meet me for breakfast tomorrow morning."

"Promise. Come on. I'll walk you out." Ginger intertwined one hand in his and led him out of the kitchen, through the living room where he shook her dad's hand again, and out of the front door.

His footsteps were heavy. When he reached the porch, instead of walking down the stairs, he stopped and turned to face her. Still holding Ginger's hand, he searched her eyes. "Is it crazy I don't want to leave?"

"Stay."

Chapter Twenty

Fingers linked, Brock and Ginger stared into the starlit sky while they rocked back and forth on her porch swing, comforted by the one-off creaking and occasional insect chirping. The intermittent breeze cooled the warmth circling through him. The sunset and the dim porch lighting made the atmosphere more intimate. Legs crossed, Ginger turned slightly toward him.

Brock tucked a strand of hair that danced in the wind behind her ears. She normally wore her long black hair pulled back into a ponytail, but this evening she allowed it to flow freely. A look that made her frame appear smaller.

He clicked his tongue and shifted in his seat. "I think I convinced your dad that I'm a good guy. Did I convince you, too?" One side of his lips turned upward at the twinkle in her eyes. Not from the porch lighting. A natural sparkle. Something he noticed every time she looked at him.

"Why don't you convince me now?"

Brock took both of her hands in his. "You make me want to care about someone other than myself for a change. And honestly, before now, I didn't think that I could feel this way again, but I want to see where these feelings lead me."

"And that proves you're a good guy?"

"Maybe not much, but it proves that I'm not as selfish as you've pegged me to be."

"The jury is still out on that one, conferring in the chambers."

"What must I do to convince the jury?"

Ginger shrugged, squinted, and pouted. "If I knew the answer to that, I'd feel a lot better about this." She wagged her finger between the two of them.

"You can't tell me you're not feeling everything I'm feeling when we're together. We still share a connection."

"That's the problem. I feel all of it, but I just can't trust it. Not right now. Not yet. How do we know we're not just clinging on to the past and we're somehow blinded by how things used to be between us?"

"I don't have an answer to that. All I know is even when we're apart, you're all I think about. I want us again, Gin. I want to date you exclusively to see where this goes. To relearn every part of you." He held her hands securely, tracing circles with his thumbs.

"I want us again, too, badly, but it scares me to think that I could fall for you so deeply just to repeat the past." Ginger shook her head and combed through her hair with her fingertips.

"I understand, but you should know I love you, Gin. Past, present, and future."

She sniffed. "I've come to realize I do still love you, but I don't think I'm ready. I need more time."

Ginger looked down at his thumbs moving gently across hers and then away into the distance. He slid closer and squeezed her rhythmically drawing her attention back to him.

"I get it. I do. I'm not rushing you. I'm not going anywhere." Not if he had anything to do with it, but he'd be lying to himself if he said her rejection didn't hurt. Maybe he was moving too fast, but he couldn't help himself because the moment felt right. He pulled her close and placed a kiss on top of her head.

Brock pushed the swing back and forth with his foot a while longer until Ginger suggested they call it an evening. She needed to make sure her dad took his medicine, and she needed rest if she planned to meet him in the morning.

"Alright. I see where I'm not wanted."

Ginger chuckled.

They stood, and Ginger walked with him to the edge of the porch. "Don't be like that. You don't want me to miss our breakfast date, do you?"

"No. I can't have that. I'll see you in the morning." He pulled her into one last hug. He would've bet money their hearts were synchronized as they've always been.

She waved goodbye with promises from him to let her know when he arrived home.

Brock climbed into his car and started home. He glanced into his rearview mirror until he could no longer see Ginger standing on the porch.

His heart still hadn't slowed because it pumped only for her. The memory of Ginger in his arms made it difficult for the organ to find its resting rhythm. While they hadn't agreed to start a new relationship, they were still on the path of getting to that place where they could be with each other exclusively again. And although that wasn't the solution he hoped for, Brock held on to hope that they'd find their way back to each other—where they were meant to be.

∞

When Brock's headlights were out of her driveway, she heaved a calming breath and turned to go back inside the house to see what Dad really thought of Brock.

"Must have been one heck of a goodbye. Lasted an hour. Is that how long it takes these days?" Her Dad called to her when the front door closed behind her. She went straight into the family room and took the closest seat on the sofa next to his recliner.

Ginger folded her legs under her bottom. "Alright, Dad, whatcha got for me?"

He slipped his glasses down the bridge of his nose and peered through them, squinting at his smartphone screen. "Seems his family is doing well. Like he said, his father still owns that law practice, and his oldest brother also works there. Mom is a retired teacher and volunteers as the church secretary."

Ginger rested her chin in her palm. "And you know all of this, how?"

He waved his phone in the air. "My good friend, Google. Spent the last hour checking his digital footprint while you were out on the porch finding it hard to say goodbye."

Ginger laughed. "You're something else."

"No, I'm looking out for my daughter. I see the way he looks at you—the same way he did many moons ago. He's in love."

"Dad, I wouldn't go that far." A moment ago, he confessed his love for her, but he didn't say he was *in love*. And for Ginger, there was a difference between the two. They weren't there yet. Their past permanently parked between them.

If he broke her heart once, how did she know he wouldn't do it again?

Kenneth removed his glasses, perched his lips, and lifted one eyebrow. "Do you know how long it took me to fall in love with your mother?"

"Can't say I do, but I have a feeling you're about to tell me."

"One week. Freshman year on the campus of Texas Southern University. I remember it like it was yesterday. The end of welcome week. A group of us were gathered around in the union partying the evening before the first day of class, and she accused me of stepping on her foot. Her spankin' brand-new pair of white Reeboks. Mind you, the place was crowded. Loud. Folks everywhere, yet I was the one she accused."

Ginger smiled at the image in her mind. She could imagine the death stare her mom gave him. The same stare she'd given whenever Ginger was in trouble—the stare to let you know she meant business. Soul stabbing and sharp. And if she folded her arms across her chest, it was a done deal.

"I apologized anyway. I don't know if I did or didn't. But she had the most beautiful eyes I'd ever seen. Stole my li'l eighteen-year-old heart out of my chest. I walked her back to her dorm that night and every night after. Never had eyes for anyone else. Married her as soon as we graduated, and if I had the opportunity to do it all over again, I wouldn't change a thing. Even knowing that her death would be sudden, I'd marry her."

"I don't think I knew that. I mean, I know you all dated in college but not since the beginning of freshman year."

"Yeah," Her Dad looked toward the framed wedding photo that hung above the fireplace and smiled. "She's always been my sweetheart." Turning his attention back to Ginger, he shifted in his seat and cleared his throat. "The point I'm trying to make is it's easy for me to see that in Brock because of my own experience. He's a goner." He chuckled and shook his head.

"I don't know about that, Dad."

"Mark my words." He pointed a finger at her. "I had my reservations about him before this evening because I don't want you getting hurt again. But that man is as good as gone. He's troubled by something, that I can sense, but he's also scared to death of rejection. A man can't take much of that."

Ginger shook her head slightly in disbelief, thinking back to their conversation and all she knew about him. Ginger had known him since high school. She knew better. He couldn't be scared. Not a word she'd use to describe him. More like too sure of himself and perhaps a bit arrogant.

"What kind of vibe did you get from him? Do you like him?"

He returned his glasses to the bridge of his nose and exhaled a stream of warm air. "No matter who you date, I'll always worry because I'm your father. I don't know who wouldn't. But," he paused a beat, "You're a grown woman, and I believe we raised you well enough to make your own decisions. Don't decide who or who not to date based on what I think. If he treats you well, works hard, and has a relationship with the Lord, he's all good in my book. If you're looking for me to give you a green light, then look elsewhere because I'm not a traffic cop."

Ginger chuckled and rose from her seat to get his medicine. She returned with the pill box and a glass of water.

"But—" he held on to her hand after she handed him the glass of water— "for what it's worth, I think he turned out well."

"Noted." She kissed his forehead and squeezed his shoulders before retiring to her bedroom for the evening.

Ginger showered, dressed for bed, and opened the gift bag filled with chocolates from Brock. She had her pick from Texas-made caramels, chocolate-covered s'mores, and chocolate-covered pretzels. She bit into one of the caramels and moaned, savoring the creamy confection.

Her phone vibrated next to her on the bed, and she flipped it over to see a call coming through from Brock.

"Hey. Made it home alright?"

"Yeah. Thanks again for the invite. I had a great time with you and your dad," Brock said. She heard him keying numbers into a keypad of what she assumed to be an alarm system. "Where'd you learn to cook?"

Ginger flipped onto her stomach, resting her chin in her hand. She wasn't much of a cook when he knew her in high school, though at the time, she'd already proven her baking skills. "My mom, but self-taught mostly. After burning a few dishes, I got the hang of it—trial and error to learn to cook foods to my liking. Can you cook?"

"A little. I don't find it too difficult to season meat and bake it in the oven for a couple of hours and steam a bag of vegetables. And my rice cooker is magic."

"Sounds like I deserve an invite for steamed vegetables, and this baked meat you speak of."

"You know all you have to do is say the word, and I've got you."

"I'll remember that. Thanks for the chocolate. I've only tried the Texas caramels, and they are melt-in-your-mouth good. I think I may be addicted to chocolate."

Brock half-chuckled. "You know the best way to beat an addiction is to take up something else, right?"

"Sounds like you have an idea you'd like to share."

"You could take up gardening, learn to knit, play sports, or hang out with me—you know every time you got the urge to eat chocolate you could call me."

A shiver ran through her core. "That would be nearly every day."

"That's the idea. Yours is the face I want to see every day. We'd both get what we want. I'd get to see you, and you'd get help with your chocolate addiction. Win-win kind of situation."

Ginger laughed it off, but her heart raced at the idea, sending a tingle down to her toes, which she wriggled in response. *Don't be blinded by the smoke.*

"You're too smooth for me. I'll see you in the morning. Get some rest."

"I'll do my best. You, too. Good night."

"Night." Ginger ended the call and flipped over on her back, staring up at the ceiling while the day's events tangoed in her mind.

Was Brock really in love with her like her father suggested? Was her rejection to his request for exclusivity what stopped him from telling her? Tonight seemed like the perfect opportunity to put all of his feelings out there.

Yet, he didn't.

Had she given him a reason not to?

As far as she was concerned, he hadn't given her a reason to take a chance on them again.

Chapter Twenty-One

Ginger busied herself popping frozen cookie dough balls onto baking sheets. Focusing on the perfectly round circles was the most productive task she could do to keep her mind from wandering back to Brock and their breakfast date. Everything between them was going great, yet a war raged within her. She wanted to be with him, but she couldn't just fall back in love with him like the lovesick teenager she'd once been. Things were different now. She had to take things slow and allow her mind to lead.

Not her heart.

"Hey, Miss Ginger." Jessie came bubbling in, dressed in a pink Ginger's Goodies apron. "I've been busy this weekend. Couldn't wait to show you this." She held her phone up to Ginger's face. Jessie tapped through the simple cookie delivery app to show Ginger how it would work. She only needed to approve and link it to her website.

"You're amazing, Jessie. I owe you big time." Ginger put two batches of cookies in the oven for their Monday morning deliveries. She removed her plastic gloves and wriggled her fingers for Jessie to hand over the phone. "Let me see. Let me see."

Her beautifully designed logo stared back at her from the home screen. A cookie with steam floating from it flashed the words, *Order Now.* She took a seat, her head suddenly light and her legs jelly beneath her like she'd finished a wild round of jumping in a bounce house.

"Thank you so much, Jessie. Come here." Ginger squeezed her shoulders. "You are a total and complete blessing from God. You know that, right?"

"I've been told that a time or two." Jessie blushed. "It's really not a big deal, Miss Ginger. I'm happy to help. Play around with the app, get familiar with it, and let me know if there's something you'd like to change. And what do you think about adding a list of ingredients? Or maybe not a list, but enough information to emphasize they're keto or gluten free?"

"That might be a good idea. We can update them with the types of flour used. When you come back from your deliveries, let's integrate the app with the website so we can give it a test run. I'll mention it on my next social media video."

"Now that's what I'm talking about, Miss Ginger. Way to push the pedal to the medal."

"Come again?"

"Sorry. It's a phrase my dad uses all the time."

Ginger chuckled at the old expression as she removed the cookies from the oven and added another batch to ready herself for the mall opening. She couldn't be more thankful for the nudge Jessie gave her. Could the day get any better?

∞

Ramping up her social media presence must have been the key to unlock the floodgates of heaven for Ginger's business. She'd been busier than she'd ever been over the past week. The more live videos she did, the more hits she received on her website. The week would go down in history for her—roughly five cake orders per day.

"I'm going to kill myself if I don't get more help around here soon," Ginger murmured while placing another batch of cookies into the commercial stainless-steel oven. Jessie helped with deliveries mostly and worked the counter in between. Though Jessie didn't complain, Ginger could see the toll it took on her. Less upbeat. Her steps dragged, but her friendly smile remained, making every customer feel welcomed like she owned the bakery. Ginger could appreciate that.

"Jess, I'll take over." Ginger tapped Jessie's shoulder as if tagging her out of a boxing match. "Why don't you go to the back and take a break, maybe study for your finals?"

"Thanks, Miss Ginger. I don't know if I'll be able to concentrate for finals, but I will take you up on that break." Jessie groaned and shifted from one foot to the other, then flexed. "My feet are killing me."

"I know. Saturdays are the busiest."

Ginger took over behind the counter, running on autopilot. She greeted customers with her usual welcoming line, "How may I help you today?" She plastered on a smile, rang up their orders, and filled bags while they scribbled their signatures on the electronic screen.

"Any ginger cookies available?"

That voice. The one her ears craved and her heart couldn't get enough of.

Ginger scanned the area.

"Hey. Good to see you." Ginger peered around him to make sure no customers were approaching. All clear. She perked up. "No ginger cookies available. Sorry. May I get you anything else?" Her voice was light and sweet.

Entranced in his eyes, she stood there, drawing small circles with her fingers around the countertop. The music playing through the mall's sound system, the indistinguishable chatter from mall patrons, and even the soft hum from the cookie warmer all faded. All she could see was him. All she could hear was the percussion of her heart's rhythm.

"What do you have to give?" His voice low and husky, both hands grasping the edge of the counter. His eyes lowered to her lips.

Her scalp tingled from the heat that rose within her. If she wasn't behind that counter, she would've leapt into his arms, taking pleasure in the warmth, security, and the shared syncopation of their hearts she was sure to find if she snuggled up against him.

She tore her gaze away and ran a finger along her collarbone. *Don't go there. The verdict is still out on him, remember?*

"*Ummm,* snickerdoodle or chocolate chip?"

"A dozen of each." He leaned over and peered at the warmer. "I'll take a chocolate cupcake and blueberry scone as well." Brock removed his wallet from his back pocket and slid the credit card out in one smooth motion. His eyes remained fixed on hers.

Ginger accepted and processed his payment and boxed his order as she'd done for everyone else.

She handed the box to him. "You're spending a fortune on sweets."

"If I didn't, you'd think I was crazy for driving to the mall just to see your face." He accepted the box, winked, and flashed a smile that had been etched in her mind since she crashed into him over a month ago. A smile that she'd tried hard to forget on multiple occasions.

"I thought you were working today. Aren't you at the office?" Ginger's eyebrows crinkled in confusion.

"I'm working from my couch. Just figured I'd take a quick break and clear my mind."

"Yeah, Brock, but it must have taken you at least thirty minutes to get here from the Montrose area in Saturday afternoon traffic."

"Now you know how badly I needed to see you. I guess I'm selfish enough to do whatever it takes to get what I want."

"That's exactly why I need to keep my eyes on you."

"That's all I ask."

Ginger chuckled, shifted her weight against the counter and squinted. If only she could read his mind and see what was really going on inside his head.

He reached across the counter and rubbed the back of his hand along the side of her face. "Call me when you make it home this evening."

"'Kay." Ginger watched him walk away, her mouth in desperate need of that irrigation tool her dentist used.

Her heart longed to be with him, but her mind needed more time.

Time to trust her emotions.

Time to determine if what they shared was real and not some fantasy her heart conjured up.

And time to give her heart to Brock again.

Chapter Twenty-two

Ginger navigated her car into the visitor's parking space at Brock's apartment complex. It didn't surprise her that he'd choose a gated complex that rocked a luxury resort–style feel. Olympic-sized swimming pool. Palm trees. Covered parking. Private yard.

Brock met her in the parking lot looking like the grill master at a backyard bar-b-que in a white t-shirt, blue jeans, and black apron, his arms stretched wide, and his lips curled in a you're-going-to-love-this-surprise-kind-of-smile. Whatever he was up to, he was obviously proud of himself.

I've got something for you.

Her stomach had been in knots since she received the text about their date that Sunday evening. He didn't hang around after dinner with his family because he wanted to spend some time with her. Brock's muscular frame clad in an apron was the last thing she expected.

"Well, this is a new look for you. I think I like it." Ginger strutted into his arms and encircled his waist.

"Think of it as my way of setting the mood. You've got about ten minutes to gather your thoughts because it's practice time. The competition is coming up, and my kitchen is your practice zone."

"What?" Ginger stepped back and looked up at him.

"You heard me. C'mon." He took her hand in his and gently tugged her toward the entrance of his apartment.

"Brock, I—"

"No excuses. When you get on that stage, you're not gonna know what they'll ask you to bake, right? So, this is sort of that element of surprise. You have sixty minutes to bake a dessert with whatever you can find in my kitchen, but you must include…" Brock paused, whipped out his phone and hit the side key before adding, "chocolate, apples and pecans."

"What are you talking about?"

"Just go with it. I've been watching baking shows all week. It can be done, and you can do it, and you'd better get going because time is ticking." Brock mimicked the ticking sound of the clock's second hand, led her through the entry door into the kitchen, removed the apron and placed it over her head. "Can't wait to see what you come up with."

He kissed her cheek and left her standing in the middle of the unfamiliar kitchen next to the granite countertop island littered with flour, chocolate, cocoa powder, eggs, sugar, candy bars, and a host of other baking ingredients.

Ginger wasted a full five minutes staring at the covered island in disbelief. Brock had shown some interest in her baking, but never to this magnitude, and quite recently, she couldn't be sure if his interest was more about getting to know her again or something else.

But with all doubts aside, she had a competition to win, so she pre-heated the oven, washed her hands, and got to work. She'd bake her Crazy Chocolate Caramel Apple Pie Bombs. Ginger searched the countertop for yeast, relieved when she spotted it.

Brock had practically thought of everything, and the gesture brought an appreciative smile to her lips and a swelling in her heart, much like it did when they were teenagers. She whipped up a batch of dough, combining coconut flour and almond flour to keep the recipe keto and gluten free, instant yeast, sugar, salt, warm milk, softened butter, and eggs.

Pleased with her mound of dough, she then cored and diced apples from Brock's fridge and tossed them in cinnamon and sugar. She removed the caramel wrappers to set aside for her drizzle. Ginger flipped her wrist and checked the time. Thirty-seven minutes left. Her stomach clenched, and beads of sweat gathered at the nape of her neck. She stretched the dough onto the floured countertop, created her rolls, and tossed pieces of caramels together with the apple mixture and formed twelve balls. She brushed the top of each roll with butter and cinnamon and put them in the oven to bake for thirty minutes.

Only thirty-two minutes remaining.

While her apple pie bombs baked, she melted the caramel with cream in the microwave and set it aside to cool. She'd save the melted chocolate sauce preparation for the last fifteen minutes. Jamming her fists into her hips, she threw her head back and breathed a sigh of relief. She could finish this in enough time, but the stress from it all was real. Sweat rolled down her back.

Ginger craned her neck around the kitchen entryway for Brock, but he was silent and completely out of sight. She chopped the pecans to sprinkle on top of the bombs and spent five minutes clearing her work area. At the fifteen-minute mark, she melted chocolate chips, stirring in milk and vanilla extract to create her chocolate sauce. "This is gonna be so good."

When the timer sounded, she removed the bombs from the oven and quickly drizzled caramel sauce, followed by her chocolate sauce. With thirty seconds left, she tossed pecans over the dozen goodies, finishing at the sound of Brock's baritone voice echoing throughout the kitchen. "That's time. Hands up. Step away from the treats."

Brock marched into the room with his hands clasped behind his back and stepped between Ginger and her dessert. His back turned to her, he nodded, but she couldn't see his expression. He turned to face her, his face showing no sign of emotion.

"What did you make for us this evening?" He shifted an eyebrow and nodded toward the pan. The lack of enthusiasm on his face kneaded her stomach like dough. He had really gotten into character, and she wasn't sure she liked it.

"Well, there you have my Crazy Chocolate Caramel Apple Pie Bombs glazed with caramel chocolate sauce, and pecans."

"Thank you. In a moment, the judges will sample, but first, we eat dinner." The corners of his lips curled into a grin, and she exhaled. "I know it's good. I can't wait to try it. Dinner should be here shortly."

On cue, the doorbell rang.

Brock returned from answering the door with bags of Chinese takeout. They shared a few laughs over dinner, but Ginger had been anxious for him to try her Crazy Chocolate Caramel Apple Pie Bombs. When Brock moved to put away their containers and bags, Ginger plated their desserts, presented one to Brock, and waited for him to take the first bite. "You have to judge me like we're in Austin."

"*Ummm.* I don't quite know the judges' lingo, but this tastes like a cinnamon roll and apple pie got together and had a baby. You nailed it, Gin." He high-fived her, but him calling her Gin made her heart quiver. He always called her Gin right after he professed his love for her.

"Thanks, Brock, and thanks for doing this for me. I planned to practice at home, but it was nice doing it here."

"This was my way of saying I get you and I'm proud of you and I support you. You deserve to win. You're the most talented baker I know. I just hope you'll have a li'l time for a brother when you make it big."

Ginger threw her head back in laughter and took a couple of bites of the pastry after she calmed down. She'd never prepared the dessert with chocolate. She used chocolate because Brock said she had to use chocolate in her dessert, but she loved it and would add it to her recipe book.

"If I haven't forgotten you in all this time, I doubt winning a competition would help."

Brock rubbed his hands along both of her arms. For a long moment, he said nothing, but his eyes gazing into hers said more than his words could. Convinced her that he still loved her and that he'd changed. Gave her hope that things could work out for them this time around.

"Do you still have doubts about my love for you because I want to try again?"

His actions this evening convinced her of how much he cared. Her heart swelled in response to his efforts.

Ginger swallowed her fear. "I want to try again, too. I'm ready for us."

Brock sucked his bottom lip between his teeth. "I've waited a long time to hear those words."

She threw her arms around his neck and squeezed, attempting to still the trembling of her limbs as she strengthened her embrace. Brock's arms tightened around her waist and every organ in her body tingled from excitement and anticipation of where their relationship would take them.

Ginger had the love of her life back, now the one thing she had left to do was win this baking competition.

Chapter Twenty-three

Brock spent the better part of the morning staring at his computer screen. For someone who was known to work hard and often in excess, that wasn't his story today. His weekend with Ginger went so well that he could hardly concentrate on the tasks before him. All he could think about was their future. Up until this moment, he hadn't considered the depth of his love for her and how much he wanted her in his life. And now that he had her, not much else mattered. Not even the truckload of work before him. He had merger agreements to review, contract documents to draft, and a promotion to secure.

And while that promotion didn't seem too certain these days, he'd celebrate the fact that at least one thing in his life was going his way. He and Ginger sealed the deal. She was now his woman. And just maybe they could work toward the life they'd planned to have together all those years ago.

After he and Ginger returned from Austin, he planned to re-introduce her to his family. He even wanted to make that special, but he hadn't thought of how just yet. He caught a glimpse of his face in his laptop's screen. A wide grin spread across his lips. He'd officially became that guy.

The one who couldn't wait to leave work so that he could spend time with the woman he loved.

The one who thought of someone else more than he thought of himself.

The one who desired to become a family man.

Pump the brakes.

Tap. Tap. Tap.

A simultaneous mouth clicking matched the sound of the knocks on his office door, crashing his Ginger focused moment. Ace's face was the last one he expected to see. Brock worked for Decadent Dough for the past thirteen years and Ace had never came to him, so he didn't know if he should be excited or concerned.

"Ace, hey, how are you?" Air filled Brock's chest while he waited for Ace to respond.

A smile that made Brock cringe covered Ace's face. "Good. Do you have a moment?"

Even if he didn't, he wouldn't say no to Ace. The man was his boss and the one who had the power to give him that promotion he sought. "Sure. How can I help?"

Ace nodded toward the door. "Come see me in my office." He didn't wait for Brock to respond. He disappeared as soon as he made his request.

Brock released a heavy breath and closed his laptop lid. He didn't get the feeling this would be a friendly visit. The only business he and Ace had was Brock's agreement to find a mom-and-pop bakery for a merger. Decadent Dough wanted a new subsidiary and Brock promised to deliver. And he hadn't done so. He'd bet his next paycheck that Ace wanted an update—something he could have requested when he stood at Brock's door.

He stood and buttoned his suit jacket, squared his shoulders, and marched to Ace's corner office on the floor above his where the executives of Decadent Dough worked.

When Brock arrived at Ace's office, he sat behind his desk like he'd been there all day, his attention focused on his laptop like he hadn't just summoned him to his office.

"Come inside and close the door."

The office smelled of Ace's strong cologne that masked the scent of cigar smoke.

Brock did as Ace requested and made himself comfortable in one of the leather visitor's chairs across from Ace's desk.

He shut his laptop and folded his hands on top of it. "How are things going with your assignment?"

Of course, that is what Ace wanted to talk about.

Seeking businesses for mergers wasn't his line of work. He was the guy who drafted the legal contracts. But he couldn't say that. "In process. I've talked with several business owners, but none of them were interested. I'm going to expand my search area."

"Andrew is leaving in a few days. I had high hopes for you, but it doesn't seem you want his position as much as I thought you did. Almost a month ago, you were certain you could get this done, but I don't sense that same hunger. What's changed?"

"Nothing." And everything. "I just need a little more time to present a prospect."

"I think you need to revisit the baker from the competition-- Kenneth's daughter. From the looks of things, it seemed like you two had a relationship. You can get her to reconsider."

Brock shook his head. "She's not interested."

An iciness that Brock had never seen in Ace's eyes stilled him. "You don't understand. I wasn't asking. Get her to reconsider. That's the business I want to present to Dawn and Shawna."

Fire burned in his chest at Ace's mention of Ginger and her business. What was Ace's deal? Why would he want him to go back to Ginger with this deal if she'd already said no? Although Ace didn't know the status of his relationship with Ginger, there was no way Brock would allow the man to ruin things for him. He'd never get another chance with her if he presented another deal involving Decadent Dough.

Ginger would never hear Decadent Dough, Ginger's Goodies, and business proposal in the same sentence from him.

Brock swallowed the response he wanted to give. In fact, he didn't have any more words for Ace. So, he nodded and stood. Ace would get his bakery, it just wouldn't be Ginger's Goodies. When Brock reached the door, Ace called out. "I don't have to say what would happen if I don't get Ginger's Goodies, do I?"

Instead of returning to his office, Brock went outside the building to get some fresh air and clear his mind. From where he stood, he could see Katy Mills Mall. And because Ginger's business was inside the mall, he couldn't get the reprieve he needed.

All he could think about was her and what he could do to keep Ace from trying to destroy what she built.

When had things changed from him finding a new bakery to that business specifically being Ginger's Goodies?

A range of emotions rose within him.

Anger—because now this had become personal. When Ace set his sights on Ginger, he set his sights on Brock, too.

Anxiety—the battle to find a business equally as good and unique as Ginger's was paramount. If he didn't locate another bakery soon, he may be out of a job.

Dread—the look in Ace's eyes caused an uneasy feeling to settle in the pit of Brock's stomach. He'd never seen Ace that way until today. What would Ace do if he didn't get what he wanted?

What was going on with Ace and what was Brock missing?

∞

The final baking competition was less than twenty-four hours away, and to help Ginger relax, Brock invited her to hang out on the Azul rooftop of The Westin in Downtown Austin. Twenty floors above ground, the Azul rooftop lounge promised an atmosphere where they could wind down for the evening talking about everything and nothing with a beautiful background to set the mood.

The sun set, casting hues of orange across the sky. Brock chose seating under the cabana near one of the fire pits instead of the lounge chairs by the pool. The heat wasn't a factor given the wind blowing in their direction. A local band would start their evening gig on the rooftop in an hour, so that gave them at least that much time to talk before the band started their set.

Brock and Ginger were dressed more casual than the other guests, with Ginger wearing skinny jeans and royal purple V-neck and Brock dressed in blue jeans and a burnt orange polo shirt.

He reached for her hand and drew her closer to sit with him in comfortable silence. "This is beautiful, isn't it?" Brock was the first to speak.

After an audible release of air, Ginger agreed. "Yeah, and I'm sitting here with a cheater."

"What?" Brock threw his head back in laughter. "Don't tell me you're still hung up on losing that bowling match. Never took you for being a sore loser."

"You were clearly cheating. Stepping over the line. Distracting me when it was my turn."

"What did I do to distract you? I recall being still and silent. Out of sight really."

"That's not how I remember it. I'm pretty sure you flexed your muscles that one time my ball went directly into the gutter. It couldn't have rolled two seconds on the floor."

"What I'm hearing is you need bumpers." Brock continued to laugh, tension easing from his body. He took his career frustrations out on those bowling pins earlier that evening.

"I'm glad you find it funny. Too bad I couldn't rematch you. Don't want to risk hurting myself and not being able to participate tomorrow."

"Excuses. You know I'll rematch you any time, right? We can go straight to the bowling alley after the competition tomorrow. Balance it out for you. Victory at the competition and another L for you at the bowling alley."

"No, I'd rather do something you're not allowed to cheat at." Ginger folded her arms across her chest.

Brock pulled her closer to his side, and whispered, "Ah, come here. I'll let you win from now on. Scout's honor."

"Is that your way of covering yourself in case you lose?" Ginger tilted her chin and glanced up at him from the corner of her eyes. Brock drank in and committed to memory the way her eyebrows were arched perfectly with lashes some women would buy. Eyes that met him in and out of his dreams. The slight point of her nose, which he could still feel next to his, even though it had been almost a week since he'd kissed her. And lips he couldn't forget even if someone paid him to do so. Pouty. Pretty. Perfect for him. And yet he couldn't ignore the warning in his gut that maybe their reconnection was too good to be true.

"I guess we'll never know. What I do know is that I don't want you upset with me. I only want to put smiles on that pretty face."

"Stop trying to butter me up, I'm not a piece of toast." Ginger turned away and pursed her lips.

Brock turned her face toward him with his index finger. His eyes dropped to her lips. His lips followed—a paperclip to a magnet—and pressed his lips gently against hers, lingering for several seconds after the kiss ended. When he pulled away, he'd left her with semi-permanent smile. "No, not butter. More like honey."

Brock stood and extended his hand palm up when the band started playing. "May I?"

And there on the rooftop, Ginger snuggled deeper into his embrace. They rocked back and forth in each other's arms to a tune neither of them recognized. But the music and the moment felt right.

Brock held her, remembering the way their bodies swayed together at every dance during their senior year of high school.

Remembering her as his place of peace.

Remembering the love shared between them.

No matter what happened at the competition tomorrow, he needed her to know that in his arms she'd find whatever she needed.

∞

Inside the Neal Kocurek Memorial Austin Convention Center, Ginger, Kenneth, Brock, Lisa, and Jessie followed pink and purple signs to the escalator. The signage led them to a space much like the local competition, but the room was designed in a grander fashion than before. Intimidation and insecurity crept in when Ginger entered the room.

Did she walk into a studio for the Food Network? The room setup was the same as last time except amplified. Ginger's heart and stomach dipped like a five-pound sack of flour as she took in her surroundings. Cameras attached to tripods were set up at every turn. Four baking stations were aligned across the front of the room. Two teams were already stationed in their matching aprons. *O Taste and See* hung from the ceiling in neon lighting.

And the room smelled of baked goods even though they had yet to start the competition.

She glanced around at her supporters who gave her a reassuring you-can-do-this smile.

"I'm looking forward to seeing what you wow us with today, Miss Ginger." It was Cinnamon, the same hostess from the local competition. Her southern twang set her apart from every other televised baking show host.

Ginger and Jessie claimed their assigned cooking space. Ginger watched several baking shows faithfully and hoped the structure would be reminiscent of one of them. The only information the contestants received was there would be three rounds, and after each round, someone would be eliminated. First round was judged on taste alone. Second round would be judged on taste and presentation. For the third round, the remaining contestants would be given three people to assist.

It was time.

"This twenty-five-thousand dollars will be the icing on the cake. All of your dreams are right within your reach, Miss Ginger, and I'm glad I get to be here to help," Jessie whispered and squeezed her shoulder.

"How's everybody doing this morning?" Cinnamon stretched her arms wide and addressed the audience and cameras. "I hope you love pies, cookies, and cakes as much as I do because you're in for a treat today," she continued and then introduced the competitors.

Cinnamon checked her watch. "It's still breakfast time, and our judges can use a little something to complement their morning Joe. Bakers—" she pivoted to face them— "let's give our judges a treat, cinnamon streusel muffins."

The crowd cheered.

"Wait. What's that?" Cinnamon cupped her ear toward the judges who were amused by her personality. "One of our judges has a gluten allergy, and we'd rather not send anyone to the hospital this morning. Bakers, you have sixty minutes to dazzle us with your gluten-free cinnamon streusel muffins."

Cinnamon sang, "Starting…" She paused for dramatic effect. "Now."

Gluten free gave Ginger an automatic confidence boost. Her specialty. The bakers raced to the pantry to gather their ingredients. Though a wave of confidence washed over Ginger, she'd never actually prepared cinnamon streusel muffins before. She had to use her basic baking knowledge and substitute where possible.

Ginger prepared the coffee cake batter and called out instructions to Jessie for the cinnamon streusel, mixing it until it became like wet sand.

Forty minutes left for baking, cooling, glazing, and plating. Cinnamon and the judges visited with each of the baking teams, asking about their choice of flours or any special ingredients they were using to make their muffins stand out. Ginger was cautious about who she shared her baking secrets with—competition or not, this was her livelihood. She couldn't share what she considered proprietary information.

Time's up.

First to present was Ginger. Again, she didn't share her secrets, only much of what was general information when it came to baking gluten free. She gritted her teeth, hoping her explanations were good enough for the judges.

"Mmmm," judge number one, celebrity chef Faison, commented. He bit into her muffin and sipped his coffee. "I can eat this every morning. Moist and flavorful. Perfect. Thank you, Team One." Ginger nodded and smiled. Faison's gelled mohawk reminded her of a famous rock star, not a celebrity chef.

Judge number two reminded her of her father, from his looks down to his compliment. "I don't think I've eaten a muffin this good in my entire life."

"I can't say anything bad about this muffin. It's succulent and melts in my mouth. I can taste the use of coconut flour, but it's not overpowering. You've done well to keep the muffin from tasting dry." Judge number three, Allison complimented. "Well done." Considering Allison was a Food Network TV star, her comments swelled Ginger's heart the most.

It may have been a good idea to hear the judges' comments about the remaining contestants, but Ginger's head was too high in the clouds to care. She just created a new item for her morning menu.

She advanced to the next round. Baker Two was eliminated.

The contestants took a break and moved their remaining muffins to a designated area for the audience to eat. Ginger personally handed one to her father, Lisa, and Brock and waited for their opinions.

"What do you guys think?"

Lisa sang and hi-fived her. "Honey, you have to put these on the menu. You know I'll be first in line."

Kenneth ate his muffin in two bites. "I may be a little biased, but trust me when I say this is delicious. I'll be requesting these later this week."

Ginger gave her father a peck on the cheek and turned her attention to Brock.

"*Mmmm...* I could wake up to these muffins every morning. You are amazing. And Jessie, you're doing a great job up there as well."

Wake up to them?

Ginger's thoughts went to a place she didn't have time to settle in, so she reeled in her imagination of her and Brock's future together. Today she had to focus on winning twenty-five thousand dollars. She squeezed Brock's shoulder and winked. "Thanks."

"Brock's right, Jessie. Your support is keeping my nerves at bay. Ready for the next round?"

"Of course." Jessie nodded and followed Ginger back to their baking station. Cinnamon claimed her spot in front of the camera, announcing round two.

Chapter Twenty-four

Cinnamon sauntered across the platform. "Weren't those muffins delicious? I don't know about y'all, but I can stand to have a few cookies."

The audience cheered and Brock's heart turned flips for Ginger. *Come on Babe, you got this.* He fist bumped Kenneth who smiled just as wide and proud. Ginger was one step closer to winning.

"I'm going to a Fourth of July party in a few weeks, and I signed up to bring cookies," Cinnamon sang and shimmied. "Bakers, you have one hour to give the judges' taste buds a firework show with your best cookie. The flavor is yours to choose, but they must be red, white, and blue. You will be judged on texture, presentation, and of course, deliciousness. And your time starts…now!"

Brock, Lisa, and Kenneth shot Ginger two thumbs up. She could bake cookies in her sleep.

∞

Cinnamon announced that Ginger's red, white, and blue Turtle Snickerdoodle cookies were the judges' favorite for round two and she and contestant four, Reginald Honeycutt, would face off in the final round.

The competition paused for lunch break.

However, Ginger didn't want to leave the premises and risk something happening that would prevent her from returning. Kenneth, Lisa, and Jessie stayed behind with her while Brock made a run for tacos.

The room was mostly empty except for the camera crew and the other contestant who stayed on the opposite side of the room.

"You two are doing great up there. How are you feeling?" Lisa leaned forward, holding on to Ginger's knee.

"Like a dream come true. I'm so close to opening a new shop, I can feel the keys in my hand." Ginger smoothed her thumbs across her finger. "This competition has been easy. Hopefully, this last leg is as easy as the first."

Jessie leaned over and nudged Ginger's shoulders with her own. "No matter what they throw at us, we've got this."

"Your mother would be so proud of you, sweetheart. You're doing such an amazing job up there."

Ginger leaned in to wrap her arms around his neck. "Thanks, Dad."

"Let's go introduce ourselves."

Kenneth remained seated while Ginger, Lisa, and Jessie crossed to the other side of the room to talk with Mr. Honeycutt—a local baker who wanted to use the money to expand his restaurant—a dream like hers. The white-haired gentleman looked like he could be Food Network star Guy Fieri's father. His assistant was his wife, a chef.

If nothing else, Ginger was inspired by them because they never gave up on their dream. Twenty years in the making. She looked up to see Brock had returned with their food, excused herself, and left to meet him.

Lisa and Jessie followed.

"What's the first thing you plan to do after you win today, Miss Ginger?"

Ginger's taco was half-raised to her mouth, but she lowered, folded her bottom lip between her teeth and thought for several seconds. Doubt crept in. "You know, I don't know. Mr. Honeycutt is pretty good, so it isn't going to be easy." Ginger lowered her gaze back to her taco. That gnawing sensation rumbled at the pit of her belly. Not from hunger, but from what would happen if she didn't win. Returning home without the winner's check had always been a possibility, but not one she'd allowed herself to think about. Her thoughts centered around purchasing and renovating that vacant building in Katy. Where would not winning leave her business? Sure, over the past few weeks business had picked up, but not enough to get her the building, at least not right now. Ginger took a large bite out of the taco and chewed until her food slid down her throat. Were they still waiting for an answer? No one had said anything else, and their eyes were stuck on her like cake on an ungreased pan.

"So, I'd rather not jinx it." She couldn't finish her taco.

Lisa wrapped an arm around Ginger's sagging shoulders. "I think you're in a pretty good spot. Keep the faith, sweetie."

"Well, Miss Ginger, even if this doesn't work out for you, I don't think you have anything to worry about. Business back home is booming, and if you keep up what you're doing, it's all good. There will be other opportunities for you."

Brock took an opportunity to encourage her. "I think what Jessie is trying to say is that you and your business are the bomb.

No matter what happens, you're gonna be alright. Besides, you've got us…and we believe in you. Just keep believing in yourself."

"Well, aren't you all sweet."

Kenneth took her hands in his. "Everything they've said is true. Hold your head up and remember that God's got you. We may not always know His plan, but we must trust it. Sure, Mr. Honeycutt is good, but you are too. So go on that stage and finish strong."

Ginger threw her arms around her father's neck. "Thanks, Dad. I love you."

"I love you more."

The event's theme music started, notifying them the competition would resume in five minutes.

Acupuncture needles could've been strategically placed along Ginger's legs based on the tingling sensation shooting through them during the walk back to her designated baking area. Ginger sucked a large gulp of air into her lungs and released it slowly. Jessie covered her trembling hand with her own and shot a reassuring smile. The next couple of hours would shape her future one way or the other.

"Have you all taken a tour at the state capitol building?" Cinnamon asked the audience. She paused for the murmurings. No clear answers could be heard.

"Well, if you haven't, you're in for a treat this afternoon. Our teams are going to build the state capitol with one thousand cupcakes." The crowd gasped and she continued, "There are no restrictions on the ingredients you may use, but remember that you will be judged on uniformity, flavor, and appearance."

Gasps and cheers erupted from the crowd.

"That's right," Cinnamon continued, her attention shifting between the camera and the teams, "you have three hours to create the state capitol, starting now."

Three additional assistants joined each team prepared to bake cupcakes. Ginger tasked two of the assistants with helping Jessie create the cupcake batter while she and the third assistant discussed the display he would build after the cupcakes were prepared.

Ginger perspired more than normal, thankful her deodorant wasn't giving up on her. She'd made a teapot-shaped cake in the last competition, surely creating the state capitol couldn't be that difficult. The additional sets of hands were a blessing. There was no way she could've done it without them.

Down to the wire, her breath ragged, and her hands less steady. She stepped away from the cupcakes when the buzzer sounded, wringing her fingers behind her neck. So much depended on this one moment. *Lord, I need this so bad. I must win. No, scratch that. I need to win.*

Chapter Twenty-five

Ginger listened to the judges' critique Mr. Honeycutt's display. Phenomenal. Breathtaking. Delicious. Through the extensive pressure and mounting anxiety, she'd forgotten what the judges said about her state capitol cupcake tower. Her pulse raced fast enough for her to feel an aching in her wrist. *Get a grip.* The judges left the room to make their decision, and Ginger mentally worked to prepare herself for the outcome. She wouldn't cry under any circumstances. Win or lose. She learned what she was made of through this experience.

She couldn't recall how long the judges had been away before they filed back in the room and took their seat. Cinnamon, who she assumed would make the announcement, stood next to the judges' table with a bright smile coloring her face and handed the microphone to celebrity chef, Faison.

"Ginger Evans, you have blown us away today with everything you've created." Ginger's entire body tingled when her name poured from his lips. The incessant pounding of her heart was almost unbearable, but she had to hold on until the end.

Faison continued, "Mr. Honeycutt, you also have amazed us, and as hard as it was, there can only be one winner."

He smiled and darted his eyes between Ginger and Mr. Honeycutt. The extra seconds he took to make the announcement drove Ginger crazy. And her stomach agreed based on the funnel cake of knots it contorted into. Faison took a deep breath. "Contestant four, Mr. Honeycutt, congratulations. You are the winner of the *O Taste and See* baking competition."

Ginger's knees buckled, and she gripped the table to brace herself. She clenched her jaw to fight the tears welling in her eyes. No, she wouldn't cry. At least not here.

She held a congratulatory smile she didn't feel when Mr. Honeycutt received his trophy and posed for pictures with the oversized twenty-five-thousand-dollar check.

That was supposed to be her right now. Grinning with a smile as large as that check. Readying herself to put her plan to buy the building in motion.

Ginger swallowed what felt like glass in her throat, sucked in a deep breath, and walked over to offer a congratulatory handshake.

"Congratulations. I'm happy for you." Not as happy as she would've been for herself, but that was the polite thing to say. Good sportsmanship and all that jazz.

Mrs. Honeycutt squeezed Ginger's chin and held her gaze. "Sweetheart, this is not the end of the world or baking for you. You know that right?"

Ginger nodded. She got motherly vibes from Mrs. Honeycutt, so no matter how much she didn't want the pep talk, she accepted it.

"Promise me you're going to go home and keep pushing toward your dream. Henry has done many of these competitions, and if he'd stopped the first time he didn't get the outcome he'd hoped for, he wouldn't be standing here right now."

"Thanks."

"No. Promise. You aren't allowed to have a pity party. Pull yourself up by your bootstraps and do what you must do to make your dreams come true. Henry and I looked you up during the lunch hour. You've got a lot going for yourself. This—" she waved her hand around the room— "is just one day. One opportunity. One event. You have a business to run, so keep doing your thing. I hardly know you, but I'm impressed and proud of you."

Tight-lipped, Ginger replied, "Promise. Thank you for that."

Mrs. Honeycutt pulled Ginger into an embrace.

Mr. Honeycutt added and tapped her shoulder while she was still in Mrs. Honeycutt's embrace. "She's right. Keep working. Don't let one competition stand in the way of what you're meant to become."

Ginger pulled away and offered a half-smile, still working to keep herself under composure.

"I was you once. I'm giving you the same advice I wish I could go back in time and give myself. Take care, sweetheart, and come visit us at Yummy Honey if you're ever in town again," Mrs. Honeycutt said.

Ginger nodded and turned away. Facing her support group, she blinked and swallowed hard repeatedly. She clamped her teeth shut for fear that if she loosened her jaw, only tears would come, accompanied by the ugly cry that wanted out. No, she wouldn't do it. She'd smile politely and accept her father, Lisa, Brock, and Jessie's well wishes and sulk in her hotel room.

Jessie squeezed Ginger's hand. "I'm so sorry this didn't work out the way you wanted, Miss Ginger, but you have to know you're still amazing."

Ginger offered a closed-lip smile and nodded, swallowing the lump in her throat that may as well have been a rock.

She locked eyes with her father who was making a beeline to her side. He didn't use any words to comfort her, instead he wrapped his arms around her and squeezed, competing with her willpower to withhold her tears. Ginger latched on. After a minute, she tapped his arm to release her. They shared a nod, and she backed out of his embrace, only to turn and find Lisa with her arms wide.

"Oh, honey!" Lisa pulled Ginger into a bear hug. Her arms were the only thing holding her together right now.

Holding in the tears.

Holding her knees back from buckling beneath her.

Lisa whispered against her hair. "I'm so sorry. I believe God must have an even bigger plan for you. Do you believe that?"

Ginger nodded because she still refused to speak. The oversized knot in her throat wouldn't let her even if she wanted to do so.

Lisa loosened her grip slightly as if to test whether Ginger had her balance. Confident Ginger was steady, she pulled away, gripped her shoulders, and searched her eyes. No words were exchanged. Enough had been said with Lisa's encouraging smile. Lisa looped her arm through Ginger's and clasped her hand.

Brock finally vacated his seat and locked eyes with her before he advanced to her side, encircled his arms around her waist, and squeezed just as tight as Lisa did. The slow, steady rhythm of his heart brought about the comfort of a cozy blanket on a cold winter evening. A cozy blanket she wanted to snuggle into and hide from the world, but there wasn't much time for that. She'd cry and sulk a little tonight, but tomorrow she'd get back on her grind.

This was not the end.

∞

"Miss Ginger Evans, what a performance this afternoon," Ace called to her. Ginger had finally gathered enough nerve to leave the convention room and came face-to-face with Ace Steele. Where had he been hiding? She didn't notice him inside the room. Had he come to support Jessie? Ginger turned and plastered on the kind of smile a person gave when they only talked to you because they didn't want to be rude.

"Thank you, sir."

Ginger looked to Jessie, thinking she'd join her grandfather, Ace, but she stayed by her side.

"I'm sorry it didn't work out for you, but I'd love to talk to you about another opportunity." The man clapped and rubbed his hands together like a predator who'd just discovered his next unsuspecting meal. Though she was all about new opportunities for Ginger's Goodies, Ace's dark, beady, greedy, slit-transformed eyes made her uncomfortable.

Ginger forced the politest leave-me-alone smile possible, and before she could turn him down, Jessie stepped in.

"Grandpa, maybe this isn't the right time. I think Miss Ginger would like to rest. She's had a long day. We all did."

"Nonsense, Jessie. Give the adults a few minutes here." He dismissed her with a wave, but her feet were cemented next to Ginger. Ace's gaze targeted Ginger again. Her stomach separated and formed tiny knots under his unwelcomed scrutiny. "I think Miss Ginger here knows a good deal when she hears it. I have two good friends from Decadent Dough who are ready to offer you more than you would've gained from winning this li'l competition." Ace flicked his hand, devaluing the event.

Decadent Dough.

Kenneth stepped in front of Ginger. "Look, Ace, read the room. My daughter isn't interested in entertaining you right now."

"She seems smart enough to know a good deal when she hears it. Let her be the one to tell me she isn't interested. Seems you still have a problem with allowing the women in your life to speak for themselves."

"Don't go there, Ace."

Ace chuckled and though Ginger couldn't see his face, her skin crawled when the sound reached her ears. "This is my turf, Kenneth, and don't you think for one second you'll be able to stop me from getting what I want, especially when I have Brock here working for me willing to do whatever it takes to get his promotion. His assignment was to get Ginger's Goodies for Decadent Dough. Why do you think he's here?"

Ginger's heart dropped into her stomach and remained there. Heavy. Hurting. Her worst nightmare unfolded before her. She turned her attention to Brock and jammed her fists on her hips.

She spoke through gritted teeth and her eyes shot fire at him. "How could I have not seen this coming? You just couldn't take no for an answer, could you? Thank you for proving that you're the selfish, egotistical jerk you were twenty years ago." Ginger spun on her heels to leave, but halted at Brock's tug of her wrist.

"Ginger, please. I promise this is not what you think it is."

"Well, do enlighten me, Brock, because it sounds like you've been in cahoots with Ace behind my back."

"Can we go to a private place and talk?" The plea in Brock's eyes matched his calm voice, but if he thought that would soothe or sway her, he thought wrong.

"There's no way I'll ever go anywhere with you again. I can't believe I fell in love with you again, you treacherous lying snake."

"I love you, Gin. I did not and would not betray your trust like this." Brock spoke through clenched teeth in a hushed tone.

"Brock, please. This has been all about your promotion since the moment we reconnected. Tell me Ace is lying."

"Ginger, calm down and listen to me."

"Don't tell me to be calm when you're trying to steal my business from me. So, excuse me if I don't have the luxury of being calm or having everything given to me on a silver spoon. You've hardly worked for anything in your entire life. You just smile or throw your name around, and everyone gives you what you want. Well, not this time, and never again from me."

"If you would stop looking down your nose at me for once and listen to what I have to say, you'll see that none of what you've said is true."

"You've already proven me right with this little deal you have going with Ace."

"Ginger, Ace is my boss."

"Exactly. Tell me he's lying, Brock."

Brock huffed. "He's twisting the situation. It's not what you think it is."

"You've said that already. The truth is that you're here doing what you were hired to do. Was getting me to fall in love with you again also part of the job?"

Ginger's nose flared, and it took everything good within her to keep from wrapping her hands around Brock's neck and squeezing until it felt like cookie dough between her fingers. She tugged at her father's arm, who was still standing toe-to-toe with Ace in an argument that she didn't hear because she was in the middle of her own fight with Brock.

His shoulders sagged. He'd rubbed a palm over his face in frustration, but she didn't care. He didn't have the right to be upset when he was the one who caused the problem.

"Dad, Lisa, let's go." Ginger hooked her arm into Lisa's and pivoted away from the group.

"Ginger, Babe." Brock grabbed her hand this time and she hated the connection was still there. Still caused her heart to create an entirely different rhythm. "Please, just hear me out."

Ginger gritted her teeth hard enough to push them further into her gums. "Don't ever touch me again. Find another fool."

Let them fall.

If she held the tears in any longer, her head would become a river. She'd lost more than the competition today. She lost the love of her life.

Twice.

Chapter Twenty-six

The familiar feeling of failing at love ripped through Brock's core. A place he swore he'd never return. But he couldn't help it, and now there was no way to salvage his decimated relationship with Ginger. Brock shoved his hands in his pockets and watched helplessly as Kenneth guided Ginger toward the exit. Ginger gripped Lisa's arm and stormed out of his line of vision. She should be on his arm right now—that was the plan.

He should be the one to console her after the competition didn't go as planned.

"What was that, Ace?" Brock's nostrils flared, and his chest inflated like a hot air balloon. If Ace wasn't his boss or his elder, he'd be nursing his jaw and spitting out blood or maybe even a tooth right about now.

That vicious smile Brock had come to hate stretched across Ace's lips. "Oh, I'm simply working on closing a deal you can't seem to seal. You're weak for allowing your feelings to interfere with business." Ace whipped his phone from his pocket and glanced at the screen. "I'll give Ginger some time to cool down. She'll be changing her tune soon. Money talks."

Jessie took a step forward. "Grandpa, I really think you should lay off Miss Ginger right now."

"If I ever need your opinion, Jessie, I'll ask for it." Ace dismissed Brock and Jessie, turned his back, and took a call.

"I can't believe this is happening." Brock jammed his fist into his palm. But oh, how he wished it to be Ace's face. Every muscle in his body tensed. His strides through the corridor to exit the convention center were like walking on needles. The pain in his heart reverberated throughout his body.

Jessie jogged alongside him to match his stride. "So, what's your plan? What are you gonna do about Miss Ginger?"

Brock snorted. "What plan? She's made it clear she doesn't want to see or talk to me again. That's over."

"You've got to be kidding me. Are you too much of a pretty boy to fight for the woman you love? So, you're just gonna let her go like that? That's it. Nothing else?"

Brock kept straight ahead and hoped Jessie would take the hint. He'd hate to take out his anger on her. "Not much else to say or do. She's made up her mind."

"That's the problem with men like you. You're too stuck on yourself. Used to women chasing you."

Brock shot her a sideways glance. "What are you? Nineteen? What do you know about men?"

"I know a dumb one when I see him." She stopped walking and folded her arms across her chest, and for the life of him, he didn't know why he stopped, too.

"You're the one with the bright ideas it seems. And since I'm so dumb, what do you think I should do?" Why was he entertaining Jessie? There was nothing he could do to come back from this perceived level of betrayal. And the hurt in Ginger's eyes stung in a way no bumblebee ever could. To know that he lost her heart twice—the heart he coveted—seared his soul into pieces.

"Now that I have your attention…" She picked up her stride again, but at a much slower pace, gesturing with her hands between the two of them. "I'm not really sure, but you shouldn't give up so easily. She wouldn't have been so hurt if she didn't care about you. And I don't like seeing her hurt like this."

Brock huffed. "If it makes you feel any better, I haven't completely given up on Ginger. I know her well enough to understand she needs time."

Brock steps slowed even more, and he thought aloud. "Something else is going on here, though. I've told Ace Ginger wasn't interested, so it just seems odd that he'd keep pursuing her business, especially when she didn't win the competition. Why not make an offer to Mr. Honeycutt? And that tiff he was having with Mr. Evans. What was that about?"

Jessie interrupted his stream of thoughts. "Oh, he went to school with Mr. Evans. He mentioned it once when he came over to my apartment. Come to think of it, he asked a lot of questions about Ginger and her business, but I figured it was because he was looking out for me. He even encouraged me to learn her recipes so that I could practice."

Brock stopped and stared at Jessie for several moments. "I think your grandfather has been using you from the beginning, from the very moment he recognized Ginger as Mr. Evans' daughter, but the why doesn't make sense."

Jessie bucked her eyes and whipped her hands over her mouth. "Oh no, Brock. I think we may have a big problem. He recorded me."

"What do you mean?"

"You know how Ginger does those social media videos?"

Brock nodded.

Jessie scrunched her eyebrows and bit her bottom lip. "He recorded me baking one of her cookie recipes. I walked him through the entire process. Oh goodness, I messed up. I gotta tell Miss Ginger."

"No, I know you want to help, but at this point, she'll think you were intentionally helping Ace. Just let me handle it and do your best to stay away from him, if you can."

"Oh, that's easy, he's hardly ever shown any interest in me until now. I always figured it's because we were related through marriage."

"I'm sorry he's dragged you into this, Jessie, but I'll take care of it from here. Go get some rest."

Brock strode toward the exit, his blood sizzling through his veins. His temple throbbing because of all the ways he came up with to repay Ace for what he'd done and planned to do when it came to Ginger. Ace crossed the line when he brought her into whatever he had going on with her father.

Brock vowed to get to the bottom of the situation, and after he finished with Ace, the last thing he'd need to worry about was a promotion, he'd need a new employer.

Chapter Twenty-seven

Ginger sulked in her hotel room and feasted on room service's chocolate cake. The fudgy deliciousness worked its magic for a while. Every bite gave her momentary satisfaction and filled the gaping hole in her heart—at least until she thought back to the last time she'd eaten a slice of chocolate cake, and images of Brock danced in her mind. Then she was sick to her stomach.

By six the next morning, Ginger dressed, packed her luggage, and headed downstairs for the complimentary breakfast. Surely, she could avoid Brock and Ace if she ate breakfast at the break of dawn on a Sunday. Her original plans were to hang out in Austin for most of the day with Brock, but he ruined that. As soon as she arrived in her hotel room last night, she made the flight change to the earliest flight available. Lisa and her dad were on an afternoon flight, and though there were empty seats, she just wanted to be alone. Ginger held her breath when the elevator arrived at the lobby and the double doors separated. She surveyed the area. Empty. Quiet. Peaceful. She released a long stream of air and stepped into the corridor.

Fried bacon and syrup beckoned to her, and after parking her rolling suitcase at a nearby table, she followed their call to the empty buffet lined with steaming stainless-steel chaffing pans. Ginger filled her plate with eggs and bacon and took advantage of the nonexistent line to prepare a Belgian waffle. She claimed her seat and blessed her food. Whereas most people would be lonely in the reticent sizable room, Ginger was comforted.

No one checking in to make sure she was okay.

No one searching for the right words to comfort her.

No one recognized her or even cared about who she was.

She could just be.

Almost heaven until the elevator dinged and another woman strode into the area alone, probably with the same idea as Ginger. She tossed Ginger a friendly smile and headed for the buffet. Her hands trembled with thoughts of Brock stepping off the elevator. An encounter with him would begin and end in another fight—a fight she didn't have in her. At least not where he was concerned. *Let me hurry before I run into him.*

"Hi. Ginger, right?" The gorgeous woman who'd stepped off the elevator moments ago approached her table. Her friendly smile was contagious and made it hard for Ginger to brush her off.

"Yes, I'm Ginger, and you are?"

"Oh, sorry. I'm Dawn. Dawn Bradford. I would shake your hand, but you're eating. Mind if I join you? I don't want to impose, but it's so quiet, and I could use the company."

Ginger hesitated, but Dawn's smile never faded, and her eyes were soft, pleading even, almost like she was using them to transform her no into a yes. She drew in a calming breath and relented. "Sure. Why not?" She was almost finished anyway, and wouldn't hesitate to leave Dawn at the table alone if it meant getting out of there before she could spot Brock.

"I watched the baking competition yesterday. You were amazing." Dawn took a bite of eggs. "Tell me more about Ginger's

Goodies." She flicked her long, silky ponytail over her shoulder, her eyes glued to Ginger's.

"We're in the food court inside of Katy Mills mall, west of Houston, and we specialize in keto, gluten free, and paleo pastries." Ginger usually had no issues talking about her business, but the way things were going, she couldn't be sure of anyone's motives anymore, so she kept her answer brief.

"That sounds amazing. How did you get started?" Dawn rested her wrist on the table, fork in hand, poised to listen.

Ginger closed her eyes and inhaled deeply, thinking back to the conversation she had with her mother that changed her life. She'd been encouraging, but adamant about her making room in her life for doing what she loved, because God didn't give her the talent to hide it under a basket, her mom would say. She chuckled at the memory and swiped at a tear that was quick enough to escape. "In a nutshell, I started baking when I was little girl and fell in love with it. When I was in college, I'd made a promise to my mom before she died that I'd open my own bakery one day. My father loaned me the money and voilà."

"And how long has it been since you started?"

"We're two years old."

Although Dawn was friendly and Ginger loved talking about her business to anyone who would listen, something about Dawn didn't feel right, possibly because Brock's betrayal was as fresh as an open wound.

Ginger diverted the attention from herself. The least she could do was show some interest in Dawn. "Do you live in Austin? What inspired you to come to the baking competition?" Ginger sipped her coffee and gave Dawn her undivided attention, not that there was much else on which she could focus.

"I guess I'm sort of a baking snob. I like to keep up with events like this, and if time permits, I attend. Since I live in Houston, I was also able to see you in action at George R. Brown as well. I wanted to introduce myself to you then, but didn't have the opportunity. But when I walked in here and saw you sitting alone, I couldn't pass up the chance to chat. It's always inspiring to see young, talented, women like us doing our thing." Dawn slid closer to the table, settling in like an old girlfriend.

"Thanks, Dawn."

"I'm sorry you didn't win though. I was cheering for you. So, what's next?"

"I'm heading back to town any moment now to be the young, talented baker that I am." Ginger sipped her cup to hide the suspicion that was sure to be noticeable in her eyes by now. Warning signals shot through her brain like fireworks, and she couldn't help but think Dawn had some sort of hidden agenda. "So, it was nice to meet you, Dawn, but it's time I head to the airport."

"Is it okay if we meet up for coffee one day to finish our conversation? Call me crazy, but I feel like we have a connection, and I'd like to talk about collaboration opportunities with you."

The warning bells were now as real as Dawn's voice. Ginger tugged at her ear and leaned closer to the table. "You never told me what you do for a living. Do you own a bakery as well?"

"Sort of. My twin sister and I inherited our grandfather's business. Baking was his thing. I only deal with the dough that is green if you know what I mean. We solely operate from the business side of things and leave the pastry making to the true bakers. If you're interested at all in talking more about investment opportunities, let's have a chat." Dawn slid her business card across the table to Ginger, and without reading it, she scooped it off the table and tucked it into the side pocket of her purse.

"Thanks, Dawn."

"You're welcome."

"I need to be going now."

The elevator dinged, and her stomach churned and sank when Brock stepped off dressed in jeans and a red polo shirt that looked like it had been made specifically for him the way the sleeves hugged his arms.

Dawn stood. "May I give you a hug? I'm celeb crushing over here."

Ginger chuckled. "Sure. It was great to meet you."

"My pleasure. And remember what I said about calling me if you're interested in investment opportunities. No pressure. Just a woman who wants to see another woman succeed."

"I appreciate the offer. Take care."

It was too late to pretend like she didn't see him because once their gazes locked, he wouldn't release her. Too bad for him, she was strong enough to break free. He wouldn't get the benefit of persuading her with his charm and lines he spent last night cooking up. Ginger hustled away from her table, maneuvered through the tight spaces with her rolling suitcase, and shuffled out the automatic exit doors.

Away from Brock.

Away from the competition.

Away from everything she'd set her hopes.

∞

234

"It takes a woman to get the job done. I might have just saved your job at Decadent Dough. You can thank me later." Dawn stood behind him in the breakfast buffet line and ran a long, red-painted fingernail along Brock's arm.

Brock raised his eyebrows, and she clarified.

"I just spoke with Ginger. We're going to have coffee soon." Dawn patted his shoulder and strutted back toward the elevator.

Brock spent most of yesterday evening mulling over his conversation with Jessie. The only rationale he came up with was that Ace's interest in Ginger's Goodies had something to do with her father, Kenneth. And from the looks of it, Ace and Dawn were working together. There was no way Ginger would work with Dawn, unless Dawn neglected to share that she co-owned Decadent Dough with her twin sister, Shawna. And Ginger had already made it clear that she wanted nothing to do with the company.

Brock couldn't shake the incessant pounding in his head. Of course, Ginger would find a way to turn the whole situation with Dawn back on him, too. When he sought out this promotion, he had no idea he pulled on a thread that wouldn't stop unraveling.

He didn't have the stomach to eat anymore. Brock advanced to the coffee station, and while he prepared a cup of the steamy feel-good liquid, Lisa caught his eye, and he froze. Would she give him the benefit of doubt? If Lisa wouldn't budge, he'd need another plan, or give Ginger the permanent space she requested. And as much as that thought crippled his ego and his heart, he'd honor her wishes.

Brock pursed his lips to speak when she passed by, but he may as well have been a ghost because Lisa didn't even acknowledge his presence, and she nearly brushed his shoulder as she passed. He sucked in a deep breath, gathered his thoughts, skipped ahead of the buffet line, and joined Lisa's side.

"Lisa, can I talk to you?"

Lisa piled her plate with bacon, eggs, sausage, pancakes, and hash browns, and hummed along to the music that played softly through the sound system, moving along the buffet line as if he wasn't there. At least Ginger thought enough of him to speak her mind, but Lisa, on the other hand, had been blind and deaf when it came to him. When Lisa found a table in the near empty eating area, Brock slid into the seat across from her without invitation.

She bowed her head to give thanks for her food, then a hint of emotion simmered in her features.

"Why are you here, Brock?" If he didn't know any better, he'd think the issue was with Lisa as opposed to Ginger, but her anger with him was a testament of their closeness. It was then that he realized his chances of coaxing her to his side were near zero, but he had to try.

"Lisa, look." If her eyes could shoot lasers, he would've been burned into pieces by now, so he measured his words and softened his tone. He rested his elbows on his thighs, hung his head, and took a deep breath before he continued. "That situation with Ace didn't go down the way Ginger thinks it did. Yes, I work for him, but I'm not working with him when it comes to Ginger's Goodies. Ace has some hidden agenda and I plan to find out what it is. Now, after she told me she didn't want to do business with Decadent Dough the first time I mentioned it, I let it go. My interest in her is solely about her and not Ginger's Goodies."

"And why should I believe anything you say?" Lisa stuffed a forkful of pancake into her mouth and chewed.

"I'd mentioned to Ace that I wanted a promotion, and he promised it to me if I could bring a company who would be interested in a merger acquisition deal with Decadent Dough. When I ran into Ginger again and brought up the idea to her, she turned it down. I never brought it up to her again. In fact, I don't even mention Decadent Dough to Gin because of how I offended her. Lisa, I swear I wouldn't betray her like that."

"Umm hmm. So, now that Ginger is out of the picture, where does that leave you and your promotion? Did you find another company?"

"Nah, not yet." And Ginger wasn't completely out of the picture based on Dawn's assessment of her this morning, but that was information he'd keep to himself. No need in bringing that up when he didn't have all the facts. "But to be transparent, I'm not sure I still want the promotion."

Lisa took another bite of food and chewed slowly, taking too long to respond for Brock's taste. "Okay, but I don't understand what you want from me."

"I want you to talk to Ginger, so she'll know I'm innocent. She won't listen to me right now, but as her best friend, she'll listen to you."

"Sorry. Can't do that."

"May I ask why?"

"First of all, this is between the two of you. I'm not in the business of swaying her to do or think one way or the other. Secondly, you're only concerned about yourself and how you look in all of this. Not once did you ask me if she's okay or what you could do to help her through this or how she's holding up since she lost the competition yesterday. Everything you've said to me has been all about poor Brock. In case no one has told you, I will: The earth does not orbit around you."

"You sound like Ginger." A pitiful chuckle slipped from his lips, and he hung his head once again. He knew Ginger wasn't okay and that her heart had been ripped out of her chest when it came to losing the baking competition, and probably when it came to him too. He couldn't bear the look of hurt in her eyes ever again, especially knowing that he'd caused it. So no, he didn't have to ask if she was okay because he already knew the answer to that. Wasn't that understood?

"Sorry I can't help."

"Be real. You're not sorry. You had your mind made up before I sat here."

"You're right, I did, but I'm nosy enough to want to hear what you had to say." She smirked and lifted the coffee cup to her lips. Her eyes sparkled a bit too much for his liking as she peered over the cup at him.

"So, what do I have to do to win her back?"

"See, that's where you have this all twisted. Ginger is not some jury or court case to win over. This is her life. You're messing with her livelihood, and until you can truly understand what it means to be the *little guy* as you guys like to call it, then you should leave her alone and let her live her life. Make this a lot more about her and a lot less about you, and perhaps you'll be able to see more clearly." Lisa sipped the final drop of coffee, crushed the cup, and stood. "I don't see this working out for you until you squash that ego."

There was no denying why Lisa and Ginger were best friends; they were kindred spirits when it came to telling him off. Brock remained seated at the table where Lisa left him. He closed his eyes and pulled prayer hands to his forehead. For a split second, he considered praying because who could help him win Ginger back and with the mess unfolding with Ace but God?

But he hadn't talked to God in years. Did God want to hear from him? And if He did, surely God wanted him to pray about something other than this stuff, right?

As quickly as the thought of praying entered his mind, it left, and Brock curled his hands into a fist. He didn't see a way out of this mess. Maybe the best thing to do was to leave Ginger alone as she and Lisa had adamantly suggested.

With food being the last thing on Brock's mind, he stood to leave and return to his hotel room until checkout. Even if Ginger never wanted to talk to him again, he would prove his innocence and Ace's sole guilt by the time this was over.

Kenneth halted his tracks and his stomach knotted as images of the dinner he shared with Kenneth and Ginger flooded his mind where he proclaimed he'd never hurt her.

Kenneth gestured toward the table Brock had just vacated. "Have a seat young man."

Brock sat and mirrored Kenneth's seated posture with his elbows resting against the table and fingers linked.

When the smile he'd become accustomed to seeing from Kenneth was replaced with a scowl and wrinkled eyebrows, Brock braced himself for reprimand. "I don't know how deep your involvement is with Ace when it comes to my daughter's business, but I think it goes without saying that if you cross her, you cross me."

Brock interrupted him. "Sir, I don't know what's going on with Ace." Brock shared his first business proposal with Kenneth and how Ginger turned him down. "But I can tell you that I love Gin, and I wouldn't do anything like this to hurt her."

Kenneth stared him down for a moment as if choosing whether to believe him, then his gaze softened, and he relaxed his eyebrows. "I think I know what's going on here."

"Please do enlighten me because I didn't betray Ginger. She has to know I love and care for her enough not to hurt her like that."

Kenneth crossed his arms under his chest and sighed. "Ace and I went to college together. He tried many times to go out with Lily, even though we were together." Kenneth chuckled at the memory. "He was so mad she wouldn't leave me for him, thinking his parents' money somehow made him a better man than me. He was a jerk then and still is now. Whatever he's up to has everything to do with his disdain for me. And he had the nerve to say Lily would still be alive if she were with him, because he could've paid for any medical treatment she needed. I swear the only thing that stopped me from putting a hole in his face was the fact I didn't want to embarrass my daughter."

Brock knew that sentiment all too well. Ace had a busted face coming.

"So, is that what you two were going at it about yesterday?"

"Right. But keep an eye on him. I don't know what he thinks he's going to do, but he made some vague little threat this wasn't over, and he'd get the last word."

Brock had the mind to ask Kenneth to help him with Ginger and to explain all of this to her, but Lisa's words hung in the back of his mind. "I'll do my best to take care of this. He won't do anything to hurt Ginger's Goodies if I have anything to do with it."

Kenneth stood and extended his hand to shake Brock's. "I know you'll do what's right son, and pretty soon Ginger will see that, too."

"Thanks, Mr. Evans."

He strode toward the elevator bank, a little more confident than he was before he talked to Kenneth. And relieved that Kenneth didn't fault him as his daughter did. In the deep recesses of his mind and heart, Brock hoped Kenneth would convey the truth to Ginger. But no matter how much he hoped, Kenneth wouldn't get involved.

Brock had to handle this situation on his own. As much as he wanted to honor Ginger's wishes to leave her alone, he couldn't handle losing her for good.

Chapter Twenty-eight

Ginger leaned against the wall and watched her father work the counter at Ginger's Goodies like he'd been doing it for the last two years. Smiling and engaging her customers that same way she would, but with more charm. She covered her heart with her palm and smiled at the scene before her– her father bagging pastries and telling jokes to an older woman who seemed to enjoy the attention with her head thrown back in laughter. Her phone vibrated in her pocket, and she whipped it out to check the message. It was Brock again. She'd been ignoring his calls and text messages for the past three weeks, with pleas to talk things through. As far as she was concerned, they didn't have anything to talk about. She hit the side key to dim the screen when her phone vibrated again.

I'm coming to see you.

Ginger heaved a heavy sigh and shoved the phone into her back pocket. With her father working the counter, it would be easy to get rid of Brock. She walked up alongside him and patted his shoulder. He introduced her to the customer.

"Honey, this is Mary. She was telling me about how much she loves these cinnamon streusel muffins."

Ginger reached across the counter and shook her hand. "Thank you, and it's nice to meet you, Ms. Mary."

"Oh, it's nice to meet you, my dear. My daughter has brought me several of your pastries and she purchased my birthday cake from you. She watches your video tips online every week, so you're like a celebrity in my eyes. Since I'm out shopping today, I made it a point to stop by and support you."

Ginger's smile nearly reached her ears. "Thank you, Ms. Mary. Please come by to see me anytime you're in Katy Mills and keep me in mind whenever you need a cake, cookie or pastry platters. I'd be glad to help."

"I'll do that." Mary shifted her attention to Kenneth and offered her hand. "And it was a pleasure to meet you, Kenneth. I hope to see you again, too."

She sauntered away from the counter, leaving a whiff of floral perfume, and Kenneth's gaze followed her.

"Alright, Dad, don't let that charm get you into trouble. Ms. Mary seems like she's looking for more than muffins. And what were you saying to her that was so funny?"

Kenneth chuckled and ran his hand up and down his belly. "Nothing you would find funny. It was an old folks' joke, as you like to call it."

"I'm pretty sure I've never said that, but," Ginger rested an arm over his shoulder, "I will say it's nice having you around to help while Jessie focuses on deliveries."

"Anything for you."

Kenneth volunteered to help at Ginger's Goodies for a while since business had been good to her these days, something that put a smile in her heart given her recent competition loss. He'd been acting strange since his encounter with Ace Steele in Austin, but assured her everything was okay, and she should put her energy into her business.

"Since you're managing so well, it's time for me to take a break. I'll be back in fifteen minutes."

Ginger rounded the counter and came face-to-face with Dawn Bradford who was dressed just as casually as she was when she intruded on Ginger's breakfast three weeks ago, but with a pair of red bottom pumps instead of the ballerina flats she'd worn then. Her oversized designer tote hung on one arm, and the other she shoved in Ginger's direction.

"Hey, Ginger. So good to see you again. I thought I'd stop by to see if you've given any thought to our conversation." Dawn reached out and squeezed Ginger's arm, a pretentious smile spread across her lips. "Got a minute?"

"Nice to see you, Dawn. I'm actually taking a break, so I have a few minutes to talk."

"Oh, good. I promise not to take too much of your time."

They sat at a nearby food court table.

"Alright, so what can I do for you, Dawn?" Ginger thought back to their conversation in Austin. She hadn't even taken the time to look at the woman's business card. In fact, she'd forgotten about the card tucked into the side pocket of her purse.

Dawn waved her off and crossed her legs with her hands overlapping the other at her knees. "So how have you been, Ginger?"

Ginger fought to keep a straight face, but couldn't stop the involuntary scrunching of her eyebrows. The fact Dawn pretended like they were best friends turned her off. The only thing they had in common was their race and gender. She perceived Dawn, like

Brock, as an opportunist and was all about what she could squeeze out of people. Come to think of it, maybe Dawn and Brock would make an excellent couple. Ginger returned the same exaggerated smile Dawn gave her.

"I've been well. Business is very good these days."

"I have no doubt about it, which is why I'm here. I've done a little research on you, combed through your website and watched your social media videos. Our company has partnered with a non-profit organization called Reach for the Stars, whose goal is to educate underrepresented entrepreneurs through eight weeks of classes. The icing on the cake is a grant, which I've already submitted your name for consideration. What do you say?"

"That sounds amazing, but what's the catch." Ginger hadn't taken any entrepreneurial classes, and she could use the grant to help fund her building.

"No catch. However, we can't tell you the dollar amount of the grant until all recipients complete the course. Could be more or less if everyone doesn't finish the classes. Imagine walking through the bread aisle of the grocery store and seeing Ginger's Goodies on the shelves next to Little Debbie and Hostess. And imagine how many little girls you'd inspire to pursue their dreams." Dawn painted the picture in the air with her hands, and Ginger couldn't help but grasp on to it.

Ginger rested her weight against the table and hugged her elbows. "I must admit it sounds good, but I'll need time to think and pray about it."

Dawn sucked the air between her teeth. "I added your name at the last minute, so I need an answer from you today."

Images of refurbishing that old building in Katy to transform into her new storefront came to mind.

"I'm in."

Dawn reached for Ginger's hand, but the move was interrupted by Brock's snarl.

"Don't buy anything she's selling."

Ginger's eyelids fluttered, her mouth flew open, and she jumped at the sound of his voice. The sound her ears missed like sunburned grass missed water. But she also cringed. Her stomach quivered and weaved into knots with her heart following suit.

Dawn's once friendly expression turned grim. She gritted her teeth and jabbed a finger in his direction. "Watch it, Brock, or I'll have you fired. This has nothing to do with you, so back away while you still have the chance."

Brock gripped Ginger's arms, his eyes pleading with hers. "As hard as it may seem, I'm asking you to trust me, Gin. I can guarantee you nothing good will come from doing any business with this woman."

Ginger yanked her arms out of Brock's grasp and clenched her teeth. "Keep your hands off me. You have no right to interfere in my life. I thought I made myself clear in Austin." Ginger bumped his shoulder as she marched back toward her shop.

Against her wishes, Brock followed. "Despite what you think, I care about you and your business, Ginger. Don't throw it away."

Ginger spun on her heel to face him. "Where was all of this caring when it mattered the most? Wait." Ginger folded her arms under her breasts and tapped her foot. Her head crooked out of alignment with a go-ahead-and-feed-me-your-lies expression etched in her features. "What do you gain by this little act of yours?"

Brock took a deep breath. "Yes, I've made mistakes, but this has nothing to do with me and everything to do with you. Ace is using Dawn to get to you. Don't fall for it." His voice was calm, and though she hated it, comforting.

After several moments of silence passed between them, Brock turned to leave. Dawn popped up, blocking his path.

"You may as well head back to the office and pack up your stuff. I just got off the phone with Ace, and he's not happy about this little stunt of yours." Dawn waved her phone around, the screen illuminated with call ended and Ace's name. She hiked an eyebrow, and a told-you-I'm-in-charge-here smile tethered on her lips.

Brock gritted his teeth. "It doesn't matter Dawn, because I quit."

"Good. Your belongings will be waiting for you downstairs at the security desk. And Ginger, I'll be in touch."

Brock gripped Ginger's arms, forcing her to look at him. "Whatever lies Dawn fed to you, are just that, lies. Don't do it."

"And how would you know this?"

"Because she's co-owner of Decadent Dough, with her sister, Shawna, the same company you refused to do business with a couple of months ago when I brought it up. There's something strange happening because of Ace's history with your father and I believe he's trying to get revenge in some way."

"Brock, do you know how ridiculous you sound?" And even if he was right, she wasn't doing business with Decadent Dough, she'd be involved in the Reach for the Stars non-profit program.

However, Brock now had her a bit concerned, but she wouldn't tell him that.

"Maybe I don't have all the facts yet, but would you please stay away from her? I'm asking you to trust me one more time, Gin."

Brock's intense gaze nearly melted her like butter on a hot dinner roll, but she couldn't trust her feelings when it came to him.

"Brock, I think you should leave."

He dropped his hands and shoved them into his pockets. The rise and fall in his chest and the way his eyes glistened put a squeeze on her heart, but she recovered.

"Babe," he tapped his chest, "Deep in here, you know I love you and would never hurt you the way you think I did."

"Good-bye, Brock."

When Brock strutted away and his frame was no longer in view, she swallowed the knot in her throat. It took everything within her not to cry. She was done crying over him.

"That was almost better than television. Are you alright?" Kenneth peered over his frames and asked when Ginger took her place behind the counter and Brock and Dawn were long gone.

"Dawn and I were talking about a business opportunity, which sounded pretty good by the way, and Brock appears out of thin air demanding I stay away from her and insisting Ace is using her as a puppet."

"Not to mention he just quit his job. What does your gut tell you?"

"I'm not quite sure. Right now, what I want for my business is overruling anything my gut has to say."

"In other words, you need to pray and proceed with caution. If she's promising you something too good to be true, then it probably is. And you know I'm here if you need someone to talk things over with, but you shouldn't be too quick to dismiss what Brock says about Ace. He's had it in for me since our college days. Didn't think he'd be still holding on to his grudge because your mother chose me."

Ginger folded her arms across her chest and cocked her head to the side. When her dad mentioned his and Ace's history, it never occurred to her that the man would try to use her to get back at her dad somehow. "Is that why you're here, Daddy? To see if Ace shows up?"

He pulled his lips into a tight line. "Well, to be truthful, that's part of it. That devilish look in his eyes concerned me back in Austin. You can never be too sure with someone like him, so I'll be hanging around here for a while."

"Well, you won't get much complaining out of me. A bodyguard and free labor. What more can a woman ask for?"

Kenneth parted his lips to speak, but instead he offered a fatherly smile, kissed her cheek, and stepped away for a restroom break.

Ginger plopped down on the stool behind the counter. An exasperated breath streamed from her lips. Her heart returned to its normal rhythm, and she gave herself permission to relax.

No customers.

No Brock.

No Dawn.

Nothing fighting for her attention or her will.

Ginger ran her hands up and down her pant leg until every other part of her leg cooled. "Lord, please let this Reach for the Stars organization be the right decision. If it isn't, I need you to show me because I don't want to let you or my mom down."

That was it.

On top of the general pressure to make the right decision, she feared if she chose wrong, she'd disappoint her mom and the hopes she had for her.

She couldn't let that happen.

Chapter Twenty-nine

There was no longer a place for Brock at Decadent Dough. Not when his superiors wanted to destroy everything the woman he loved worked for.

Not when they threatened his career if he didn't help them.

Not when they wanted him to be involved in their bad dealings.

That was not the career he wanted for himself.

Not now.

Not ever.

After Ginger pushed him away, he spent the next thirty minutes walking through the mall to calm down. Mentally, he wasn't in the position to walk back into Decadent Dough's office. He didn't trust himself not to be disrespectful nor present himself as the stereotypical angry black man. Because right now, anger consumed him.

He'd spent the last thirteen years of his life and career with Decadent Dough working countless hours and going beyond his duties to climb the corporate ladder—a ladder that seemed to grow taller the more he climbed.

And today he'd had enough.

Enough of politics.

Enough of the games.

Enough of everyone entangled with the company.

While he'd enjoyed his career at Decadent Dough and hated to see it slip through his fingers like sand, there was nothing left for him there.

Ace confirmed his feelings when he walked back into the office. A brown cardboard box filled with his few belongings waited for him at Ms. Janet's desk. She looked at him with sad eyes.

Brock ground his teeth, his jaw muscles flexed. He was prepared to find Ace to professionally tell him off. While he knew his time there had expired, he wanted to be the one to say so. But he didn't have to look for the man, because he entered the lobby seconds after Brock arrived, as if he smelled him come inside.

Ace approached Brock and stood a foot away from him. He stuffed his hands into his pockets and tilted his head to the side. That devious smirk on his lips made Brock's back itch. And although his lips were curled into an evil smile, fire still burned in his eyes. "Your promotion is off the table."

"That's fine because I came to tell you that I'm no longer interested."

Ace huffed. "It's just as well. You don't have the balls to do what needs to be done. I assume Dawn told you that your services are no longer needed here."

Brock matched Ace's stance and stuffed his hands in his pockets. When thoughts of what Ace tried to do to Ginger's business lingered in his mind, he wanted to connect his hands with Ace's neck. Lava pumped through his veins. Irritation and rage coursed from his head down to his feet. He lifted his chin and glared at the man. "She said as much and it's just as well because I quit." He bit back what he really wanted to say—that Ace disgusted him. He didn't want to work for anyone who would intentionally destroy someone else's business because of a personal vendetta. Or that he needed to grow up and leave the past behind him. Or that Decadent Dough would be better off without him, Dawn, and Shawna tearing down what their grandfather built. While he never planned to return to Decadent Dough, his parents had taught him not to burn bridges, so he clamped his mouth shut.

Ace huffed, like he'd won the battle. His smirk, which irritated Brock, never left his face. "Janet, please make sure Brock has all of his things. If he ever returns, call the cops." And with that, Ace disappeared from the lobby.

Brock turned to pick up the cardboard box filled with his personal belongings, which consisted of his law degree, a photo of him and his family at his law school graduation, and his personal leather portfolio his mother purchased for him as a gift.

Ms. Janet's eyes still spoke sadness. "I'm sorry things didn't work out here the way you hoped. You're one of the best lawyers we have."

"Thanks, Ms. Janet." He was sorry and not sorry at the same time.

"Are you planning to go work at your father's firm now?"

She took care of everyone in the office, so it was quite natural that she wanted to make sure that he'd be taken care of after he left the company. However, the truth was that he hadn't thought that far ahead. All he knew was that he couldn't stay. But after everything he'd gone through in the past couple of months, working with his father and brother didn't seem like the worst idea.

You can practice the law you want and let your family handle the tax stuff.

Ginger's suggestion came rushing back to him. Come to think of it, if his father would have him, that was exactly what he would do.

"We'll see what happens."

Ms. Janet rounded the desk and hugged him. He'd never had any physical contact with her before now, so the hug felt strange and like comfort coming from a grandparent all at once. "Take care of yourself, Brock. I know you'll do well with whatever you choose. It was a pleasure having you around here."

She released him. Brock picked up his box. "Thank you, Ms. Janet. Take care."

When Brock walked through the glass entry doors for the last time, relief and a sense of peace like he'd never known before washed over him. He couldn't see it before, but this was the promotion he needed. When he stepped onto the elevator and pressed the button for the ground floor, he looked up to see Ms. Janet's friendly face. She stood in the lobby and watched him like a parent seeing a child off to school. He hoisted the box in one arm and waved a final good-bye to her.

When the elevator doors closed, Brock released a soul cleansing breath.

Today was the start of his new life.

∞

Ginger dressed in her black skirt suit and red blouse. Red represented power and the strength she'd mustered that morning. She and Dawn talked a few times over the last couple of weeks, now it was time for her to sign the paperwork to accept the grant terms stipulated by the Reach for the Stars organization. The elevator chimed. Ginger exited and entered the double-paneled glass doors with red and two yellow stars in the glass.

Ginger stepped closer and smiled at the receptionist. "Good morning. I'm Ginger Evans. I'm here for a meeting with Dawn Bradford."

The older Caucasian woman was heavy set with a pair of red glasses on the bridge of her nose. She offered a bright smile. "Hi Ginger, please have a seat. Dawn will be with you in about ten minutes. Would you like a bottled water while you wait?"

"No, thank you." A nagging feeling puddled in Ginger's stomach. "But I do need to run to the ladies' room."

The receptionist pointed. "Right outside the door to your left."

"Thank you."

Trust me rang in her ears repeatedly. Honestly, Ginger believed Brock had her best interest in mind, but she had to choose herself and do what she thought was best for her business.

Lord, if this isn't the right decision, I need you to give me a sign, like right now. Before I sign those papers.

Inside the bathroom stall, Ginger hesitated to exit when she heard two women enter, compelled to hang around in her stall until they left. She preferred complete privacy while freshening up, so, she waited. Her ears perked up when she realized she was the topic of their conversation, and she peered through the slit in the stall opening.

"What do you think about Ginger?" A woman who looked identical to Dawn asked. Ginger assumed her to be Shawna, Dawn's twin sister.

Dawn shrugged and reapplied lipstick. "Eh, she's alright, I guess. A little too goody-goody for me. I'm ready to get this over with."

Shawna turned and rested her rear against the vanity. "The whole gluten-free and keto thing she has going can be really good for Decadent Dough."

"Oh, absolutely. I'm sure we'll be able to get our hands on her recipes in no time, and Ginger's Goodies will be history, at least that's Ace's plan. He's been trying to use that li'l clueless granddaughter of his to get his hands on her recipes, but it's not working fast enough. That old fool had a video of her making Ginger's keto chocolate chip cookies, walking him through every step, and he somehow deleted it."

"Doesn't he have backup?"

Dawn waved Shawna off. "Pssh. You'd think so, right? Anyway, he's been trying to play Jessie this whole time by encouraging her to practice at home so he could get a little closer to," she used air quotes, "making Ginger's old man feel his pain."

"He has a little vendetta against her father and plans to stick it to him by taking his daughter's business down. And with things not moving fast enough with Jessie, my charm worked perfectly. You should've seen the way Ginger's eyes sparkled when I mentioned the business classes and grant." Dawn licked her lips and spread them into a mischievous grin.

"You and Ace are two peas in a pod."

Dawn shrugged. "The way I see it, we both get what we want, though I could care less about Ace's issues as long as Decadent Dough wins in the end. Next on my list is Brock Pearson.

Oh, those eyes sent me into a tailspin at our last meeting." Dawn fanned herself, rolling her eyes. "That man is hot."

"You're so bad, but I think there's a company rule against fraternization. Besides, I believe he's taken. I'm pretty sure he was in Austin with Ginger looking like a lovesick puppy."

"Look at me." Dawn ran her manicured hand along the side of her body. "I'm about to take her business and her man. Brock won't even remember her name once I get a hold of him, and you know I don't care about any rules. What's mine is mine, and I'm about to write my name all over him. She hates him now anyway, so I'll be there to mend his broken heart." Dawn and Shawna laughed in unison.

Ginger gasped for air, gripped the bathroom stall handle, and yanked it open. Her blood had to be clotted somewhere because her fingertips were cold. Had she been holding her breath? Everything Brock warned her about now made sense.

Ginger marched over to where Dawn and Shawna stood. Their coffee skin paled in a way she didn't think possible. Her insides quivered, but she presented a calm and strong appearance. Ginger folded her arms across her chest and stepped close enough to Dawn to where they were eye-to-eye and Dawn could feel her breath.

"You don't know who you're messing with, do you? But I'll let you in on a little secret." She stepped even closer and crooked her head to the right, the way she always did when she was prepared to tell someone off. How she managed to be so calm and keep her voice from shaking as much as everything within her had amazed her, but that boosted her moxie. "I don't need you, your business, your money, or your sponsorship, and honey, you can have Brock.

Snakes belong together." Ginger sealed her delivery with the same pretentious smile that draped Dawn's lips at every opportunity.

Ginger strutted out of the restroom with her head held high, relieved, and thankful God had answered her prayer instantly. She stopped by the office just to tell the receptionist she was leaving and headed back toward the elevator bank. She'd caught a glimpse of Dawn and Shawna coming down the hall and smirked. She was finally free of them and the entire Decadent Dough fiasco. She didn't need Decadent Dough or anyone else to invest in her. She'd do what she'd done all along: invest in herself.

Chapter Thirty

Two weeks after the Dawn and Shawna fiasco, Ginger regained her rhythm of baking for the lunch crowd and for the delivery orders that had already come through on the app. Removing a fresh batch of cookies out of the stainless-steel commercial oven, she transferred them to the countertop warmer immediately.

She'd spent the last five weeks sulking over the competition, the mess with Dawn, and feeling discouraged about the fact it may take a lot longer to grow her business enough to where she could finance her own building. And today, of all days, Jessie was sick.

"Hi. Excuse me. Ginger?" A short Caucasian woman with a chin-length brunette bob approached the counter with a noticeably large black portfolio in her arms.

"Yes. How may I help you today?" Ginger plastered on a smile—an expression opposite of the discontentment and discouragement lingering within her—but she couldn't greet customers with a frown.

"I'm Sharon Steinhouser, a food critic here in the Houston area."

"It's nice to meet you." Ginger's smile was now more authentic. She knew exactly who Sharon Steinhouser was—a woman with tons of influence in the baking community. Ginger froze in anticipation of her reason for stopping by. Did she want to place an order for a large function? Was she getting a cover article in the *Houston Chronicle*?

"I attended the live tapings of the *O Taste and See* competition, and I must say I'm impressed with you, and I'm not the only one. Your social media videos are a hit, and I think you're on to something."

Ginger immediately thought about her first interaction with Dawn and couldn't help but wonder if Dawn sent this woman over to sucker her into another scheme. Whatever she was selling, Ginger wasn't buying.

"I also work with the producers of *Baking Bundts & Breads,* and they're interested in offering you a baking show of your own."

Ginger bucked her eyes and her mouth hung open for a few seconds, but she regained her composure. Ginger couldn't allow herself to fall into another trap. *Lord, haven't I had enough already?*

Sharon must have sensed her skepticism, so she continued. "I wanted the pleasure of coming down here to share the good news. There are several things that need to happen before the offer is official, one of which is a screen test." She raised the portfolio and double-tapped. "The details are inside. I suggest you secure a lawyer to review the fine print."

Ginger accepted the portfolio, but still didn't speak, uncertain of if any of what Sharon said was real.

Sharon flipped her wrist to check the time on her watch. "I guess I'll be going so you can get back to work, but look over the documents, and call me within the week so we can schedule the screen test."

Quiet like a television whose sound had been silenced by the mute button, Ginger nodded.

"I know this must be quite a shock for you. I understand." Sharon chuckled. "Have a great day, and I look forward to hearing from you."

Ginger turned slightly to watch Sharon walk away but still, no words would come. Her entire body tingled, but she couldn't allow herself to get excited.

Not yet.

∞

With Jessie out, Ginger closed her shop to deliver the last cake order for the day. Ginger input the address into her GPS for a delivery to Tina Sullivan. The address seemed familiar, but not the name. And as exhausted as she was, she couldn't spend any time figuring out how she knew the address. All she wanted was to crash across her bed after she'd dropped off the cake.

On her route, she called Lisa on her Bluetooth speaker.

"Hey lady, what's up?" Lisa answered.

"Today is not April first, so why am I getting punked?"

Lisa chuckled. "Oh, goodness. What happened this time?"

Ginger shared Sharon Steinhouser's visit with Lisa. "I really think the folks at Decadent Dough are behind this."

"I'm looking at her social media page now, Gin. I think it may be for real. Have you looked her up?"

"I'm familiar with her, so I didn't need to. I mean, think about it. Her visit was just too coincidental. I'm tired, Lisa. Tired of folks trying to take away something I've worked so hard for."

"Well, seems to me, this could be a blessing. At the very least, get a lawyer to read over the documents she sent. Even call to talk to her and investigate her social media. This could be legit."

Ginger blew an audible breath. "She can be legit and still be working for Decadent Dough."

"Possibly, but don't block your blessings. Get a lawyer ASAP."

Ginger wanted to believe Sharon Steinhouser had good intentions. In fact, she needed to believe her. And after talking with Lisa, she had peace about it, so she'd take Lisa's advice.

"Thanks, Lisa. I'll call you later."

"Ok. Love you. Keep me posted."

Ginger ended the call. And although she had peace about Sharon Steinhouser, her stomach flip flopped when she pulled into the semi-circle driveway of Brock's parents' house. She double-checked the address. Yeah, she was in the right place. If Jessie didn't have to leave work early because of a stomach bug, she wouldn't be in this predicament right now.

Relief coursed through her when she didn't see Brock's car. She had to get this delivery over with quickly just in case he showed up. Ginger rang the doorbell with her elbow but couldn't help looking over her shoulder every five seconds for Brock's car to pull in the driveway. That would be just her luck.

"Ginger." Della, Brock's mom, answered the door. Her wide smile made Ginger feel welcomed. Brock shared the same snub nose and chestnut eyes. "It's so good to see you. Come on in."

"Oh, no I don't mind waiting outside. I'm just here to drop this off to Tina Sullivan." Ginger raised the cake box.

Della flicked her hand. "Nonsense. I'm not going to wrestle you down, take the cake, and bury you in the backyard."

Ginger sucked in a breath and raised her eyebrows at the darkness of Mrs. Della's statement.

A pretty younger woman, who looked to be close to Ginger's age, appeared next to her. And squeezed Mrs. Della's shoulders. She also wore her friendly smile. "Momma Della, you're scaring the poor woman. I'm Tina." She pressed her hands into her chest. "I ordered the cake. I can pay you the remaining balance in just a second. Let me get my purse."

Ginger stepped into the foyer. Her stomach warned her she'd regret going inside the house, but Tina ushered her into the kitchen, and Ginger instantly fell in love. The twelve-foot island with green granite countertops that included a four-foot baking center with a pop-up KitchenAid mixer caught her attention. Ginger's mind churned like butter with baking ideas.

"Mrs. Della, this is gorgeous." Ginger resisted the urge to run her hands along the countertop after she set down the cake.

"Thanks, darling. Since I retired, I've done quite a bit of remodeling, but if you think this is something, let me show you the backyard."

Ginger's thoughts rewound back to Della's earlier not-so-funny-backyard-burial joke and declined. "No, thanks. Don't want to get buried back there. It's time for me to get home."

Tina interjected, "It really is gorgeous, Ginger. You should see it. It'll only take a couple of minutes, and I'll come, too."

Ginger chewed her lower lip for a second and looked between the two of them. She hadn't spent time with Della in ages, so she agreed. A few minutes couldn't hurt.

Della and Tina led Ginger to the backyard, which Della referred to as an oasis. A kidney-shaped pool encompassed most of the area. Palm trees were planted strategically along what was left of the yard outside of the travertine decking and wooden pergola, which had a built-in outdoor kitchen. Two seating areas were on either end of the pool. Under the pergola was a warm brown rattan sectional with cushions that matched the color of the swimming pool water. A flat-screen TV hung in the center above the outdoor fireplace. On the opposite end of the pool were two white chaise longue chairs. A small round table with an umbrella that matched the cushions was positioned between them. An at-home retreat.

"*Oooh,* watch this." Animated, Della held a remote and pushed a button, turning on the colored pool lights.

Ginger gushed, "This is absolutely amazing. How do you spend time anywhere else?"

"It's hard, trust me, but I'm out here every chance I get. Come, let's sit under the pergola."

Della strolled under the pergola and sat. She patted the seat next to her for Ginger. Tina, who had remained quiet throughout the tour, sat on the other side of Ginger. Della shifted her elbow against the back of the sofa, resting her chin on her hand. "Let's talk about you. How've you been?"

Mrs. Della's energy made Ginger feel at home, almost forgetting that she needed to leave. There was a good chance Brock might show up and she didn't need to see him. They hadn't talked to each other in weeks. And that's the way things needed to be between them right now—silent—because her heart and mind were just a bunch of jumbled up emotions.

"I've been good. I live with my father in a newer area of Katy now, Cinco Ranch." Her parents had moved during her sophomore year at University of Houston. "My mom died my last year in college, so I moved back home when I finished school to look after my dad."

"Oh, honey I'm sorry to hear that." Della squeezed her hand like they were old girlfriends sitting around catching up on each other's lives. At least that's what it felt like for Ginger and she welcomed the connection. When she and Brock broke up, she cut off contact with his mother, too. When they'd dated, she'd enjoyed the time she spent with Brock and his family—church, picnics, family reunions, and even a few trips out to Galveston Island and Destin, Florida.

"When did you learn to bake? I don't think I knew that about you when you and Brock dated in high school."

"My mom taught me when I was a little girl."

"Your mother was a special woman and I'm sorry to hear she's no longer with you, but she lives in there," Della tapped Ginger's chest with her forefinger, "because everything she's taught you is alive and well in your keto cakes. I swear it's taking everything in me not to order from you every week."

"Thank you for saying that." Ginger clasped her hands. "Well, I'm here when you need me." While she hated to end their catch-up session, she had to leave. She knew it was only a matter of time before Brock walked through the door. That was the kind of day she'd have. "I should get going now." *Before Brock shows up.*

"Oh, here's your payment." Tina handed her cash.

"Thanks for your business."

"Ginger," Tina blurted and halted Ginger's move to stand. "I watch all of your videos where you offer baking tips and I have to tell you they've helped me a bit. Bryce can attest to that." She chuckled. "How'd you get into keto and gluten-free baking?"

Ginger chuckled at the memory before addressing Tina's question, almost forgetting she was in a rush to leave to avoid running into Brock. Although he'd been right about Ace, she wasn't sure how she'd handle things between them.

"Back in college, I had a friend with a gluten allergy. She'd gotten sick and I baked her a batch of gluten-free-get-well-soon cookies. She loved them and I started baking cookies to give away as gifts. My mom and I started a recipe book shortly after that. And the keto pastries started when I tried the keto diet five years ago and didn't want to give up my goodies. The pickiest of eaters, my dad, loved them and I just went from there."

"That's a nice story. You have a fan over here. I've been watching your videos every week since Brock told us about your live streams."

At the mention of his name, her stomach quivered, and she was pretty sure her face responded involuntarily.

Ginger stood.

Please don't let Brock be sitting in that house when I through.

"I'll walk you out." Tina leapt to her feet and led the way.

When they arrived at the door, Tina rested her hand on the knob and turned to Ginger. "I'm sorry, Ginger, I know it's not my place to say anything, but Brock is sick about losing you."

There lay the real reason she'd been lured over. "Tina, thanks for your concern, but Brock will be okay and so will I." She offered her friendliest-let-me-out-of-here-smile.

Tina shot pleading eyes at Della, who gave a slight shake of her head, as if to say, pull back.

"Thank you again for your order, and please keep me in mind whenever you need a cake, cookies, or any pastry. I'll be glad to help out."

If she could've ran, she would've. Tina escorted her through the house and back to the front door where Brock stood on the other side when she opened it. Ginger's heart jumped into her throat.

Chapter Thirty-One

"Gin?" Brock's eyes melded with hers. He was unable to swallow, think, or come up with anything intelligent to say.

"Hey, Brock. Bye, Brock, Thanks, again, Tina." Ginger raced to her car in a one-woman marathon.

Brock stepped inside and shut the door behind him. His voice croaked. "What was that about?"

"Fool," Tina said, smacking his shoulder, "are you just gonna let her leave?"

"Yes, because that's what she wants. She's made it clear she wants nothing to do with me. I'll honor her wishes."

"Momma Della, your son really is a fool." Della entered the house, and Tina jutted her thumb over her shoulder in his direction.

"What'd he do now?"

"It's not what he did, it's what he's not doing. We've done the hard work for him by getting Ginger over here and holding her long enough for him to make it, and he's just gonna let her walk away." Tina shook her head and tossed her hands in the air. "I'm so done with him."

"Trust me, Tina. Ginger needs more time. Where's Dad?"

Brock found Bryce and his father, Derrick, in the kitchen. His dad pulled him into a hug, patted his back, and rubbed the top of his head, just as he'd done many times when he was a kid, before he broke the embrace.

"How are you, son?" His dad leaned against the counter with his arms folded, head cocked to the side.

"I'm alright, Dad, I guess. Considering I quit my job and got fired simultaneously, I feel pretty good. I suppose you and Bryce may have been right when you said something seemed off about what Ace was asking of me to get the promotion. There's no way I could work with him knowing what he was trying to do with Ginger's business."

Brock took a seat at the breakfast table. Bryce and their dad followed suit.

After he gave them a rundown of the Ginger-Ace-and-Decadent-Dough-debacle, Bryce slapped his shoulder. "I hate things didn't work out the way you wanted them to."

"Thanks, bro, but I'm pretty sure it worked out for my own good. I'm not trying to roll with anybody like Ace."

"So, you're here to talk to me about a job?"

"Yes, sir." The two words had never been so painful, yet Brock looked his father square in the eye like he'd taught him. "Do you have anything open?" The words tasted like failure, daggers to his own heart. Words he'd never thought he'd have to say to his father because after all, he was supposed to be making his own way.

"All you ever needed to do was ask."

"Thanks for having my back, Dad."

"Brock, I built that firm for you and your brother. When your mother and I first married, I worked my tail off."

Brock and Bryce nodded. They were aware of how hard their father worked, even when they were in elementary school. Dinner was sometimes late to accompany his schedule.

"I know you think you understand, but you don't. I was fresh out of law school. Hungry. Eager to climb the ranks. I worked seventy- and eighty-hour weeks. Taking on any assignment thrown my way. Had a hard time saying no because I didn't want to look like I wasn't capable."

Brock leaned forward in his seat, his demeanor mirroring his father's. It sounded like the story of his life.

"When Thaddeus McKnight, the head partner at the time and my boss, called me to his office and asked me to falsify federal tax return information, I knew it was time for me to make a change. I had to decide what kind of man I was going to be. If I would be able to look at myself in the mirror. If I would be a man my wife and sons could be proud of."

Brock asked, "So, what'd you do?"

"I quit and started my own firm. It hasn't always been easy, but I don't expect easy. What I do expect is to sleep peacefully at night knowing I've given honest work that God, myself, and my family would be pleased with. And to you, son, that's what you must ask yourself. What kind of man do you want to be? I'm not foolish enough to think you'll want to work with Bryce and me for the long haul, but it's time you made the tough choices. The honest road may not get you quickly to the top or make you millions of dollars, but will you be okay with that?"

Brock nodded.

"This isn't anything you have to answer for me, but something you need to answer for yourself because, my son, your integrity is what will guide you. I'll be praying for you." Derrick patted his hand and moved to get up from the table.

"Will you pray for me now?" Brock had been so far away from God, he wasn't sure God would listen to or honor his petition, but surely, He would listen to someone like his father who had been faithful in his spiritual walk.

"It'd be my pleasure, son." Derrick slid his chair around until the table no longer separated him and Brock. Bryce adjusted his seat until they formed a circle, then Derrick began to pray. "Father God, thank You for Your goodness and mercy. We come before You now lifting up my son, Brock. I ask that You bless him with Your wisdom and guidance. Lead him along the path that honors You, and give him the courage to follow. Strengthen his spirit and his faith. And show him Your hand over his life. In Jesus' name. Amen."

"Amen."

Bryce left the table to grab a bottle of water from the fridge. Derrick stood and encircled Brock in his arms. "For what it's worth, I'm proud of you, son."

"Thanks, Dad."

"Now on to other business." Bryce cracked a crooked smile, walked over to Brock, and nudged his shoulder with his own. "Tell me, what'd you do to bribe Ginger to go out with you again? After that big blowup y'all had years ago, I didn't think you two would ever get over your stubbornness and talk to each other. Plus, based on the last time we talked about you and her, I didn't think you heard anything I said."

"Whatever. I did the same thing you did to get Tina to go out with you."

"I doubt it. I laid down the law with Tina. Flat out. Told her I was feeling her and to meet me in the quad that evening around six if she wanted to hang out. The rest is history."

"Dad, is this what you teach your employees to do?" Brock jutted a thumb in Bryce's direction. "Tell lies?"

Derrick dismissed them with a wave of his hand. "My name is Wes, and I ain't in that mess."

"I don't seem to recall it happening that way," Tina announced as she entered the kitchen. "But since you're handsome, I'll let you slide right now." She swatted Brock's shoulders again. "The real problem is this bonehead right here."

Brock flinched. "Stop that, Tina. What'd I do now?"

"It's what you didn't do."

Bryce laughed and took a swig of water from his bottle. "Oh, is this about him letting Ginger walk out the door?"

Tina tossed her hands in the air. "Exactly. I just can't deal with Brock right now."

"Why are you so concerned, Tina?"

Tina planted her fists at her hips and shifted her weight to one foot. "Great question. I guess I shouldn't be concerned about your love life—or lack thereof—if you aren't, huh?"

"Chill. I'm just giving her time to cool down. She's not ready to talk to me just yet. Is that better?"

"Hey, don't make this about me. This is about you doing what you need to do to get her back." She leaned against Bryce, rubbed her growing belly, and looked up at Brock. "Just don't do any more crazy, selfish stuff."

"Is that what she told you?"

"She didn't say anything you don't already know. Just clean up your mess because I want a sister-in-law soon."

Brock, Bryce, and Derrick all yelled a resounding, "Oh!"

Brock backed away toward the kitchen exit. "On that note, I'm out of here. See y'all later. Dad, when should I report to the office?"

"I'll see you tomorrow morning at nine sharp."

Brock saluted him, found his mom who had retreated to her oasis, and talked with her a while before leaving. Now that the competition, Decadent Dough, and Ace were part of their past, he prayed he and Ginger could find their way back to each other.

Chapter Thirty-two

With her father gone to the bowling alley to meet with his friends, Ginger enjoyed time alone on the front porch swing. The summer heat didn't bother her. The patio covering provided enough shade. And as much as she tried not to think of Brock, sitting there reminded her of him. The last time she sat there, she was in his arms.

Everything reminded her of him, like the black BMW traveling down the street that seemed to be slowing down as it approached her home.

She downed her glass of lemonade. Perhaps she was hotter than she thought and hallucinating.

Nope.

The car pulled into her driveway.

It was him. He stepped out of the car wearing a blue tee shirt and blue-and-gray plaid shorts. He could make anything look good. His shades covered his eyes, so she couldn't read his expression. He trekked the path leading to where she sat. His smile grew wider the closer he got.

She sat, unable to move, in utter disbelief he'd driven over to see her without calling first. Well, he did call. She didn't answer. Had she not made herself clear? Their relationship was over.

When Ginger was within reach, Brock pulled her to her feet, dipped his head, and moved his lips against hers—a firm grip on the small of her back and the other supporting the back of her head. She wanted and needed to break free from his muscular arms and kissable lips, but she'd be lying to herself if she said she didn't miss him—miss this—despite the hailstorm that followed him into her life.

Brock pulled away and rested his forehead against hers, wiping away a stray tear from her cheek with his thumb.

"I'm sorry," Brock said between breaths. "Not for kissing you, but for everything that happened with Ace and Decadent Dough."

Ginger released a semi-steady breath, gestured for him to sit, and reclaimed her seat. Her shoulders slumped, and she rested her hands between her knees. Part of her wanted to send him away. And the other piece of her heart desired he kiss her again.

Ugh.

Did he think he could just pop up, kiss her senseless, and everything would be alright? Apparently so, or else he wouldn't have done it.

"It's not exactly your fault. I heard everything from Dawn's lips, so I know about Ace's scheme. It's just he convinced me you were involved and to think you'd do something like that…was unbearable. Maybe that was a sign for us, well for me, that I don't truly trust you like I should. I mean, this started with you propositioning me about working with Decadent Dough, and things were going so well between us I kept wondering when it would all fall apart."

Brock turned her to face him. "Really?"

Ginger averted her gaze to the live oak tree in the center of the yard. "Yes. Maybe I'm not as ready as I wanted to be, but I do love you, Brock."

Brock tilted her chin to look him in the eyes. "Gin, I love you, too. I would never allow anyone else to hurt you. That's why I quit and got fired at the same time. I couldn't stand by and watch someone else try to hurt you and not do anything about it. And if you can't trust anything else, trust my love for you."

"What about your promotion?"

"Gin, I don't care about a promotion if I have to hurt someone else to get it, especially if that person is you. To be completely transparent, I was headed down a dark path that would've been difficult to get out of if I'd kept going. I realize that now. And I've been praying about you and for you and us over the last couple of days."

"Praying? Really?"

Brock nodded. "It's because you're back in my life I considered the person I was becoming. More importantly, I want to like the man I see in the mirror, and I don't want to disappoint God with my choices."

"Who are you, and what have you done with the real Brock Pearson?"

Brock chuckled and took her hand in his. "You've been a good influence on me."

"How so?"

"I recommitted myself to my relationship with God. For so long, I separated myself from Him mostly because of what happened to our relationship when we were younger. I was angry, and that drove me to shut a lot of people out—keep them at arm's distance—but somehow you finagled your way around it."

"Stop it!" Ginger giggled and brushed against his shoulder with her own. "I'm happy for you, Brock. That's really good news."

"I should be thanking you. You wasted no time telling me off when I presented that deal to you."

Ginger thought back to that day and sucked the air through her teeth. "You had that coming. I've always blamed your self-centeredness as the reason we broke up, and you had the nerve to come in my face with that. I think I'd been waiting to tell you off for years."

"I was an egotistical idiot. How can I make it up to you?"

"Your list of things to make up is getting pretty long. I don't know."

"Seriously, Ginger, I'm asking for the opportunity to try." He placed her hand over his heart, the erratic rhythm matching her own.

Brock stood and pulled her to her feet, linking their fingers. "I'm in love with you, however, I won't pressure you to be with me if you aren't ready. Is a week enough time for you to think and pray about us?"

Ginger nodded.

"And as hard as it'll be for me, I won't call. I won't text, and I won't stop by your bakery. Next Monday, I'll wait for you at the Cracker Barrel down the street from Katy Mills before work at the same time we've always met for breakfast. If you've decided you're ready for us, come, and if not, I'll have my answer and I'll back off."

Brock pulled her into his arms and squeezed like it could be the last time he held her. He gently wiped away tears from both cheeks with his thumbs. Cradling the back of her neck, he dipped his head and pressed his lips firmly against hers.

"Hope to see you next Monday," he whispered in her ear, the sound vibration sent a tingle trickling through her body.

Brock left her standing there motionless and speechless, the same way he'd found her, except her heart was a lump of putty.

Chapter Thirty-three

A man of his word, Brock refrained from reaching out to Ginger for one week. The separation had been like that of a nursing infant without his mother. Throwing fits of rage wasn't his style though he wanted to do so a day or two.

Work kept him company throughout the week. His new job at The Pearson Group wasn't half as bad as he thought it'd be. He joined at an opportune time because one of their clients was working on a merger deal. His father tossed the reins to him, and Brock convinced the client to allow their firm to oversee it. He thought back to an earlier conversation he had with Ginger about him doing the kind of work he wanted at his father's firm. Perhaps if he hadn't been so stubborn and hellbent on forging his own path, he could've had a healthy career from the beginning.

He found himself back at a place he once was over twenty years ago, where he'd completely opened his heart to Ginger. The question now was if it was enough for her to trust his love for her.

Brock dressed a lot slower than normal the morning of his potential meeting with Ginger while he contemplated what the next few hours could mean for them. Would she really walk away from him for good? Not knowing suffocated him, and he opted not to put on his tie until he made it to the office. He also left the top two buttons of his white dress shirt open and slipped into his navy-blue suit jacket, sprayed on Ginger's favorite cologne and headed for the door. His mouth was too dry for his usual coffee, so he opted for a bottle of water on his way out.

God had heard more from him this week than He had in the last twenty years. Brock prayed on his drive to Cracker Barrel. *God, thank You for being God. Knowing all things and having control of all things. I place my relationship with Ginger in Your hands. Soften her heart towards me and help us to work out our differences. Amen.*

When he pulled into the parking lot, her car wasn't there, but that didn't alarm him because he always arrived before she did. He waited for her at the entrance for ten minutes before he went inside without her and got seats at their usual table.

After another twenty minutes, he checked his phone for messages. Maybe she was on her way, and something had happened that prevented her from being on time.

Nothing.

He checked e-mails to pass the time, his eyes darting to the door every time a customer came inside. Still, no sign of Ginger. After ten more minutes, he surmised she wasn't coming and placed an order for bacon, eggs, a biscuit, and black coffee, though he'd lost his appetite. He'd only eat to distract himself from the pain hitched in his chest.

Rejection was more bitter than his coffee without cream and sugar. Although he'd always known it was a risk she wouldn't come, deep in the pit of his belly, he didn't believe she'd give up on them. They were connected like a moth to a flame.

∞

The offer Ginger received for her baking television series was triple the amount of the baking competition grand prize and included money for her new set, which would be housed in the new building she planned to purchase.

Thoughts of the last conversation she had with Brock on her front porch replayed in her mind all week long. Several times, she wanted to go to him and profess her love, believing they could work, but she decided against it. What if being with Brock was a wrong decision like the one she was about to make with the Bradford sisters—a decision that would ultimately come back to haunt her?

She'd set her alarm clock to rise early and meet him at Cracker Barrel but couldn't bring herself to go. Instead, she went to work, baking cookies and pastry platters for the standing deliveries.

"You are such a chicken. I knew I'd find you here." Lisa waltzed into Ginger's Goodies commercial kitchen and held her position at the swinging door entrance.

"What are you doing here?" Ginger covered her chest to steady her breathing.

"I came here to see if you'd gone to meet Brock this morning."

"You mean to tell me you rolled out of your bed an entire hour early to come up here and check on me? You could've called."

Lisa folded her arms across her chest. "Sure did, and it looks like I was right. Are you really okay with not ever seeing Brock again or running into him two years from now and he's happily married with someone else?"

Ginger suppressed the bile that rose in her throat at the thought of Dawn hanging on Brock's arm.

"Since when did you become an advocate for him?" Ginger turned her attention to removing the chilled dough from the refrigerator to make blueberry scones.

Lisa walked over, snatched Ginger's wrists, and pulled them away from the dough. "I'm an advocate for you. I could care less about his thoughts and feelings. I know you're in love with him, and have been for as long as I've known you. So why the hesitation?"

Ginger shrugged. "I don't know, really. Just not sure if it's entirely right or if I trust him the way I should. I mean, when Ace insinuated Brock was involved with that mess, without hesitation, I believed the worst about Brock. That is not how a good relationship should work."

"I don't totally blame you. Ace was convincing, and you'd just received the results from the competition. Your emotions were all over the place. Who knows if you would've reacted the same given different circumstances?"

"Lisa, I've told myself the same thing, but I shouldn't have those feelings about someone I'm in a relationship with in the first place."

"Well, yes and no. You and Brock have history and probably quite a bit you still need to work through but that'll take time. Now, I told Brock I wouldn't get involved, but you got me getting involved because you're over here looking all weepy eyed. *Ugh!* If you love him, go to him."

"Lisa, it's not that easy. Too many uncertainties. I don't know if it'll work." Ginger frowned and shifted her weight from one foot to the other under Lisa's scrutiny.

"That's sort of the beauty and excitement of it all, don't you think? Not knowing. Life would be boring if we knew exactly how everything would work out."

Ginger shrugged.

"If you love him, Ginger, go—now."

Ginger contemplated whether she'd really be okay with Brock out of her life for good. She sighed. "I don't know, Lisa."

Lisa folded her arms across her chest and for the next several minutes they engaged in a stare down with Ginger's mind running rampant with different possible outcomes. Finally, she released a heavy breath and relented.

"Since you're here early, I take it that means you've come to work. If I go now, you'll have to take over for me until Jessie gets here. All you need to do is take the cookies out of the oven when they're done. I don't need you burning anything. Don't touch the scones, Jessie will know what to do when she gets here."

"No worries. I know my limitations." Lisa tapped her shoulders. "Just go."

Ginger squealed, untied her apron, and put it around Lisa's neck. "Wash your hands first, please."

"Go."

"Wash for thirty seconds."

"Get out of here."

Ginger squeezed Lisa tightly. "Thank you for the chat, sis."

"A good friend knows what you need to hear. Now, go."

Ginger boxed a half-dozen of Brock's favorite cookies and tied a pink ribbon around the box.

After she'd made it outside and into her car, she checked the time on the dashboard. If Brock stayed the entire time of their usual breakfast, he should be leaving in about five minutes, the amount of time it would take her to get there. She started her car and navigated the back streets, avoiding traffic signals. Ginger pulled into the parking lot, spotted Brock exiting the building, and parked behind him to block his exit.

When he turned to check his clearance, he locked eyes with her, and a mix of emotions flooded his eyes. From rejection to excitement to confusion and back to exhilaration.

Ginger got out of her car and went to him. Brock stepped out of his car and stuffed his hands in his pockets. Ginger knew he only did so to refrain from touching her.

"Brock, I'm sorry I didn't come. I guess I needed a few more hours to consider." Ginger released a nervous chuckle. "The truth is, I'm scared, and I don't know if this will work out this time, but I do want to try because I want us. I love you."

He peered into her eyes, searing down into her soul. "That's all I needed to hear because I love you, Gin. Always have and always will."

Brock cupped her cheeks and pressed his lips against hers. And Ginger, overcome with emotion, allowed a stream of tears to flow helplessly down her cheeks. It was a kiss filled with perfection, purity, and promises for the future.

Epilogue

The last seven months were the craziest, busiest, but most adventurous Ginger ever had. Once she signed the contract for her own baking show, *Baking Keto and Gluten-free with Ginger,* everything moved quickly—from buying the building to having it renovated for her business and the show. Ginger purchased a one-story three-bedroom house in old Katy and had it transformed into the perfect coffeehouse and bakery. The living room and master bedroom were renovated into the customer dining area. The former kitchen, dining room, and one bedroom had been completely gutted and transformed into her commercial kitchen used to film the show. She also had a second kitchen added for day-to-day business. The third bedroom served as her office space. Hardwood floors were installed throughout, and the main customer dining area was painted yellow with Ginger's Goodies plastered in pink letters.

Brock's parents' kitchen served as inspiration for the kitchen used for show tapings. It held an oversized granite island, stainless-steel double wall oven, butler's pantry, and a stainless-steel built-in refrigerator and freezer combo.

One month before Valentine's Day, Ginger had her first taping. Sitting in white folding chairs across the room, her support team was there for the entire five hours it took to film apart from

Bryce and Tina who were at home with their newborn baby girl. Ginger had baked a thousand times before, but it felt different with seven cameras pointing at her face and bright lights beaming down on her. It didn't help she had at least fifteen pairs of eyes on her listening to her explain every baking step.

With her hair pulled into a high ponytail and dressed in a pink blouse and blue comfortable skinny jeans, Ginger inhaled deeply and waited for the director to cue her in. A nervous smile covered her face—a smile that became more authentic when she caught a glimpse of Brock and he mouthed, *I love you.*

"Hello, and welcome to *Baking Keto and Gluten-free with Ginger*. I'm Ginger, and today I'm going to share three easy recipes to help you steal your Valentine's heart. So, ladies, let him know he can skip the flowers this year and woo you with one of these tasty treats." Ginger told herself this recording was an extended video of what she did every week for her social media page, and it helped her relax.

"Let's start with the flourless chocolate cake. Who doesn't love chocolate on Valentine's Day or any day of the year for that matter?" She chuckled. "And if your love has an allergy to gluten, then this is perfect for you. No flour or flour substitutions. All you'll need is bittersweet chocolate, roughly chopped, one stick of butter, one cup of sugar, four large eggs, a three-quarter cup of cocoa powder, and one teaspoon of instant espresso powder."

"I know it seems like I've said a mouthful, but we're going to work this out together."

Ginger worked through the instructions, step-by-step. Though introverted, it wasn't visible by watching her in her comfort zone—the kitchen.

"Now you want to pour this into a springform pan and let it bake for about thirty-five minutes. While this is going, we're going to move on to what I like to call turtle shortbread cookies. If you're like me and you're in love with all things caramel, this is the one you want to go for. These are great for dinner parties or even mid-week treats for yourself."

"We'll start with our shortbread layer." Ginger dazzled the studio audience and camera from beginning to end, Brock's gaze locked on hers equally as long.

The director cut several times for restroom breaks, makeup touch-ups, and to wipe the beads of sweat from her forehead, special thanks to the overhead lights and her bout of nerves.

"You're fabulous up there," Lisa commented to which everyone else agreed.

"I'm proud of you, baby girl. So proud. Your mother would be too." Her dad kissed her cheek.

"I don't even deserve to have such an amazing woman like you to be by my side. You're doing great."

"Great job up there, boss," Jessie added and squeezed her with a sideways hug.

Ginger finished the tapping, renewed by the compliments of her family and friends. Tomorrow she'd have a ribbon cutting ceremony and soft opening of her new bakery location.

∞∞∞∞

Ginger posed in front of the Ginger's Goodies gold-plated sign hanging on the front door of her building. First alone, then with her father. Lisa also joined in the photo ops. She snipped the pink ribbon strung in front of the door, and her family and friends yelled for her to give a speech. No one seemed to care about the breeze brought on by the cool February temperatures.

With trembling fingers, she wiped away warm tears from her cheeks. "I have God and each one of you to thank for supporting me along the way. I don't know if I'd be standing in front of this building if it wasn't for a nudge from one of you at some point in my life."

She paused for a moment and looked at familiar faces in the crowd. "I'm so grateful for the love you all have shown me, and I can't think of anything that will make this day more perfect, so thank you."

"I can." Brock slipped his phone into his jacket pocket and moved to stand next to her.

"What do you mean?"

"I can think of something." Brock knelt on one knee and pulled a tiny velvet box from his suit jacket.

Ginger was now visibly trembling. Her peacoat kept her warm, but these tremors were caused by the man who made her heart act out of control and could cause her stomach to churn with one look and could make her feel like the ground disappeared beneath her feet when he kissed her.

"Ginger Evans, you have turned my life upside down in the best way. I never understood how much I needed love until I laid eyes on you again. I never want to be without you, and I'll do my best to show you how much I love you every day. Will you marry me?"

Ginger's eyes blurred from the overflowing tears. A permanent grin etched her features. Her father didn't seem surprised, as he nodded his approval. From his smile, she knew he'd had a long conversation with Brock.

"Yeah, she will," Lisa yelled, and the crowd burst into laughter.

"Oh my gosh, Brock. You know I will. I love you so much."

Brock slid the ring on her finger and pulled her down onto his knee, expressing his appreciation with a thank-you-for-loving-me-and-I'll-love-you-forever kind of kiss. When he broke the kiss, Ginger lifted her left hand to the crowd and showcased the diamond.

"The future Mrs. Brock Pearson, y'all."

"I love the sound of that."

THE END

Dear reader,

What did you think of Brock and Ginger? This story has been a long time coming and I'm so excited that you've finally had the chance to read it.

In the story, Ginger and Brock had to work through their past to find their way back to each other. Although they were in their late teens when they dated and broke up, their love was real and I'm happy they were able to work through their immaturity (even when they believed they were mature).

One of my favorite things about Ginger was her desire to pursue her dreams. She didn't know how she would get there, but not knowing didn't stop her from trying. And while Brock was on a similar path, he was also on a dangerous path—at the brink of ruining someone else's dream to get what he wanted. I'm happy he changed. I don't believe God would want us to destroy what anyone else has, in order to get what we want.

My message of love for you today is, never give up on your dreams—that is one of the biggest themes in *Batch of Love*. And above all else, trust God in the process.

I hope you enjoyed *Batch of Love*. Please take a moment to let me know what you think by leaving a review on Amazon/Goodreads/Bookbub.

Until next time,

Natasha

About the Author

Natasha fell in love with love around the age of twelve because of artists like Babyface, Boys II Men, Whitney Houston, and New Edition. Around sixteen when her mother purchased a romance novel and left it lying around the house untouched, Natasha read it and a spark for the written word had been ignited.

Natasha believes that writing is one of her purposes and contributions to the world. She feels accomplished when she can get a few words written and like blah when life gets in the way. Her hope is that at the end of every novel, readers will feel like they've been wrapped in a cozy blanket with a mug of their favorite coffee/tea/warm drink.

When she isn't reading or writing, she is likely working out or watching movies with her family. Natasha resides in Richmond, TX with her husband, Eddie Frazier, Jr. and their three children, Eden, Ethan, and Emilyn. Her greatest joy and commitment is to her family who she hopes to inspire above all else. One of her many mottos in life is: Faith removes limitations. Natasha and her family attend Parkway Fellowship in Richmond, TX, where she volunteers as an Usher. Natasha is also a member of the Houston Area Alumni Chapter of Jackson State University and Alpha Kappa Alpha Sorority, Inc.

Connect with Natasha online:

Bookbub @NatashaDFrazier

Instagram @author_natashafrazier

Twitter or X @author_natashaf

TikTok @author_natashafrazier

Facebook @craves.2012

Website: www.natashafrazier.com

Also by Natasha D. Frazier

Devotionals

The Life Your Spirit Craves

Not Without You

Not Without You Prayer Journal

The Life Your Spirit Craves for Mommies

Pursuit

Fiction

Love, Lies & Consequences

Through Thick & Thin: Love, Lies & Consequences Book 2

Shattered Vows: Love, Lies & Consequences Book 3

Out of the Shadows: Love, Lies & Consequences Book 4

Kairos: The Perfect Time for Love

Fate (The Perfect Time for Love series)

With Every Breath (The McCall Family Series, book 1)

With Every Step (The McCall Family Series, book 2)

With Every Moment (The McCall Family Series, book 3)

The Reunion (Langston Sisters, book1)

The Wrong Seat (Langston Sisters, book 2)

The Missing Link (Langston Sisters, book 3)

Non-Fiction
How Long Are You Going to Wait?